THE TRUTH ABOUT TRULY

LYNDA MEYERS

HALLWAY
11

For my Family.
You mean everything.
And I do mean, everything.

the *truth* about truly

PROLOGUE

"Life is short. Break the rules. Forgive quickly. Love truly. Laugh uncontrollably, and never regret anything that makes you smile."
M.T.

F INN

BASEBALL, as I'm sure you're aware, is generally considered a singularly American tradition. However, for us Brits and the Irish alike, we've been playing games with balls and sticks and running 'round bases for centuries. In fact, if you want to get technical, even the name "base-ball" was first coined in an English poem from the mid 1700s.

At any rate, it wasn't like I hated the game, or even hated America, which, at that point in our fledgling relationship had treated me quite well. I just–didn't want to be there, really. Crowds weren't exactly my thing, although if you take into account that I was running one of the more successful new nightclubs in Manhattan, I admit it seems a bit backwards.

I'D GONE to Yankee Stadium with my friend David, who literally yanked me out of my office at the club and assured me a good time. I don't know how to tell you what happened when he told me where we were going. I just knew I had to go with him.

I guess I should back up a bit.

Three weeks earlier I'd been at my apartment, asleep, when an entire dream sequence blew through my mind. You know those dreams that feel so real that they creep inside you and make you wonder if you're crazy? That kind of a dream. This one was so real I could smell it.

It was about a girl with dark hair and fair skin and a gorgeous smile. Here's where it gets a bit dodgy: I'd seen her face twice before, and yet we'd never met. Once in a previous dream, and then again in a vision I had at Nana's when I was back in Ireland. Both times I'd been under extreme stress. The first was after an accident at sea that left three of my friends dead. The second was while I was having withdrawals from booze and painkillers.

But that's another story.

THIS PARTICULAR DREAM brought her closer than ever. I opened the door to my apartment there she was, in a long trench coat and navy-blue high heels and this pair of legs that went on forever. I could feel my heart begin to race as soon as I saw her. We were familiar, she and I, but I knew somehow that we had never made love. She commented on my apartment as if she'd never seen it before.

I slipped the coat off her shoulders and her scent overwhelmed me. I still don't know what it was she was wearing. I've smelled a lot of women's perfumes before and this was unlike anything I knew. Of course, it was a dream, so perhaps that particular scent doesn't actually exist. Or maybe it isn't a perfume at all. Maybe it's just *her* scent. At any rate, it's stuck in my nose and even now the mere thought of it makes me catch my breath.

In the dream I poured us some wine and we danced in the middle of my living room. I ran my fingers across the skin on her shoulders and down one arm, then followed with my mouth. If it's possible, she tasted even better than she smelled.

I was caught completely in her atmosphere. The colors faded away. The apartment faded away. I picked her up and carried her to my bed, but it was all very dream-like, as if we were encased in light. All I could see was her face. Her eyes. Her body underneath me. Something clicked into place when we kissed, like I was diving inside her and exploring from the inside out.

We made love for hours. Or at least, what seemed like hours in the dream. When the room came back into focus it was daylight and she was in my arms, and I knew only one thing: I never wanted to let her go.

THE DREAM HAD BEEN GNAWING at the corners of my mind, just far enough outside of reality to dismiss it, but real enough that I could feel the electricity course through my skin when I remembered the details. This was a woman from my dream world, and yet she was so real to me I could have sworn she existed in this world as well. It was a strange sort of existence that often felt like accessing both realms at once.

The Celts have a name for this. They call it walking between the worlds. I didn't know if that's what I was doing, I only knew that my experiences over the past several years had raised a lot of questions that didn't have traditional answers.

But for now, back to the original story.

. . .

3

DAVID and I were at Yankee Stadium. He was trying to cheer me up, I think. Not that I was depressed. More of a flat preoccupation with the business side of my life and absolutely no desire whatsoever to explore the life and culture of New York.

Ok, maybe I was a little depressed.

We got there and he ordered me a beer and a hot dog. He said these were the things you did at baseball games in America, so I went along with it, even though it was terrible and I ended up giving my hot dog to him to finish.

The beer wasn't much better. It was terribly flavorless and served in a plastic cup that a toddler could crush with one hand. Ridiculous, I know.

"You're going to love this. I promise." He said, taking a bite of my hot dog. "Look at all these people!"

The stadium in Dublin was about this size, and I'd been to football games there. Fans are fans, and these fans seemed as loyal to their teams as any other sport. Honestly, I was bored already. No offense to the sport itself or its fans.

"It's lovely, really."

I took another sip of that beer he'd given me and I must have made an awful face, because David snatched my beer from me and flagged down the nearest concessions waiter.

"He'll have a Coke please."

I laughed at his obvious annoyance but took a sip of the Coke and gave him an exaggerated smile.

"There, is that better? Coca-Cola. Still iconic, still solidly American." David chopped at the air with his hand.

"But considerably more drinkable." I laughed.

"You haven't been outside the bar in weeks. It's time you had some fun."

"Alright then. Explain the game to me." I set my drink down and prepared to concentrate as David went over the rules.

I tried to get into the game, but honestly all I could think about was the paperwork and inventory that needed to be done back at the bar. After the hot dog failure, David made me try an Italian

Sausage with peppers and onions and a giant pretzel with mustard. I'm not a huge fan of mustard, so the pretzel was just so-so, but the sausage was fairly fabulous. The smell of it brought me back to Mary's place on the coast in Ireland. Mary owned a pub where I spent quite a bit of time. She was good people, Mary was.

A couple of kids sitting in front of us were arguing, the little girl clutching her doll as she pouted, and suddenly there in my mind were Declan and Bree, two precious wee ones that lived at Mary's place now. Like I said, that's a whole other story, but it felt more like a whole other lifetime.

The crowd kept cheering and David kept talking, but I was elsewhere. At the seventh inning stretch I got up to use the bathroom and as I walked through the crowds I caught a whiff of that scent. The one from my dream.

The girl. It was real?

I spun around, looking for her, but caught myself and chuckled. I was imagining things. I had to be. There were just too many memories today. Too much to pain that had to be put back away. The people in New York were fascinating to watch, though. I almost enjoyed that part of things more than the game itself, so I leaned against a post for a while, taking it all in. I still couldn't shake that feeling. Something was up, I just couldn't figure out what it was. Eventually, I made my way back down to our seats.

"Jesus, I thought maybe you fell in!" David said through a mouthful of pretzel.

"*Another* pretzel?"

"Yeah, I love these things. You want some?" He held it out to me but I shook my head and ordered another Coke. I would need to stay up if I wanted to finish that inventory.

When the game finished, we started threading our way through the crowd. I was still carrying my Coke, and a handful of napkins from our various food items. It was honestly very difficult to walk holding that flimsy cup and I was looking around for nearest trash bin to dispose of it when I got that strange electrical feeling I get sometimes when I know I'm supposed to pay attention.

My eyes searched for the source of the disturbance and I noticed two women walking a few paces ahead of us, one blond and the other brunette. That smell. That perfume. It couldn't be. When I looked at them again, the hair stood up on the back of my neck, as if the air pressure had changed and it was about to storm. I looked up, but there wasn't a cloud in the sky.

I must have slowed down way too much, because the guy behind me gave me a hard shove and told me to keep moving, which launched me forward into the shoulder of the girl. I tried to grip that cup as I stumbled and merely succeeded in squeezing its contents all over her shirt.

She stopped suddenly and so did time, as I reached over with the napkins in my other hand and tried desperately to dry her off. Her shirt was ruined, and I felt simply horrible.

Out of nowhere her fist came up and socked me right in the face. The world went black for just a moment, and luckily David caught me before I hit the ground, because—well, that would've been embarrassing. My eyes were watering so badly, all I could see was her shaking her hand out in front of me, yelling furiously. Finally her face came into focus and everything froze.

It was her. The girl from my dreams. But that was...impossible, right?

I blinked a few times, still massaging my nose, dumbfounded. She kept on yelling at me, as did her friend. David elbowed me and I began to apologize, but it didn't seem to help. A crowd was gathering around us and soon a security officer was standing there asking what the trouble was.

"This a-hole grabbed my breast, that's what the problem is!"

"I did not!" I insisted, trying to calm my voice. "Someone ran into me and my drink went flying. I was merely trying to help. I was just trying to clean off your shirt. I did *not* mean to touch you inappropriately."

The officer looked at me, massaging my nose and started laughing. "You punched him?"

"Yeah. I did," she answered. Her body language said she wouldn't mind doing it again.

"Good for you," the officer nodded, then turned to me and said some word I'd never heard before but I'm assuming it wasn't very nice. "You shoulda known better."

The officer dismissed us and walked away and so did the crowd. We were all standing there and the girl's friend started laughing. Loudly. So did David. Some mate he was. The girl looked down at her shirt and looked up at me and her face broke into a gorgeous smile. I knew that smile. I still couldn't get over the fact that I knew that smile.

I stuck out my hand. "I'm Finn, and I'm extremely sorry I've ruined your shirt. Please, allow me to buy you a new one."

"I just punched you in the face." She looked down at her hand and splayed the fingers in and out a few times. "And you want to buy me a new shirt?"

Her eyebrows went up and she was shaking her head, still smiling. I couldn't stop staring at her. She was breathtaking.

"It's...the least I could do, really. I'm dreadfully sorry."

"No, it's ok. Truly."

She took my hand and shook it. "If you're sure," I tried to smile. "I don't think I caught your name." God, I wanted to know her name. I was fascinated and intrigued and aroused all at the same time. I tried to keep my eyes trained on her face, but the whole picture was simply beautiful. I tried not to imagine her in a trench coat and a pair of navy-blue heels.

"Truly" she said again. We were still shaking hands.

"Oh, I see. You'd rather not give me your name." My eyes fell and so did my hopes. Standing before me was, quite literally, the girl of my dreams, and I'd completely blown it and she didn't want anything to do with me. "I completely understand. It's...not a problem."

Her hand dropped away, and as she let go the smell of her

7

perfume filled my senses. I breathed it in, and her head tilted slightly as she watched me.

"Her name is Truly," her friend added, with emphasis on the word *name*. "It's short for Trulane, but she hates it when people call her that, so if you don't want to get punched again, I'd stick with Truly."

The girl's eyes went wide. "That is a bold-faced lie!" She looked at me apologetically. "I don't normally punch people either. I'm really sorry. Is your nose alright?"

I wiggled it a bit, checking all the parts. "No harm done, but I must say, you've got quite the right hook for a girl. I've gotten less of a spin by some of the blokes I went to school with."

Her eyes narrowed a bit. "Yeah, well. I guess it was a reflex. Let's just call it good. We have to get going."

She grabbed onto her friend's arm, but her friend wasn't moving. She was looking at David, who was returning the favor.

"Yes. Of course," I offered. "Unless..." She waited. I wanted to know more. I needed to find out who she was. This chance, it was...one in a million. The odds were astronomical. Unless...

"...You'd at least let me buy you a cup of coffee?" That was what people in America liked to do, wasn't it? But maybe she didn't like coffee. I started throwing out other options "Or tea. Or... cocoa." It was no use. I dropped my head in defeat. I was making a fool of myself. "I obviously have no idea what you like to drink."

She was pulling her shirt out of her pants, looking down at the stains. "Well, I think I've had plenty of Coke, so something warm might be nice."

She looked back up and smiled at me again. That beautiful smile. I realized with some surprise that I couldn't hear any of the other people in the stadium. No one else existed. It was like I was in a time warp or a dream sequence, and yet, I knew it was real. And I wanted desperately to take the next step, whatever it might be.

"May we give you a ride?" I asked, as politely as I could. I wanted so much to be a gentleman after having been such a fool.

She and her friend looked at each other. Her friend, who's name turned out to be Kate, said to David "We were just going to take the subway."

"I'm going to need to change," Truly stated, wringing some of the wetness out of her shirt. It was stuck to her body beautifully, outlining the delicate lines of her collarbones and making me remember everything I loved about women.

"Perhaps we could share a cab," I offered. "We could drop by your place so you could change and then continue on?"

She was staring at me and I found myself reliving parts of my dream that I hadn't previously remembered. I swallowed with some difficulty, waiting for her answer.

"Ok" she smiled. "Why not. Kate?"

"You know me, sweetie. I'm always down."

David winked at me and we set off in the direction of the front gates. Hailing a cab isn't quite so difficult as one might imagine in the company of a woman wearing a wet t-shirt.

1

"Why not go out on a limb?
That's where the fruit is."
M.T.

TRULY

LOOKING BACK, I can't say that I saw any of this coming. I didn't understand my own story, even when I was right in the middle of it. I wonder if it's like that for most people. It's true that Finn changed my life, but it was already changing - I just didn't know it at the time.

FINN CAME into my life when I just about had things all sewn up. I was working on my first novel and had a regular stream of free-lance gigs in multiple magazines with decent circulation. I'd even published a few special interest pieces in The Times. I had a good relationship with one of the editors over there and he was considering bringing me in on a more regular basis. He liked my no-nonsense way of looking at life, and said New Yorkers seemed to like it too. I mean, let's face it—living in New York can be challenging. The only way to get through it is with good planning and a regular routine.

I'd written a piece about organizing stuff in your closet, followed up with one on organizing your financial stuff, then spread out to include menu stuff, trip stuff, "social media and other time sucking stuff". People were eating it up. They wanted to dub me "The Stuff Girl." This worked for me. I liked having a place for everything and everything in its place.

It wasn't until Kate and I were in the back of that cab and I was looking into his beautiful eyes that I'd even considered the idea of veering off the path. I'm not even sure it was a conscious decision. He invited me out for coffee and for some reason I still can't explain, I said yes. There are a lot of things I can't explain when it comes to Finn.

THAT NIGHT the guys waited while we stopped by my apartment so that I could change my shirt. The minute we hit the steps, Kate was grilling me.

"You know I'm always up for a challenge, but you? I've known you three years and you've never done anything even remotely close to this! What's going on with you?"

"I really couldn't tell you." The hard New York edge was off of my voice and I was suddenly pensive and almost shy. "There was something in his eyes." I shrugged. "Something in my heart said yes."

"Yes, he's a stalker? Yes, you want to marry him? What does *yes* mean?"

"Yes, we should have coffee! Yes, I should forgive him for

ruining my shirt. I don't know Kate, ok? Let's just see where this goes."

She leaned against the door in the hallway as I fumbled with my keys, repeating my words. "Let's just see where this goes?" Just inside the door she turned me to face the small mirror on the wall. "See this face? This girl?"

I looked. Really looked. "Yes. I see her."

"This is not a girl who says things like *Let's just see where this goes*. This is a girl who dots i's and crosses t's. A girl who makes lists and weighs pros and cons." She turned me back toward the door. "A girl with six different kinds of locks on her apartment to ward off stalkers and all but the sickest of thieves with death wishes. Who *are* you?" She smiled at me then, and I knew she was just teasing. "Hey, I'm just saying is all."

I shook my head and walked to the bedroom, searching the left side of my closet, way back to two-thousand and one, and found the perfect shirt. It was a pale-pink, peasant number with some tiny polka dots in the piping.

"Pink?" Kate says to me. "In the whole time I've known you I have never *once* seen you in pink."

"I know." I winked at her. "Just trying to keep you on your toes."

"Truly you are an enigma."

"Thank you." I nodded and held the door open. "Shall we?"

Kate just kept shaking her head as she followed me out.

"And by the way, I only have three locks – not six," I reminded her.

"Whatever."

DOWN IN THE cab Finn had been lounging with his arm across the back bench, but he sat up straight and scooted right over when he realized we were at the window. His friend David jumped out and let the two of us in before squeezing next to Kate. Four in the back of a cab is cozy at best.

Kate and David were talking and laughing in no time. I, on the other hand, had no clue what I was doing there, so I figured we should start with the basics. I asked Finn what he did for a living.

"Well, when I'm not accidentally fondling perfect strangers, I run a company that develops new technology for film making. You know, CGI and what not. Dabble in some other ideas."

Dabble? Who said dabble anymore? "Oh. Really?"

"Did you think maybe I was a contract killer or a serial rapist then?"

"You have a very dry sense of humor." I replied.

"So I've been told. I don't mean to put you off though. Do I somehow not look the part of a computer geek?"

He was ridiculously handsome, and when he smiled, only one side of his mouth hooked up, kind of like a lazy eye but farther down. "Maybe it's the accent. I can't really place it. English or Irish?"

"Both actually." He grinned at me and laid it on extra thick, changing voices mid-stream and then melding them together at the end. "Me mum is a brit and me da is an Irishman. I'm afraid I favor them both at times."

"It's a bit confusing but...charming nonetheless." I smiled at him and could have sworn some sort of light twinkled in his eyes.

"And you? What is it you do?" He turned serious to match my earlier line of questioning. I couldn't tell if he was being polite or mocking me.

"Well, when I'm not being inappropriately fondled by half-breed Irishmen, I'm a writer."

"Oh!" He feigned a concerned look and leaned toward me a little. "Does that mean my less than gentlemanly conduct will be ensconced in the pages of a brilliant novel someday?"

"I'm not sure yet. Let's just see where this goes."

Kate eyed me again. She was right of course. I kept saying that.

Why on earth did I keep saying that? I'm not a fly by the seat of your pants girl–what was I even doing?

A sigh escaped my lips and Finn looked over. "Bored already?"

"No, just arguing with myself."

His mouth curved up part way. "I hope you're winning."

"Always." He was staring at me. I hate it when people stare at me. "Let's go to a club!" I blurted.

Judging from the look on Kate's face, I'd already lost sight of the edge of the cliff. She looked at me as if I'd grown fur and an extra set of limbs.

Finn looked over at David with a raise of his eyebrows. "Who knew that unintentional abuse could bring about such sweet rewards?"

I leaned forward, shaking my head, and was about to give the cab driver an address when Finn scribbled something on a piece of paper and handed it up. The driver read what was written on it and nodded with a smirk of approval on his face.

We pulled up in front of an unassuming door with a couple of Greek Gods for bouncers and a line around the block. I sighed audibly. I had neither the time nor the inclination to spend an extra couple of hours waiting in the freezing cold. And I definitely wasn't dressed for it. Finn peeked at the line and smiled at me again.

"Shall we?"

This was turning out to be a colossal mistake. I tried to make eye contact with Kate, but she was already getting out of the cab. I knew that look–like we'd just stepped into Saks. I followed her eyes, but didn't see anything unusual. Just a bunch of freezing cold, well-dressed posers waiting to become yet another sardine in the can. I stood by the curb but didn't want to let go of the door. My instincts told me to just get back in the cab and say goodnight, but then a warm, gentle hand was on the small of my back, leading me toward the sidewalk.

Finn smiled at the Gods and they parted the waters. The ropes were unhooked and we walked through to the warmth of a techno-pop haze. The music was loud but not quite deafening. There was plenty of comfortable seating and the dance floor was spacious. Several bar areas spanned the two floors of converted warehouse and it actually seemed pretty well organized. Still a bar, but almost...civilized.

Suddenly I had a new idea for a piece for The Times. I started scanning the layout, making mental notes and pulling out a pad and pen for good measure. I quickly sketched out a couple of the seating ideas and drew a rough layout of the main floor.

"Hey, what's this place called?" I looked up at Finn, all business, and he started to laugh.

He looked down at my drawing and back at me, puzzled. "Planning a party? Good luck. I heard you've got to book this place a year in advance and the owner's a real hard-ass."

"A party?" I shook my head, frustrated. "No, of course not!" I dismissed him. How absurd. Why would I want to plan a party at a place like this? Dissatisfied, I turned to his friend David. "I need the name of this place."

I followed David's grin and it landed on a matching face to my right. "It's called Finnegan's."

The bulb now fully lit above my head, I proceeded to close my mouth and try to act unimpressed. I nodded in Finn's direction. "Is there any other *dabbling* I should know about? Diamond mines, oil refineries, that kind of thing?"

He looked like a schoolboy—embarrassed almost, although it was hard to tell if he was blushing in the dim light. It was adorable and I found my eyes trailing down to his lips as the one side of his mouth curved up. I blinked, shaking my head and forcing my eyes away from his face.

He laughed softly and hooked a finger under my chin so I'd look at him again. "Can I get you a drink?"

I composed myself quickly. He'd ignored my question about the dabbling, so I moved on. Who knows how many women he'd brought here like this, trying to impress them with his Moses act. He waited patiently for my response.

"Well, I don't know. What's good here? Do they have any specialties?"

Finn watched me with interest. I watched right back. He hesitated, then answered. "As far as I know there's not a drink on the planet they can't make. You name it, they've got it."

"Really! Well, color me happy! Let's see if they can make me my favorite."

I threaded my way through the crowd to the nearest bar. Finn was right on my heels. The bartender was an experienced looking fellow, about twice Finn's age with a sort of blonding gray hair but similar blue eyes that smiled at me before his mouth ever started its ascent. Finn leaned sideways on the bar and watched me, awaiting his victory lap.

I slid effortlessly onto a black leather stool and leaned both arms on the deep, polished mahogany. "Caipirinha please."

The man nodded and pulled out a fresh lime, which he cut into several wedges, adding them to a hefty–sized rocks glass with a couple teaspoons of sugar. After mashing them together for a couple of minutes he pulled the telltale red, black and yellow bottle of 51 Pirassununga from a shelf behind him and poured some out, shaking it with a good dose of ice before pouring it over the fruit mixture.

The way Finn watched me made me feel warm and wanted, invited to participate fully in his experience of life. He was laughing again.

"What's so funny?" I looked around for Kate, but she and David had made their way to one of the dance floors and I was alone with Finn and the two hundred or so other blurs that surrounded his face.

"I don't know. Just didn't peg you for a girl who'd spent time in Rio."

I took a sip of my drink and found it perfect. The slow burn that always followed the sweet, tangy smoothness made its way down my esophagus and somehow landed south of where it belonged. I didn't like where this was going.

The bartender tilted his head slightly as he looked at me. "How is it?"

"Oh! It's great! Thank you!" I started to reach into my purse for a twenty but he shook his head. I looked at him, then at Finn.

"Shall we go find a seat?" A glass of clear liquid had made its appearance on the bar next to Finn and he scooped it up in one fluid motion.

"Ok. Sure." I nodded.

Finn tapped the top of the bar twice and grinned at the bartender. "Thanks, da."

There was that hand on my lower back again. I was beginning to feel like the proverbial sheep being led to slaughter. "Da? Nice, Finn. Nice."

He laughed heartily then. "I thought you'd like that one."

We slid into a comfortable booth. "So this is your dad's place then?"

"It's a joint venture."

"Oh yeah? Who started out smoking the joint?"

Finn laughed out loud. "He provides the money, and I provide the planning and *urban design* that makes it a hit."

I looked around again and remembered the article idea. He'd planned this out? It was really well done. Definitely a hit.

"How long do you make people wait out there in the cold?"

He glanced toward the door. "As long as it takes to keep critical mass but not overwhelm it. People like to know it's popular, but they want to be able to breathe as well."

I hooked my thumb toward the doors. "And that's where Venus and Apollo come in?"

He grinned at me. "Yes. Exactly." His arm was still up on the back of the seat, and I liked that it was above me, even if we weren't touching. His other arm was up too. It wasn't like he was trying to put his arm around me, but I found myself wishing he would. I shook my head again. This was completely absurd. Where was Kate when I needed her? I scanned the dance floor but she was nowhere to be found.

Finn tipped his head sideways and studied me. "Who's winning now?"

I looked over. "What? Winning what?"

"The argument you keep having with yourself."

I sat up a little straighter. "I am. I told you, I always win these arguments. I don't stand a chance against myself."

His eyes narrowed and he took a sip of his drink. "So, how is it you came to be fond of Cachaca? Are you sure you've never been to Brazil?"

"Only in my mind." I took another sip, but he still wasn't tracking with me. "Ever read John Updike?"

He shook his head.

"He wrote a book called *Brazil* back in 1995. Kind of a Tristan and Isolde story line."

"Well, see now? I hadn't pegged you for a romantic either."

Ok, so that made me a boring homebody who watched psychological thrillers?

He took a slow, deep breath in and I watched his chest rise and fall. He was very purposeful when he spoke. "What does the book have to do with Cachaca?"

"I don't know, it was the beverage of choice in the story, so I tried it once and I really liked it. It felt exotic to me, even though in Brazil it's a poor man's drink." I took a long sip of my Caipirinha and this time the burn went to my head.

He watched me with some amount of amused concern. "You know, they say Cachaca is like Tequila in some ways. Too much can cloud your judgment."

I nodded. "So I've heard." Finn wasn't the only one who kept things close to his chest. He didn't need to know my history. I was feeling self-conscious, and more than a little angry with Kate for deserting me.

"I like your shirt."

I shot Finn a look. "Excuse me?"

"Your shirt. It's much better than the other one."

"You mean the ruined one?"

19

His eyes rolled back and his head followed. He did seem genuinely sorry. "Are you certain you won't let me reimburse you for it?"

"Positive."

"Pink. Hmm."

I shook my head. "What is it with you and this shirt thing?"

His head pulled back as if I'd pushed into his personal space. "I just didn't peg you for a pink girl."

It was my turn to raise my eyebrows. I wondered if he knew he was actually going backwards in the point-making game?

"But I like it. It creates this...fascinating contrast." He rolled his hand in a circle as if to frame my head.

I looked down at my shirt. It was pale pink against my winter-white skin, which at this point in my fluorescent light existence was almost translucent.

"I'm sorry, did you say contrast?" I had to raise my voice a bit because the music had ramped up.

Just then David and Kate plopped down, obviously exhausted. She looked over at Finn. "Your friend's a great dancer! I haven't had this much fun in ages!"

Finn smiled and raised his voice to match the increase in volume. "David dances professionally."

It was Kate's turn to be surprised. "Really! Where?"

David shrugged. "Mostly off Broadway. Trying to break in still."

Kate nodded, satisfied. She'd studied at the School of Performing Arts, but never really ventured out past graduation, and hadn't gotten picked up by a dance company. Instead she taught at one of the modern dance studios on the Upper East Side and helped with choreography at the high school in her neighborhood.

"Well, Kate graduated from PA!" I offered with a grin. She kicked me under the table.

"No kidding!" David leaned forward and they ascended into their own little version of dancer's heaven, leaving Finn and I sitting there, staring at one another.

"Can I get you another?" He was staring at my empty glass.

My eyes were already having a little trouble staying focused. I knew I'd lose my cool if I had another and we ended up alone together, but at the time I didn't really care.

"You bet."

"Well, aren't you a brave one?"

"And what is it you're drinking over there? Water?"

"Vodka. And I'll join you in a second round if you don't mind."

I smiled. "I think I'd mind if you didn't."

He was gone in a flash and David followed his lead after getting Kate's order. As soon as they were out of sight, Kate was right in my face.

"What the hell are you drinking?" She picked up my glass and sniffed it. "Oh, no you don't. What are you, crazy? You never order that crap anymore. Don't you remember the last time you drank that poison?"

"Of course I do." I could tell I had a dumb smile on my face already. Kate looked over at the bar. Finn and David were talking to Finn's father. "He is fine. I'll give you that."

As I was watching he looked over at me. Neither of us smiled or made any overt gestures, yet our faces entered into an entire conversation. He just stared and I couldn't break my gaze loose. I couldn't figure out if he was playing me or if I'd somehow entered a parallel universe. Maybe he was right. Maybe he would need to be ensconced in a brilliant narrative someday.

The two of them walked back toward us with drinks in hand, but if I didn't get up and move a bit I'd be sorry when it came time to drink that second round. Before Finn reached the booth I slid out and took the two glasses from his hands, setting them down on the table behind me.

I grabbed his hands, and they were both cold. He must drink his vodka chilled. "Do you dance?"

"Not if I can help it, but I'm willing to embarrass myself if you are."

I pulled him toward the dance floor. "Who said I was going to embarrass myself?"

Before we could weave our way through the crowd the song slowed down and I eyed him suspiciously, scanning the room for the DJ's box. "Did you do that?"

He smiled smugly. "Do what?" In one fluid motion he dropped one of my hands and wrapped his securely around my waist, spinning me toward him until we were face to face. His hand was warm again, surprisingly warm, and I was thankful for whoever dimmed the lights on the dance floor, certain that my cheeks now matched the color of my shirt.

I too had danced much of my life, but the way he moved me around made me feel like an extension of his arms and legs. We flowed easily together, like two rivers into the same ocean.

If this was foreshadowing, I was in for an awfully long fall.

It's important to note here that I wasn't looking for a relationship. At that moment I can honestly say it was pretty close to the farthest thing from my mind. Kate was right. The last time I had Cachaca I'd ended the night with a guy that turned out to be the biggest mistake of my life. Fast-forward two years, including the nine months I spent in therapy, and I was just getting my life back on track. I didn't need a distraction, but then again, I'd forgotten what it felt like to be held by someone who wanted to match his rhythm with mine.

The idea was tempting. The guy was quicksand.

2

"Go to heaven for the climate.
Hell for the company."
M.T.

I pulled out of his arms and took a deep breath. I knew I needed to tell him this wasn't right, but when I looked up he wrapped his hands around my jaw and gently pulled me into his mouth. The falling commenced then, as he released one of his hands to pull my hips back toward his. We moved along with the music and my body ignited, sending sparks in all directions. This was not good. I hadn't even touched that second drink.

I struggled to resurface. It was an epic battle for control, one I hadn't seen the likes of since–well, I'm not sure I've ever had to fight that hard. Control had always come fairly easily–part of the hardwiring that happens when you live like I do.

Finn sensed the hesitation, and stepped back, studying my face. "Let me guess. You want to get out of here?"

I looked up, genuinely surprised. He'd obviously misread my

struggle. I just stood there, blinking. If he thought I was going home with him after one kiss–

He shook his head as if I were clearly mistaken. "No, I mean maybe you'd like to get some air."

I'd assumed his presumption and guessed wrong–something else that hardly ever happened. He didn't wait for my answer, but took my hand and led me up a stairway, under a roped entryway guarded by another of the Mount Olympians and through a door that opened onto a small rooftop atrium. There was just enough room for a couple of chairs and a small table. A dim, yellow-covered globe fixture sat suspended over the doorway, casting a soft light onto the small space.

It was cozy. Private. Exactly what I needed. But, how did he know that?

Finn squeezed my hand gently. "No one will bother you out here. Stay as long as you like." He turned to leave but thought better of it. Taking off his jacket, he draped it around my shoulders.

I felt like a small child and must have looked the part, because he smiled indulgently and then he was gone. The door closed behind him and I blew out a deep breath, dropping into one of the chairs. What the hell was I doing? I wrapped his jacket tightly around my shoulders and tried to sort through the events of the evening. All of my usual arguments crumbled in the face of reality. The guy seemed too good to be true. Maybe *that* was it...he wasn't real.

Or maybe, just maybe, he was the measuring stick against which my life felt pale and drawn. Sure, I had a system. What I didn't have was a clue how deep this rabbit hole might go. That I was, in the space of a few hours, suddenly willing to follow him down it was absolutely terrifying.

~

I SAT with my knees pulled up, looking up at the stars through the soft yellow glow. It was cozy. Private. Exactly what I needed. But, how did *he* know that?

This guy was unraveling my nerves and I couldn't get my bearings. It was like he'd grabbed onto the one snagged thread in my sweater and sent me spinning.

There were some rocks set into a planter on the table. I picked one up and started scratching into the surface of the slate tabletop. Soon I had the rough sketch of a small flower with rounded petals, much like a child might draw.

When I was a kid I used to love picking up rocks or sticks and trying to draw with them. I would hunt for the kind of rocks that would crumble like chalk as I pushed them around on the driveway or the sidewalk. I fancied myself quite the artist, back then. I scribbled with crayons, and painted with those little orange watercolor trays in coloring books with flimsy pages that warped with the drying.

When I discovered words, I started drawing my pictures in story form. I drew pictures with my words through long, hot summers, stormy cold winters, and every argument my parents ever had. I seemed determined to draw my life in pictures.

Stories upon stories. I was in love with story. But who was the hero in this one? Was it me? Or was there a knight that I hadn't seen hiding out along the edges of the forest?

I DON'T KNOW how long I sat there on the roof, but when Finn found me I still had my legs pulled up, completely wrapped in that jacket, staring out into space.

"When I said you should stay as long as you like, I didn't mean until you turned into a Popsicle."

I looked up at him and smiled weakly. "Sorry. Have I been out here long?"

"Come on. Let's get you warm."

He led me inside and through the other door and it led to a comfortable office with a couch, a pillow and a blanket.

"Do you want your coat back?"

He smiled, shaking his head. "Not until you're back to room temperature."

I sat down on the couch. The room was warm but I was still shivering. He grabbed the blanket and held it up behind me. "May I?"

I nodded, and he wrapped the blanket around me *and* the jacket until we were one big lump, then pulled the lump toward him as he leaned back onto the couch. I tucked up my feet and sank in.

"Thanks."

"What kind of gentleman would I be if I let you freeze out there? Besides, we should probably be getting back to Kate and David before they send out a search party."

I nodded in agreement. "Were you waiting in here the whole time?"

He looked up at the desk. "I had a little work to catch up on."

"So, this is your office?"

"Yes."

"And the pillow and blanket? It doesn't double as your apartment, does it?"

He chuckled softly, as if it wasn't exactly an outrageous thought. "No, but on the particularly late nights sometimes I don't feel like going home."

I looked over at the desk. A strange sort of organized chaos existed between the stacks of papers and the filing bins and pencil tins. He could have definitely benefitted from some of my articles.

"Are you all right then?" He looked down his chin at me.

I didn't know how to answer. I wasn't sure an answer existed.

"I'm fine."

"You're quite the debater aren't you? I thought you said you never lose these arguments?"

"Yes well, apparently *hardly ever* might have been more accurate. I haven't lost one in quite a long time."

"I don't know whether to be offended or flattered." He grinned.

I hated the fact that I'd revealed so much after such an insanely short period of time. What was I even doing there? I stood up, breaking out of my cocoon and handing him back the blazer.

"Who said the argument was about you?"

He stood too, but dropped the blazer back onto the couch and took my face in his hands. His kiss was warm and satisfying and I was lost all over again.

"You did." He whispered, reaching his face past my lips and into my ear. On the way back he kissed my neck and I shuddered involuntarily. He had me and he knew it. I was speechless. The music was thumping somewhere in the distance, and when I opened my eyes, his were smiling back at me. He picked up his jacket and slipped it back on. "Shall we go find David and Kate then?"

I tried to swallow, my mouth searching for that second drink. "Yeah. Definitely."

We walked out into the heat of the haze and I had to readjust my thinking. Kate and David were on the dance floor just below us and she caught my eye as I came down the steps. She whispered something in David's ear and the two of them made a beeline straight for us, but she grabbed onto my hands and started pulling me along behind her, apologizing to Finn on her way by.

We pushed our way through the mob toward one of the bathrooms and Kate locked the door behind us, trapping me in there with her. She was all kinds of wobbly, and slurring badly.

"Hey...so...you...weren't supposed to disappear like that." Her fingernail was dangerously close to my eyelid.

I pulled my head back slightly. "Hey, so...how many Kamikazes have you had Kate?"

"*Me?!* You're the one drinking poison!" She stumbled back against the stall door.

"I've had one drink Kate, and that was a while ago. I'm perfectly fine. You, on the other hand, are almost ready for bed."

"I know, right? Is it that obvious? Man, that boy can *move!*" She moved her hips in repeating circles, not that I needed the visual.

"David?"

"Yes, David! Who did you think I was talking about?"

I ignored her question. It was late, and I was in no mood. The two debaters in my head had caused a bloody war that was threatening its way toward my heart, and there was no way that was happening. Not on a first date. Not again. I don't know how I let myself get so caught up - and after only one drink! I guess it took getting out of his immediate atmosphere to realize it, but there in the bathroom stall it became crystal clear.

"Kate I have to go."

"What? You can't leave now! Where were you, anyway? Did you *sleep* with him?"

"No, of course not! I was gone for like, five minutes."

Kate blinked a few times and up came the fingernail. "I may be ahead of you on the drinks, but you've been gone for at least an hour."

I scoffed at her and pulled out my phone. She was right, of course. I'd left her alone with a new guy for longer than thirty minutes, which was a breach of our standard agreement. She had a right to be mad, but I just couldn't stay.

"He got to you, didn't he?" Kate was straightening her shirt and tucking herself up in preparation for reentry.

"Kate, don't be ridiculous."

"Look at me." She pulled at my face. "*Look* at me!"

I can bullshit the whole world except for Kate. When I finally looked at her she smiled sadly. "Ok. Let's get you out of here."

"What about David?"

She waved her hand at me. "I'll give him my number. Absence makes the heart grow fonder, right?"

"I didn't think it was his heart you were after." I winked as she turned to let us out of the bathroom.

"It's not. But with any luck a little hard-to-get will make his other parts grow fonder too." She stopped with the door half open. "So what are we going to tell them?"

"How about the truth?"

"Oh man. This is worse than I thought!" Kate laughed. "Why don't you let me do the talking?"

"Maybe because you're slurring?"

She punched at my arm and missed. I love Kate.

When we got back to the table the two of them were sitting there much like they looked when we were getting into the cab earlier. Not really expectant, just kind of mellow and almost... natural. It was so surreal, like the four of us had been performing this routine together for years.

I think that's the part that threw me the most–the total lack of expectation that bordered on apathy. Neither one of them seemed in a hurry to jump in the sack, and that could only mean one of two things: either they were getting it plenty regular as it was, and it really didn't matter to them, or... it really didn't matter to them. I was banking on the former, because the latter seemed utterly ridiculous.

As soon as we got to the table, the music slowed down again and David pulled Kate toward the dance floor. Her protests were quickly hushed by something he whispered in her ear. So much for her doing the talking.

"Nice timing. Your handiwork again?" I nodded upward, referring to the change in tempo.

Finn just shook his head and stared at me. He patted the spot next to him in the booth and said simply "Why don't we sit this one out?" He never took his eyes off me.

My heart dropped into the pit of my stomach and strange tears threatened at the corners of my eyes. Once again I found myself fighting for control, but he didn't say a word. He just waited for me to talk.

Finally, I couldn't stand the silence. "Finn I..."

He sighed and looked down at the table, as if he'd lost some sort of bet with himself.

"...Appreciate the drink, but really have to get going?" He was fiddling with his glass, waiting for my reply. When I couldn't form the words he looked up. "It's written all over your face. You're terrified."

I swallowed hard.

"I thought we were getting on fairly well?"

"You don't understand."

"No, I'm fairly certain you're the one who's confused." He said quietly.

I felt the color creep up my neck. For a writer, I wasn't very good at coming up with the right words at the right time. "I just wasn't expecting...this. I wasn't ready for this. I'm not—ready for this." I sounded like an idiot and I knew it.

Finn put his elbows up on the table and leaned in close. "Look, it wasn't like I tossed my drink all over your shirt on purpose, but something happened here tonight and I don't think we can ignore that. I don't think I *want* to ignore it. Now if you do, then I'll be the gentleman and step away, but I think you're making a big mistake."

He was dangerously close to kissing me again. I watched his eyes travel there and back, but he kept his distance steady. "I'd like to see you again." He slid a business card toward me. "But it's going to have to be your call."

The card had been in his hand the whole time. *How could he have known that I was going to...?* I just sat there, the watered down Caipirinha still sitting on the table between us.

I looked down at the glass. "I don't suppose you've slipped a roofie in there and I'll wake up tomorrow with no memory of the next few hours?"

"A what?" He looked puzzled. It was perfectly, annoyingly adorable. This hole was so, so much bigger than I thought.

"Never mind." I picked up the glass and downed the entire thing. When I looked up at Finn he had a sort of hopeful smile on his face and I had to laugh out loud. I pocketed the business card and slid a little closer to him. "Thanks for ruining my shirt." I leaned over to kiss his cheek and he met me there in the middle instead. Sweet and soft, my lime mixed with his Vodka in an unforgettable mélange.

I couldn't have written a better exit scene, so I shimmied my way out of the booth and stood up. I didn't dare open my mouth again, so I simply smiled and turned around. Kate ran over to me as I was leaving and grabbed my arm. No sense mincing words. I just gave it to her straight.

"I'm going home. I'm going to bed. I don't want to talk, and I don't want company, so if you want to stay, stay. Have a blast! Call me in the morning." I was still walking toward the door and she was trying to pull me back.

She looked over her shoulder at David, who was still waiting on the dance floor. Finn had already disappeared from our booth. "Are you sure?"

"Positive. Have fun." I kissed Kate on the cheek. "Call me tomorrow."

She grinned and hugged me. "I will. Thanks!"

It never took much encouragement for Kate, and she and David seemed fairly well matched. Why should my stupidity cost her a good time? She was gone before I'd finished waving her off. I shook my head, smiling in spite of myself, and made my way toward the door. Time to let another frozen soul take my place in the fire. Maybe Finn would have better luck with one of them. He'd certainly be better off, he just didn't know that yet.

I was unprepared for the cold wind that hit my face as I walked outside, but no sooner had I slipped into my jacket than one of the bouncers was touching my shoulder and pointing me toward a warm, waiting cab.

"For me? You shouldn't have."

"I didn't." He opened the door for me and I ducked down onto the seat. He stuck his head in after me. "The driver will wait till you get inside."

"He'll what? What are you talking about?" Adonis closed the

door on my question and tapped the top of the cab twice. As we drove away I saw Finn standing in the shadow of the building, watching, hands stuffed in his pockets.

I should have known better than to slam that second drink, but it was a necessary kind of numb. Besides, I felt strangely sober. The swimming in my head had considerably less to do with Cachaca than this puzzle of a man who would stand in the shadows and yet see me home safely.

The passion was still there, lingering. I could feel it like an ember in my belly. Finn had blown on it–stirred the ashes, and it was growing warmer by the minute. He was right, of course. I was terrified. Unfortunately, mixing fear with passion is often what drives me forward–usually right over the cliff and toward certain death.

But oh, what a sweet death it would be...

3

"It usually takes me more than three weeks
to prepare a good impromptu speech."
-M.T.

I'm not an expert at a lot of things, but there are a couple of areas where I totally excel—like organization. And avoidance.

I'm the kind of person who prefers simple, logical, preferably painless solutions to a problem, and Finn was definitely a problem. I figured if I could put enough focus on something else, it would squeeze out all the extra space in my heart and mind, leaving no room for a new relationship.

It seemed like a perfectly brilliant plan when my subconscious conceived it. Once I thought it through of course, I realized it made no sense at all. By then it was too late.

I spent those first few days after we met focused one hundred percent on my writing. I almost had myself convinced that there was no Finn–that the man standing in the shadows was merely an apparition–a reflection of my lack. The antithesis of my need for control.

The Times called and offered me a biweekly column on a three-month trial, so I started writing and I didn't stop for nearly forty-eight hours straight. I stayed holed up in my apartment eating Nutty Bars and bad take out, drinking vitamin water and vats of coffee, sleeping on my keyboard and on my couch and waking up constantly from strange dreams, with words drowning in my head, begging to be rescued from the depths. I couldn't write fast enough.

I was writing article specs, special interest pieces; I even worked on my novel with renewed vigor. Of course, just as Finn predicted, a new character showed up in my fiction: a mysterious foreigner with a chivalrous heart.

It was bad.

It was worse than bad. It was pathetic.

By the third day when Kate knocked on my door, I still hadn't showered and I must have scared her pretty good, because she started snapping pictures on her cell phone and pushing me toward the bathroom.

She sniffed at me. "Have you been drinking?"

I just stared at her. "What? No! Of course not!"

"Oh my God. Oh. My. God! Look at you!"

"What is your problem? And why are you taking pictures?"

Her eyes were huge. "What are you *wearing*?"

I looked down at my favorite sweats and moccasins. "I'm comfortable."

"You look homeless."

"I'm writing."

This stopped the clicking of her phone's camera, at least temporarily. "You're writing? Really?"

"Yes. Really. And I'm on a roll, so don't...*judge* me."

"Ok ok. I won't judge, but answer me one question: When's the last time you left the apartment?"

"It's cold out."

Her head tilted in disbelief. "Just answer the question!"

I didn't. Answer, that is.

34

"You *have* been out since the other night." She looked toward my kitchen area. The dirty dishes betrayed me. Another photo was snapped.

"Hey! Stop that!" I tried to swipe her camera but she pulled her arm away just in time.

"Just...go take a shower. We're going to dinner."

"I already ate."

"Yeah. I can see that." She shut me in the bathroom. "Chinese, Pizza, Mexican...Any other take-out genres I've missed?"

I turned on the shower. "Don't forget Nutty Bars!"

I could hear her crinkling wrappers on the other side of the door. "Right. How could I forget? Some organizational guru you are! Look at this place! It's like a *bomb* went off in here."

The shower did feel pretty amazing. Through the warm rain I could hear Kate banging around my apartment. I couldn't make out what she was saying, but she seemed really pissed off, so I decided to take my time.

When I finally emerged in my towel she was sitting on my couch eating a Nutty Bar. She'd cleaned up a bit and it did feel a lot better in there.

"They're good, right?"

She just stared at me. "Well, at least you don't *look* like a hermit anymore."

"I'm not a hermit! Don't be ridiculous!"

"Have you even seen another human since..." She picked up the jeans that I'd been wearing the night of the Yankees game. "Since we went *out* the other night? Jesus Truly!"

When she lifted my jeans a card fell out of the pocket. Finn's card. I stopped toweling my hair.

There was a moment of awkward silence and I swear I saw an actual light bulb turn on above her head before she looked up. "Has he called you?"

"No."

"Have you called him?"

I shook my head.

"Why not?"

I resumed my toweling. "Come on. You know better than to ask me that."

Kate was turning the card over in her fingers. "I mean, I'm sorry...I knew you were upset the other night, but Truly, he was perfect! What *happened*?"

I ducked into my room for a bra and some underwear, and then came back for the jeans. I could say they were my only clean pair, but that would be a lie. Suddenly I just wanted to be wearing them again.

I told you it was pathetic.

I picked up the pink top – also still crumpled in the spot I'd left it, and walked it into the bedroom laundry. I tried smelling it, but there was no hint of him. I don't think he was wearing cologne that night, yet I vividly remembered how he smelled. Warm and clean and somehow soft, but not like *Downy-soft*. His softness came from someplace else. Someplace I'd never been.

And frankly, it still scared the hell out of me.

No amount of take-out food was going to get me over that hurdle, and I knew it. I was just procrastinating, which is something I absolutely disdain in the rest of my life, yet have a special knack for when it comes to relationships. My therapist says there's a link there – a thread that needs to be pulled on. I say leave the poor thread alone.

I tossed the shirt and picked out a black sweater, then headed back to the bathroom for a couple of hair tricks. I was going to skip the makeup until I saw my face in the mirror and realized I looked like my mother when she was going through chemo–kind of pasty and swollen. Kate was right. I did look like a hermit. I did my best with a quick coating of tinted moisturizer, a little blush, mascara and some lip-gloss, but it was no use. I sighed. Maybe we could pick a restaurant with mood lighting.

"So? Where do you want to eat?"

When I came back out again Kate was paging through The Times. "I don't know. I'm not really hungry anymore. I just ate that

Nutty Bar." She peeked out from behind the newspaper, grinning. Kate was a good egg.

"Hey. Don't knock Little Debbie. We have a special kind of relationship."

"Yeah, but you can't keep running to Little Debbie every time you get scared. You'll end up big and fat." Her face twisted into a pathetic mess. "And *lonely*."

I grabbed her arm and pulled her up off my couch. "How could I possibly be lonely with friends like you around, hmm? Come on, we're out of here!"

I reached into my pocket and fingered the card. High noon was fast approaching. I could feel it in my bones. And after that? Taps.

I'd probably be better off marrying my therapist.

4

_____

"Sanity and happiness
are an impossible combination."
M.T.

After my mom died, things got a little rough. My dad couldn't really handle it–and by 'it' I mean my little sister and me. I was thirteen when mom got sick, fourteen when she died. My sister was only twelve, but in Queens, twelve is more like twenty, and fourteen might as well be thirty. For about a year mom was in and out of the hospital and it was just Jenny and me after school every day.

At first she tried to be good, helping me as much as she could to make dinners and wash dad's work shirts, but we had to take her off laundry duty when she turned all dad's light blue, embroidered shirts a speckled kind of pink. It was like a stain he wore every day–a stain that told everyone down at the shop just how bad it had gotten at home. I tried to get those stains out but I didn't know how, and we couldn't afford to buy him all new shirts, so there was nothing to be done. Never mind that Jenny's dance uniform got ruined in the same load. We couldn't replace that either. With mom not working we were barely making it.

IT WASN'T the cancer that killed her in the end. She developed some weird kind of clotting reaction that caused her to bleed out of every pore and orifice she had. It was fairly disgusting, not to mention frightening. They did everything they could to reverse it, pouring blood and fluids back into her just as fast as she was losing it, but it didn't seem to matter. She got weaker and weaker, and one afternoon as I was sitting there in the hospital room, trying to work on my Algebra, she just slipped away. No fanfare, no big crash-cart scene like on TV... the line just went flat and the nurses ran in, but she'd signed some kind of order not to do anything heroic if her heart stopped, so they just stood there looking as stupid as I felt. Jenny was at dance class when it happened.

After mom died the shirts made it even worse. I know it sounds silly, but intense experiences create weird triggers, and I swear it was like her faded blood was splattered all over him. I could barely stand the sight of him coming home from work.

That Christmas I saved up all my babysitting money and went down to the shop when dad wasn't there. Jimmy ordered a new shirt for him and promised not to tell. When dad opened my gift we exchanged a look that told me how grateful he was. He smiled for the first time in months.

Jenny stormed up to her room and slammed the door. It was a normal kind of kid mistake that shouldn't have been such a big deal, but mistakes are harder to deal with when you have to look at them in the mirror every single day.

She quit dancing and started hanging out with some girls in the neighborhood that didn't have the best reputation. I tried to talk to her, but she stayed out too late on school nights and dad was too exhausted to care much. Most of the time I lied for her, saying she was at the library or a friend's house. I kept hoping she'd turn it around, but it was all I could handle trying to keep house and keep buying groceries and keep from failing school.

I guess that's when I started to get good at organizing things. I made charts for Jenny and I so we could get all the chores done. I created a budget and tried my best to stick to it, spending my weekends going to the different stores that were advertising specials to save money on the essentials. It felt better somehow, keeping things in order, like everything I was doing kept what was left of us from falling apart. Most importantly, it gave me a purpose when I really needed one.

Dad's depression only deepened. The more I took care of things the less he tried. He worked late nights at the shop and Saturdays too, trying to cover the hospital bills, but it was never enough. He came home every night around eight o'clock, drank a couple of beers, sat in his chair for an hour with the TV on, ate something I warmed up, and then went to bed. On Sundays he slept a lot and drank more beers than usual, but otherwise it was the same routine.

When Jenny was sixteen she started going out with the head of one of the gangs in our neighborhood. He was my age, two years older than her, and I tried to warn her off of him, but by then she'd stopped listening to me altogether. We were like opposite poles of a magnet, pulling our lives in completely different directions. Looking back now, I really wish I'd tried harder with Jenny, but I was just a kid. At the time I was too busy studying and applying to colleges to notice just how bad it had gotten. I guess dad and I had the same problem, we just chose different methods of dealing with it.

The great part about being from a single-parent household with a good sob story is that you qualify for a ton of financial aid. I'd somehow found a way to squeeze in work for the student newspaper and my grades were holding steady in the low nineties. I killed it on the SATs so my future was looking pretty hopeful as far as college was concerned.

Then one night in May, three weeks before graduation, Jenny

came stumbling through the front door. I figured she was high and told her to head up to bed before dad got home and saw her like that. She was holding her stomach.

"Are you sick?"

She didn't answer me.

"Jenny what's wrong? Didn't you hear me? You'd better get up to bed."

When she looked up at me she was deathly pale. She unwrapped her hands from her middle and they were covered in blood. I jumped up from my chair, spewing books all over the place and just barely caught her before she hit the ground. Her shirt pulled up as she fell, revealing a gushing knife wound under the right side of her ribs.

"Oh my God! Jenny what happened?"

She had a glazed look on her face and I grabbed the phone to dial 911. I tried not to panic and did what they told me, putting a pillow under her legs and covering her with a blanket while we waited for the ambulance.

"Carlos said not to worry, that they wouldn't dare hurt his girl." She mumbled. "They did it anyway. They jumped me and then left me for dead. He doesn't know yet Truly. You have to tell him. He'll have to answer for this. He'll have to pay them back."

"You're kidding me, right? You're bleeding to death and you're worried about Carlos? What's wrong with you?"

"But I love him,Truly. And he loves me."

"That's not love Jenny." I stroked her hair back and kissed her forehead. "That's not love."

I held her head in my arms and rocked like that for five eternal minutes until the windows reflected the spinning red and blue lights that I hoped would rescue me from the nightmare I was caught in. She was slipping away from me too. Just like that.

The paramedics came through the still open door and got right to work, asking me questions while they assessed her condition. When they saw how much blood she was losing, they scooped her up and got her right on a gurney, using words like "shock" and "liver laceration".

She was unconscious by the time we got into the ambulance. I tried to call my dad at the shop but Jimmy said he was welding a frame and he'd have to call me back. I gave Jimmy the name of the hospital they were taking us to and told him something terrible had happened to Jenny.

I sat in the front seat of the ambulance next to the driver while a man and a woman worked on Jenny. One was on the radio with the hospital telling them to prepare the trauma team, while the other was sticking an IV in her arm. She didn't make a sound, and Jenny hated needles. I looked down at my hands, covered in blood.

"Miss?"

I was rocking again.

"Miss? Hey, is there someone we can call for you?"

Was there anyone? It was a valid question. There was dad, and there was Jenny. I had a few friends at school but I hardly ever went out. My best friends were my books and my writing. Dad's parents were both dead and mom's parents lived in Missouri. I didn't even have aunts or uncles close by. It had always been just us.

Somewhere in the distance the ambulance driver was still talking to me. I shook my head. "I called my dad at work. He'll probably meet me at the hospital."

"What about your mom?"

"She's dead." I swallowed. It had been a while since I'd said it. Understood it. Felt it in the place where a person was supposed to feel a thing like that.

"Oh." He managed. "I'm sorry."

"So am I." I put my head on the window and watched the houses speed past.

Then all of a sudden, Jenny just stopped. Her heart stopped. Her breathing stopped. She just... stopped. It sent the two paramedics in the back into a panic. The ambulance sped up, but I knew somewhere in my heart that we weren't going to make it to the hospital in time, and even if we could it wouldn't matter. She was gone. Gone to be with mom. It was like Jenny just up and walked out of that ambulance, but left her body laying on the gurney. I knew it as truth and yet I couldn't connect it to a feeling, just numbness covering over everything else. Even after we pulled up to the hospital life went past in a slow-motion blur.

Jenny died that night in May. We buried her next to mom. It seemed only right. I handled all the arrangements. Dad barely spoke the whole summer. I tried to organize things as best I could so he could manage ok when I left for NYU, but by then he'd lost all three of us, one by one. Part of me wanted to stick around and just keep taking care of him, but when it came right down to it I just couldn't live in that tomb of a house with its bloodstained memories. I tried to convince dad to move to a smaller place with less bedrooms and no grass to cut. He said he'd think about it.

I was hoping that maybe when I left he'd come back to life. Maybe when the grass got so long that neighbors complained he'd step out into the sunshine once in a while. Then again, maybe I was kidding myself. You just don't recover from a series of losses like that. It's not like the chicken pox where one by one all the spots go away and never come back. It's more like tuberculosis, the bacteria brooding even in its dormancy, waiting for your weakness and scheming at ways to overpower your defenses and steal your breath away.

Till death do you part.

5

"Dance like nobody's watching.
Love like you've never been hurt.
Sing like nobody's listening.
Live like it's heaven on earth."
M.T.

K ate waited until we were about halfway through dinner before she mentioned that she was meeting David at a club afterward.

"Which club?"

She kept forking the salad around her plate and wouldn't look at me. "Finn's club."

I sucked in a deep breath and let it out slowly, just like my Bikram teacher had taught me. "Do you think he'll be there?"

She nodded as she looked up. "Probably. Why?"

"Because I think I'd like to come with you."

Kate's smile widened with her obvious approval at my having grown a small pair. "Ok then!"

"Ok then." I picked up the bottle and poured myself some more wine.

Kate lifted her glass to toast me. "To new beginnings." Our glasses clinked midair. She took a sip and I downed what was left of my portion and quickly refilled.

"You know Truly, it doesn't have to be that way."

"What way?" I asked between sips.

"The way it was before, with Christopher."

When she said his name my stomach turned to rock. I swallowed with some difficulty, willing back the torrent of black hatred that attempted to breach my carefully constructed walls. I could see his face, his near perfect features melting into control, anger and manipulation. I could see a mirror image of myself looking ghostly and thin and then Kate shook my hand.

"Hey! Leave that alone. That's over, Truly. Look at me!"

The acid in my stomach curled its way up into my throat, but I did what I was told.

"You're not that girl anymore, and Finn is *not* Christopher."

"I know that! Do you think I don't know that?"

Kate ignored my belligerence. "David says he's an amazing guy. Apparently they've been friends for a while. He says Finn is gentle and genuine, and..."

"You didn't tell David about–"

"No, of course not! But he did say Finn hasn't been himself since the other night."

Well, that made two of us.

After dinner we got a cab to the club and stepped out to find the bouncers still remembered their Moses act. Kate smiled at them as we passed through the ropes and I watched both of them check her out. Occupational hazard, I suppose. Kate was quite the looker with that long blond hair and dancer's legs.

I took a deep breath and walked through the door. There must have been a magnet attached to Finn's head because I locked onto his position without too much trouble. He was talking to some of the wait staff over in one corner, but he didn't see me and I was fine with that.

"I'll see you later Kate."

She looked shocked. "Really?"

"Yeah, I got this."

She squeezed my hand. "Ok. If you're sure."

She spotted David and left me standing there, so I decided to head to the bar.

Finn's dad turned around as I slid onto the stool. His whole face smiled at me this time. "Well, aren't you a sight for sore eyes!"

Ok I'll bite. "How so?"

He got out a rocks glass and started cutting limes. "Maybe me boyo over there won't be so gloomy now." He laughed heartily.

He'd been gloomy? I peeked out over my shoulder. He was still talking to the wait staff and hadn't noticed me yet. I looked up at Finn's dad. "I think I'd like to sit for a minute if you don't mind."

He finished making the drink and handed me the glass. "I won't be giving you away, but he's bound to notice ye sooner or later. I noticed as soon as you walked in."

"You did?"

He nodded. "Course I did darlin'. What do you take me for?"

The accent was thick but the innuendo was thicker. I couldn't quite figure out what he was getting at. After my first shower in three days I'd let my hair fall loose around my shoulders and the curls that wouldn't be tamed were in full swing given the dampness of the weather. With near colorless skin against the almost black of my hair, I looked more like a vampire than usual.

He studied me with open curiosity. "You don't have any idea, do you?"

"About what?"

"How beautiful y'are." His smile was kind, genuine.

"Me? Please." I took a large sip of my drink trying to drown the compliment.

He put his hand on mine and waited for me to look up. "You're going to have to get over that."

"Get over what?"

That's when I felt it. Like radiation boring into the back of me. My shoulders got hot, and it ran down the length of my spine until the hair on the back of my neck stood up. It was like being in the middle of an electric storm. I looked down at my hand where Finn's father was touching me and then back up to meet his eyes. "He's standing behind me, isn't he?"

He gave my hand a quick squeeze and winked before walking away. I took a deep breath and turned to find the source of the laser beam smiling at me with those warm eyes and one side of his mouth hooked up, just like I remembered it.

"Hi" I managed.

He nodded, then looked down at my drink, then looked me over as if he was making sure I was all in one piece. Satisfied, he stepped closer. "May I sit down?"

I smiled back. I couldn't help it. "Sure."

It was awkward for just a moment as he sat there straightening the napkins and condiments on the bar. "I'm glad you're here." He looked up at me. "I was wondering if you'd call."

"Yeah. Me too."

He dropped his head in obvious defeat.

"I don't mean it that way. I just mean...I'm having a hard time." I took a long drink.

"I understand." Finn nodded. That was it. Two simple words that contained whole paragraphs of explanation. Apparently he didn't feel the need to placate me, nor did he seem overly anxious to defend himself which, to be honest, is what I expect from most guys.

Somehow I knew that he really did understand me, although it didn't make a lick of sense. There was no possible way that could be true, and yet I felt comfortable and slightly off my guard, which is a dangerous place to be if you're me. I found myself wanting to reach out and fall into his arms on the dance floor, or lean into him on the couch in his office–to somehow relive the parts of the other night where we connected physically.

"What do you say we get out of here then?"

I looked at him with wide eyes. Had he been reading my mind? It was spooky. He looked back at me with an innocence that betrayed my suspicions.

"It's hard to think and talk properly with all this noise. How about a bite to eat?"

Eat? My mind was in the gutter and he was talking about sharing a meal. How had this strange role reversal happened? I shook my head. "Kate and I just ate."

"Oh. Right. Well then..."

"Dessert?" I grinned.

"Brilliant."

I smiled. "Do you mind if I pick the place?"

"Not at all."

"Ever had chocolate by the bald man?"

"What's that?"

"C'mon." I grabbed his hand and started pulling him toward the door.

The same electricity that spanned the gap between our hands arced when we touched. It was the second time in as many meetings that I'd gone from paralyzing fear to impulsive suggestion in a matter of seconds. Finn and I were walking out the door of the club before I remembered to say goodbye to Kate.

I hugged her and nodded toward Finn. "We're going to get some dessert!" I had to yell above the music.

She looked Finn up and down then raised her eyebrows at me. "Have some for me too!"

I shook my head and laughed. Talk about a mind in the gutter. "I'll call you."

"You'd better!"

Kate went back to dancing and Finn and I left. Outside we caught a cab to Union Square.

"So, I'll ask you again. Do you like chocolate?" I asked hopefully.

"Sure." He nodded.

My eyebrows went up. "Sure? That's all you got? 'Sure'? You've obviously never been to chocolate heaven."

He just shrugged. "Helps me keep my girlish figure."

I flashed back to ninety-seven pounds. I'd worked hard to get above a hundred and ten, and for the most part I didn't think about my weight at all anymore. It was like when Christopher vanished, so did the stress that kept me from eating.

I'd always been a stress puke-er, so that part couldn't really be helped. It wasn't like I tried to make myself throw up. I just worried and it happened.

Mom used to tell me stories about when I was a baby. Apparently I'd cry until I projectile vomited. Then as a toddler I threw temper tantrums and frequently ended the kicking and screaming session with a lovely Technicolor yawn.

By elementary school I could throw up nearly at will. If I had a big test coming up, I'd hurl. If I got in a fight with the popular kids, I spent the afternoon in the nurse's office. I had to run out of the church during both funerals. I even threw up when I found out I got into NYU.

Somehow chocolate was a completely different animal. Chocolate was like Tums. It soothed and settled my stomach. It even calmed my nerves. Don't ask me, I don't make the magic.

I eyed Finn suspiciously. "Well, I could eat chocolate for breakfast, lunch *and* dinner, and at Max's you can do just that."

"Dinner?" Finn looked more than confused.

I was incredulous. "Don't you date?"

"Excuse me?"

"Nothing." I shook my head. "It's just the quintessential date place."

He didn't answer with anything but a nod. I figured he'd come back with *something*, but he was comfortable in the silence—much more so than I.

"You do...date, don't you?"

I'm not sure what I was fishing for, but he wasn't biting. Of course he dated. Everyone dates. What was he supposed to say?

Yes would leave me wondering how many and how often, and *no* left me with weird questions about celibacy and sexual orientation. There was no good answer to a question like that, which means it probably shouldn't have been asked in the first place. Embarrassed, I looked down.

He put his hand over mine and it felt warm and safe. When I looked up, again there were no words, just his eyes, searching my heart, pulling out the fear strand by strand. Finally he spoke.

"I'm glad you're here."

That was it. No other explanation. He'd avoided the question completely and yet answered it entirely. I keep telling you, he's a puzzle, and I couldn't put two edge pieces together to save my life.

I think that's what did it actually–the thing that threw me under the bus and caused me to come unglued and unguarded. Every experience with this guy ran counter to everything I knew to be true about men. I could not for the life of me figure him out, and I needed desperately to know why.

Then he leaned toward me and kissed me on the lips, the gentleness of his touch somehow holding back a tsunami of sensation. "Really, really glad."

I watched him reign in his emotions, and a muscle twitched in his jaw as he held his face there and whispered "Something tells me Max isn't going to be able to top that."

The cab driver was oblivious. I guess he'd seen worse. Finn paid the man and we got out. It may have been night time, but the lights of Union Square made it seem bright and vibrant.

"You're blushing." He smiled as he opened the door for me.

"I know. I'm sorry." I shook my head, getting out.

He moved some of the hair off my neck and kissed it in one smooth motion. "Don't be." There was that involuntary shudder again.

6

"When angry, count to four.
When very angry, swear."
M.T.

I t had been at least a year and a half since I'd been with anyone, and normally it didn't bother me too much. In my case, 'out of sight, out of mind' usually worked fairly well. Being around Finn, however, brought it painfully to my attention, like an unnamed ache in places that couldn't actually be touched. Some people say chocolate is an aphrodisiac. Too bad we hadn't had any yet.

We didn't have to wait too long for a table, and in the noise of the waiting area we made small talk. I learned that he'd spent his early years mostly in Ireland, but went to high school in England. He traveled back and forth during summers and on breaks, often staying with his mother's family in the hill country outside of London, where he'd spent all of his free time "out of doors" as he called it, fishing and hunting and riding horses. I immediately pictured Mr. Darcy, then rolled my eyes at my own foolishness.

There are downsides to the constant devouring of novels. Everyone you meet somehow compares to a character you've read.

At the table we tried to decide what to order. The waiter suggested we start with drinks.

Finn looked up from the menu. "It seems you have something called a Brazilian Mocha Martini. I'll try that." He looked over at me. "In honor of the lady, who seems to fancy both Brazil *and* chocolate."

"Make it two." I added confidently. Even if he didn't date much, he definitely knew *how*.

The place was jammed. We sat there packed in like pickles in a jar. It was hardly the place for a romantic conversation, so we sipped our water and ordered the chocolate fondue for two. It's a fun thing to eat on a date, what with all the sharing and tasting going on.

"So, how long have you lived here? In New York?" I grilled him as if I were writing a piece about him for The Times.

"Almost three years. I go back and visit regularly though. Mum still lives in England and I've a sister in Ireland."

"She what? Are they divorced?" I was genuinely surprised. "Your dad seems like such a good guy."

"He is. Dad's great–very easygoing." Finn shook his head. "She just prefers the country, and she's not terribly fond of America either. Dad wanted to live his dream and open a club in New York City and she wanted to stay in England. So she did."

"I see." I didn't really, but I wasn't going to tell him that. Separate countries? Really? That was worse than twin beds in the master.

"I don't recommend it though."

"What's that?"

"Separate lives." He looked sad for a moment, as if the pain of separation had wounded his little boy heart.

My observations were interrupted by the waiter, who brought us our martinis. I sighed contentedly when he set them down.

What can I say? Chocolate makes me very, *very* happy. And this was one high class Nutty Bar.

I held up my glass, waiting for him to share the toast. "This, my friend, is a perfect blend of vanilla vodka, Frangelico, espresso and chocolate cream. Prepare to be impressed."

He started to open his mouth but whatever it was, he thought better of it.

Our glasses clinked and I took my first taste. The creamy, smooth liquid slid down my throat and lit a beautiful warm fire on the way down. I closed my eyes and smiled as I let my mouth experience all the nuances of flavor that worked their way through my palette. "Oh my God. That's amazing."

When I opened my eyes, Finn was still holding his glass in midair, thoroughly entertained. "That is one powerful drink."

I scoffed. "You haven't tasted it yet!"

He leaned forward slightly. "And yet, I think I'm aroused." He laughed good-naturedly, picking up the drink menu and pretending to peruse it. "See? It lists them right here. Cocktails and Chocolate Aphrodisiacs."

"Yes, well...that's only if you actually drink it."

He took a deep breath and smiled. "This could push me right over the edge. You're taking a big chance here."

I rolled my hand in circles. "C'mon c'mon."

He did as I asked, and a grin spread immediately across his face. "It's very good."

"Good? That's the only adjective that comes to your mind?"

"I believe I said *very* good."

I sat shaking my head, trying to understand what it was about him that drew me so intensely. "Do you mind if I ask you how old you are?"

"Not at all." He grinned. "I'm twenty-eight. And you?"

"Twenty-five."

"And your birthday?"

"Pardon?"

"Your birthday. When is it?"

This interview was making my mouth dry. I sipped my martini and was saved once again by the waiter, who set the fondue between us on the tiny table. The chocolate pot was followed by a plate filled with bananas, strawberries, marshmallows and sponge cake. "Heaven. I've arrived in heaven and there's chocolate, just like I knew there would be."

He was still smiling. Still watching me. It was starting to make me self conscious. "Could you please stop that?"

"Stop what?"

"Staring at me like that. Do I have chocolate in my teeth or something?"

He shook his head and purposefully refocused on the forks, choosing a strawberry over a straight answer, and dipping it in the molten magic of the fondue bowl before taking a bite. "Now *that's* lovely."

Ok, lovely was a little more descriptive than *very good*. We were definitely getting somewhere.

"May twentieth." I followed his lead and dipped a strawberry. "Oh my God. That's incredible." I leaned back and covered my mouth, on the off chance that I really did have chocolate in my teeth.

He tried the sponge cake next and nodded happily. "Brilliant."

I smiled, satisfied. "Now that's more like it."

"You know, neither the Irish nor the Brits are known for their culinary exploits. We're more of a war and peace, mysticism and cynicism kind of culture. While I appreciate a good meal, I'm afraid your love affair with chocolate may be lost on the likes of me."

"Who said it was a love affair?"

"Would you like me to film your next sip?" He pulled out his phone. "I can prove it to you."

I shook my head in defeat. "That's all right. I'll take your word for it."

He propped his arms up on the table while biting into another strawberry. "So tell me, what's your favorite thing to do, in celebration of your birthday?"

The question was innocent enough.

I froze.

I didn't celebrate my birthday. Ever.

Dad never remembered, and I'd just as soon forget. Jenny died about a week before my birthday, and we held the funeral the day before I turned eighteen. I didn't feel much like celebrating that day, nor any day since, really.

"I'm sorry. Did I say something wrong?"

My eyes darted around as I tried to think of something to say. I shook my head.

Finn's eyes narrowed slightly.

"I'm not much of a birthday person." I announced. "I need to use the bathroom."

He stood as I got up, still looking perplexed.

By the time I got to the ladies room I was sweating. It seemed abnormally warm in there. Perhaps it was because we'd been seated upstairs. After losing my chocolate fondue, I splashed a little water on my face and used the facilities. I put on a little lip-gloss and popped a mint into my mouth. When I got back to the table Finn looked relaxed enough but stood to get my chair and seated me again.

"Are you alright?"

"I'm not feeling very well. Do you mind if we go?"

"No problem." Finn's head tilted slightly to the side as he answered. It was abrupt and I knew it, but I still felt hot and constricted and I wasn't entirely sure why. He asked for the check and we made some more small talk while we waited, but the air had shifted somehow. There was tension and I knew it was my fault.

Outside in the cool night air I immediately felt like myself again. Just like that. Maybe the chocolate trance had strange powers that could only be broken by distance and fresh air.

"Wow. I feel so much better just being outside. I think the air was too thin in there or something."

"Would you like me to take you home?"

"To your place or mine?" I winked.

His eyes twinkled. "Let me rephrase that."

I smiled, slipping my arms around his neck. "If you're asking if I want you to put me in a cab and give the driver the correct address, then the answer is no. No thank you, actually. But I could definitely be convinced to follow an alternate plan."

He put his arms around my waist and pulled me into him. The heat was immediate and I melted just a little. "Look, I don't stand a chance at fooling you. You must know how beautiful you are, how much I want to...be with you." He swallowed with some difficulty and then kissed me. "But I can't."

I pulled my head back. "Pardon?"

"I can't sleep with you."

I looked up at him. Did he really just say what I thought he said? "I'm sorry, but are you joking?"

"I mean, I *can*. It's not like I'm–incapable or anything. He shook his head. "We've only just met. It's too soon, don't you think?"

He was right, of course. This was technically only a second date, but wasn't that my line? I wondered briefly if Kate was having this much trouble with David. Did I mention it had been nearly a year and a half?

I couldn't believe what I was hearing. His body was saying one thing and his mouth was saying another. Self-control was such a foreign concept. I was stunned–and embarrassed. I was too easy. And yet he respected me more than I respected myself.

Suddenly I felt ashamed. My cheeks turned bright red and I pulled out of his arms, walking quickly to the edge of the road, trying to hail a cab.

Finn was quick to follow. "Wait! What are you doing?"

"I have to go."

He grabbed my hand and turned me around. "No way. Not again."

All I could think about was getting out of there. My other hand was still up in the air. A cab drove up and I pulled free of him.

"Truly, tell me what's wrong!"

I got into the cab and tried to shut the door but he had it fast.

"I don't understand. Every time we get around to it you run away." He let go of the door and threw his hands in the air.

I gave the cab driver my address. He pulled away and we left Finn standing there. He was angry–I could see it in his stance. He stuffed his hands into his pockets, and I realized we'd somehow just recreated the scene from the other night–him watching me drive away in a cab.

This was ludicrous.

7

"I've had a lot of worries in my life,
most of which never happened."
M.T.

I had the cab driver drop me off at the market on the corner near my apartment. There were no groceries at my place and the take-out orgy had to stop. It was time to clean things up and get my life back on track. I bought fresh vegetables and some brown rice, oranges and milk, even some fresh flowers for my table. Oh, and two bottles of white wine, which, it turns out, is the only acceptable wine a person can drink alone. I don't know, maybe it's the fact that it's clear. It looks so non-threatening that way.

I walked the rest of the way home, beating myself with an imaginary baseball bat. It really wasn't like me to be so irrational–to snap so easily. I felt like a rubber band stretched too tight. Maybe I was kidding myself. Maybe *I* was the quicksand.

When I got off the elevator Finn was standing against the wall next to my door. The night of the Yankees game we'd stopped by my apartment so I could change, so of course he knew where I lived. The larger question, of course, was not the how but the why.

I didn't say a word, but put my key into the dead bolt and turned it, thankful that Kate had cleaned up a bit before we left. Still, it was embarrassing to have someone see my apartment in such a state of disarray. Funny how the outside matched the inside sometimes.

Then I put the next key into the next lock and turned it. Then the third. Finn watched me with amused interest, and I thought maybe he'd crack a joke about my obsessive fear of burglars.

Instead he leaned in close to my ear and spoke rather quietly. "And how many of these locks have you got 'round your heart, Truly?"

It's amazing how the fusion of those particular words caused a sudden catastrophic meltdown. I pushed open the door and he followed me inside, so I set my bags on the floor, kicking it shut behind him. "How *dare* you? You don't even know me!"

He chopped at the air with his hand. "Exactly my point! Thank you."

I was still so pathetically embarrassed by my willingness to sleep with him. In fact, I *still* wanted to, and that made it even worse. He'd wounded my pride by being a gentleman, and I couldn't forgive him for it. What kind of an emotional basket case did that make me?

"I'm not like everyone else, Truly. Can't you see that? I'm not looking for a one-night-stand. I don't want to use your body, and I'm not interested in having *sex* with you simply for the sake of personal gratification." He said the word sex as if it tasted bitter in his mouth. "Does that make me somehow unattractive to you? Or have I misjudged your depth and you're really just looking to shag and be done with it?"

I slapped him then. Right across the face, just like in the movies. I don't know what came over me. I've never slapped anyone before in my life, and now here it was the second time I'd physically assaulted him. Again I felt naked and dirty, only this time I couldn't just change my shirt.

The slap didn't make him fly into a rage like I thought it would–like Christopher would have, had I ever stood up to him. My chest was heaving and I started to cry and back away from him. Finn grabbed onto my stiff body and pulled me toward him. He wasn't angry at all–at least not at me. He was somehow infuriatingly tender, apologetic even.

He held me and whispered in my ear. "I'm terribly sorry. I deserved that. I was just trying to make a point about the opposite being true and now I fear I've done it poorly. "

Again I'd lashed out in anger, and again it was him apologizing instead of me. I was so mad yet so convicted by his words. I wanted him to go away but never stop holding me. Everywhere I turned inside myself there was paradox and it unnerved me. I was totally conflicted, completely frustrated, and utterly speechless. Tears turned to sobs, and he just stood there, holding me, stroking back my hair.

At that moment I realized that my whole world was built around control–or maybe it was built around me. I only liked worlds and people I could understand–people who played by the rules that I knew, and Finn didn't know any of them.

I hadn't cried that hard since mom died. By the time I lost Jenny I'd also lost most of my ability to feel. The strength of emotion I was fighting against seemed so ridiculously disproportionate to the situation, I became embarrassed all over again and willed the waterworks to a stop.

When I looked up he wiped my tears with his thumbs. "Are you all right?"

All I could do was nod.

"Well, that's a relief then, isn't it?" He led me over to the couch and we sat down. "Now, tell me what's wrong, Truly. Please."

I shook my head.

"I don't want to know your entire life story in one night. All I'm asking for is an explanation of what happened back at the restaurant, and I don't think that's an unreasonable request."

My stupid birthday trigger seemed so senseless in hindsight. I swallowed. I couldn't start with the restaurant. The rest of it was too real and too present. No sense beating around the bush. "I felt ashamed."

"You what?"

"I felt ashamed."

"No, I mean, I heard what you said, but...what the hell have you got to be ashamed of?"

I gathered what little courage I had and looked toward the grocery bags. "Would you like a glass of wine?"

He followed my gaze. "Not if it means you're going to change the subject."

"I promise I'll get back on track, just let me put my groceries away and pour us a glass of wine."

"All right. Can I help?"

"Sure."

I pulled down two glasses and a corkscrew and put Finn to work pouring the wine while I put the groceries away, giving me a much-needed chance to compose my thoughts.

Finn deposited the glasses on the coffee table and asked permission to use my bathroom–the same bathroom into which Kate had pushed me earlier, and which now looked like who knows what. I apologized for the state of the place, using the same lame excuses so typical to a normal person. Finn responded politely enough, but he really had no idea what a normal 'day-in-the-life' looked like for me.

On any other day it would have been obsessively neat, uber-clean, and compulsively organized. It didn't seem to make a difference to him, but as soon as he was out of sight, I was over in the kitchen frantically trying to clean and straighten things up.

I was so focused on cleaning that I forgot to figure out what I was going to say. I slid over to the coffee table and downed the glass of wine then quickly refilled it as I heard the sink water running in the bathroom.

He washed his hands? This too was a good sign! I was sitting on the couch sipping on my second glass when he came out.

Finn smiled his slightly crooked smile and I was nearly undone. In the space of a week I'd already begun to crave his warmth. I wanted it in every fiber of my being. I wanted to draw from his strength, to feed off his confidence and caring. I wanted him to take me and carry me away. Maybe it wasn't exactly sex I was craving, but it sure felt like it in all the right places.

He picked up his glass and made himself comfortable next to me. I took hold of one of his hands and felt the electricity I knew would be there. His body flinched ever so slightly and I looked up to see him once again pull the reigns back. He took a drink, swallowed, and settled in to wait for my explanation.

I puffed out my cheeks and blew the air out of my lungs. This made Finn laugh, which made me laugh, and that relaxed me quite a bit. Why couldn't I just have a normal conversation? I mean, what was so hard about telling someone the truth?

It was then that it came tumbling out: The most brutally honest speech I think I've ever made to another human being. Totally unrehearsed. Completely unlike me. Kate would've clapped. Hell, Kate might have had a heart attack.

"I'm not very good at relationships."

Finn raised one eyebrow. "You can't break up with me, you know. We're not officially dating."

He was funny, I had to give him that. "I'm trying to explain a little of my erratic behavior."

"Oh, well in that case, please, do carry on." He sipped his wine and relaxed back into the couch.

I resisted the urge to come back with sarcasm, trying desperately to stay on track. Where to begin...where to begin... "You were right."

"About what?"

"I did want to just *'shag and be done with it'* as you so indelicately put it."

I could see that I'd shocked him but he just sat there blinking, waiting for more, so I gave it to him.

"It would have been easier for me to just give in to the physical temptation of being with you than to navigate the waters of a new relationship, which frankly has me a little freaked out. I've spent the last ten years or so trying to organize my life in such a way that everything makes sense. Have you ever heard the expression 'a place for everything and everything in its place'?"

He nodded.

"Well, that's my life." His eyes darted sideways at the obvious chaos but I couldn't explain that part. Not now. I picked up my wine. "But you don't fit into any of those boxes. Not even one."

I took a deep breath and continued. To my surprise, the more I talked the easier it got. It was like journaling, in a way. Once I turned the key on the floodgates, it was just on.

"The fact that you want to take things slow and pursue a 'real' relationship scares the hell out of me. The only relationship I've ever had that lasted more than a couple of nights was with a guy who hit me and controlled me and made my life a living hell."

I started to shake. I could feel the bile rising into my throat. Finn put his hand on mine to steady it. "Is that why you have so many locks on your door? Because of him?"

I nodded, trying to keep back the tears. "I couldn't afford to move, and he had a key, so I changed the locks and added a couple more, just to make sure." Even Kate didn't know that part. She actually thought I was paranoid of burglars.

Come to think of it, I don't believe I knew any of these things about myself, at least not on a conscious level, but the minute I opened my mouth to speak it was all just laying there, like stones on a path. I followed the trail and picked them up one by one, and when I got to the end I was sitting there, looking at him, holding a box of rocks that I had no idea what to do with.

He was beautiful and honest and I couldn't help myself, but

that street usually worked both ways. I just kept shaking my head as I looked at him. "I can honestly say I've never been with someone who *didn't* want to sleep with me."

Finn leaned forward. "Now hold on just a minute. Who said I didn't want to sleep with you?" He smiled that crooked boyish smile and I had to laugh.

"A woman needs to feel beautiful and wanted."

"And you are both. I hope I've made that abundantly clear in every other way." He held both hands suspended in the air, but then closed them into fists, as if there was more to say but he wasn't willing to go there. This was obviously difficult for him. Why was he holding back? Maybe it was the British thing. They always seemed so much more 'buttoned-down' than Americans.

"You see? There it is again!"

Finn put his glass on the table and repositioned himself on the couch. "What? There *what* is again?"

We were like an old married couple. It might have been hilarious if I wasn't about to show him my twice-baked fondue. So much for the chocolate/Tums effect.

"I don't know—your...lack of passion! Your ability to practice self-control. The fact that..."

Finn was shaking his head. I could see his muscles tightening as he became more and more frustrated. "The fact that *what*?"

Tears threatened once again at the corners of my eyes. I added my glass to his on the table and put my head in my hands, covering my eyes as if it could make me invisible to the truth. "The fact that I seem to want you more than you want me!" There. It was out. Finally. God that was hard to say out loud. I wondered if birthing a child could possibly be more painful than birthing a relationship.

It was as if I'd hit him with a stun-gun. "*That's* what you think?"

I nodded, turning every possible hue of red and pink.

He sat blinking back his surprise, although whether it was directed toward my candor or my actual words was unclear—until he came at me and took my face into his hands, sliding me down onto the couch beneath him. Placing my hands up over my head, he held them there gently while his slow, deep kisses set my whole body on fire. When he had me completely at his mercy, he spoke softly.

"Please, do not mistake my self-control for a lack of passion. I assure you that my desire for you is real." He smiled down at himself. "As you can now plainly tell."

I smiled back. He had me there. I could feel him hard between my legs. There was warmth and fire and I could barely breathe. And yet, he was calm. Collected. Totally in control of his passions.

"So how do you do it?" I asked.

"Do what?"

"Stop when you want to go."

Finn shrugged, as if it was no big deal. "I just...care more about tomorrow than I do about today."

It was a good line. I might have to use that in one of my novels.

I wiggled my fingers out of his grasp and ran my hands down over his body, watching him struggle to maintain control. It was cruel of me, I know, but I wanted to test this strange sort of control. I wanted him to kiss me again. I wanted to get lost in him, and being the gentleman that he is, he obliged.

For the longest time he laid there, kissing me, drowning me in emotions that carried me deep into the undertow. I felt all those things I wanted to feel–the connection, the intimacy, the elation, and yet he never made a move to go further than a kiss. It was astounding. A half-hour or more must have gone by, with layer upon layer of emotion being pulled off and consumed.

At the end he laid next to me, holding me, and I swear to you it was better than any sex I'd ever had. Never in my life–never in any dream or fantasy or novel did I think it was possible to know such a deep and meaningful connection, and yet all we'd done was kiss. I was blown away.

Finn leaned onto one elbow, brushing the hair back from my face. "So what happened ten years ago?"

"Pardon?"

"You said that you've spent the past ten years trying to organize your life so that everything made sense?"

Geez. He was a good listener. "My mother died."

He dipped his head in regret. "I'm sorry. I shouldn't have asked. I was just trying to..."

"Get to know me, I know. It's ok."

"And how did she–"

"Cancer. Mostly."

"And the rest of your family?"

I thought back to the birthday questions, but I didn't want to ruin the moment. "Not tonight."

He kissed my forehead. "Fair enough."

The strange thing was, I *wanted* to tell him. I wanted to tell him lots of things–things I'd never told Kate. But I couldn't. Not yet. It was too soon. He was absolutely right.

And if it was too soon to let him inside, then it was too soon to let him inside.

The last thing I remember before I fell asleep was the sound of his heart as I laid my head against his chest. It was strong and steady, but he was still human, and with humans there were no guarantees. With my luck, God would eventually yank Finn out of my life too. Still, for whatever it was worth, I decided to just try to enjoy whatever time we might have left.

8

"Always do what is right.
It will gratify half of mankind and astound the other."
M.T.

I'd love to be able to tell you that I woke up from that
experience with Finn and lived happily ever after, but that's
not exactly how it went. It turns out happy is about a lot of things,
and I didn't know half of them.

Finn didn't spend the night, but apparently he held me for
several hours. I think I woke up, partially, a couple of times. I'm
still not exactly sure what happened, but somewhere in the
middle of the night he lifted me off that terribly uncomfortable
couch and laid me on my bed, covering me with a blanket. At least,
that's what happened in the dream. In the dream he also kissed
my cheek and his breath smelled sweet, which, for the middle of
the night seemed awfully suspicious.

In the morning it was the strangest thing. I found my keys on
the floor in front of the door and all three locks had been secured.
He must've figured out which key went to what and then slid them

under the door after locking me in. It was the single sweetest thing I think anyone has ever done for me. That part, at least, I know was real.

I started the coffee and then spent about a half-hour on the phone with Kate, who was waiting for the subway to go teach classes for the day. David had agreed to come dance with her for her students, so she was really excited. Her voice sounded lighter and happier than it had been in quite a while.

I told her what happened with Finn and she was as stunned as I was. When I asked about David she laughed, assuring me he wasn't nearly the prude Finn seemed to be. Neither one of us could figure out what his deal was. It just wasn't normal for a guy to act that way. Kate wondered out loud what both of us had been thinking. It wasn't as if the thought hadn't crossed my mind, it was just...

"No way. Not a chance. When he kisses me, he's all there, one hundred percent, you know what I mean? But then he just pulls back. He has amazing self-control. I don't know how he does it."

"Or why." Kate seemed especially annoyed at the idea of voluntary abstinence.

"Exactly."

"So you're telling me he spent half the night at your apartment, holding you and making out on the couch but he never touched you–other than your lips of course–and then he carried you to your bed but left you there alone?"

She made it sound so much less romantic than it felt. "Well yeah, but it wasn't like that. I mean, physically there was no doubt that he wanted to go further. He just...didn't."

"Maybe he's a gigolo. I hear they're like, the *Gods* of self-control."

The idea was amusing, if not slightly arousing. I shook my head clear. "I doubt that, Kate."

"Well, he does have the look."

"What look?"

"The strong, confident, *I-know-I-can-get-it-whenever-I-want-it-so-why-should-I-rush* kind of look."

I didn't need any more doubts creeping around my mind. "That's ridiculous Kate. Why would he be playing games with me for free when he could hire out?" What was I doing even validating such a stupid idea? "Ok I have to go. I have work to do."

"Me too. My train's almost here."

"Talk to you tonight."

"Text me if he calls you. I'm loving this, by the way. It's like an episode of the X-files or Twilight Zone or something."

"What, so now you think he's paranormal?"

"Regular human beings don't have any self control–I'm just sayin'."

"Goodbye Kate."

"Text me!"

"I will."

IT WAS Friday and I had a couple of deadlines to meet. In hindsight it was a good thing I'd written all those articles ahead while I was holed up in my apartment, playing hermit. I poured some coffee and turned on my computer.

There were six emails from editors, and that was a good sign. Two were from The Times, which I replied to immediately with attachments for this week's column and the next one for two weeks from now, already done. Editors loved that. The other four were from freelance gigs I'd queried. Two were a yes, so I attached and sent the drafts I'd prepared from the ideas I'd pitched to them. The last two said no thank you but one of them suggested something else and would I be willing to write a spec piece on the subject she suggested? I started researching the topic, found a plethora of great information, and clicked 'send' on an affirmative reply.

About an hour went by before I came up for air and took a

good look at my apartment. I had hardly been expecting company, and yet Finn had spent the night, or at least part of it.

I think.

Three hours later I had successfully returned it to the spotless, compulsively organized little flat that it was. Satisfied, I took a shower, put on some makeup and turned my creativity toward a healthy lunch.

That was when the phone rang. It was Finn and I was glad he couldn't see me because I think I smiled from the inside out when he invited me to lunch. I told him I was already making lunch, but he was welcome to come over. "Unless of course you're a greasy spoon kind of guy, because I'm making a nice, healthy, vegetable stir fry over brown rice."

"Sounds delicious. When do you want me?"

Now...All the time...Every day? "Uh, well that depends. How far away are you?"

"Not far."

"This is New York." I sighed. "Not far 23rd Street or not far Greenwich Village?"

He laughed. "Not far look out your window."

I left the cutting board and did as he suggested. Sure enough, there was Finn standing next to a tree out on the street in front of my building. He smiled at me and I covered my mouth. I think I might have even giggled. He was wearing a really nice pair of jeans and a white button-down shirt, un-tucked. Come to think of it, he did resemble something of a gigolo, right down to those soft brown leather loafers. My stomach did a back flip. I didn't even know my stomach knew how to tumble.

"Well, in that case why don't you come on up?"

"Only if you insist." He grinned up at me.

I didn't reply, just hung up the phone and waited for the buzzer to ring. When I opened the door Finn did a double take. He even sniffed at the air for effect.

"What happened in here?"

I looked around. "What do you mean?"

He started chuckling and pointing his finger at me. "Oh, I see. You're playing with me." He swept his arm around the room. "You saw me standing out there, didn't you? You didn't have to clean up for my sake, you know."

"I didn't." I was dead serious and he just kept staring skeptically. He really had no idea who he was dealing with, but I wasn't going to get into it with him partially in the hallway, so I motioned for him to come in.

"Right. And I suppose your apartment always looks like a museum? Last night was just a fluke, was it?"

"Well, now that you mention it, yes, actually." *A museum? That one stung a little.*

Finn raised an eyebrow, trying to determine if I was serious.

"Are you hungry?" I waved my knife at him. "Any good at chopping garlic?"

"I can handle myself in the kitchen." Of course he could. He was a bachelor. Or was he? I suddenly realized I was juggling a number of assumptions.

He took his coat off and laid it on the back of the couch, then picked it right back up. "Oh no, now I can't do that!" he teased. "Have you got a coat closet? Or a butler maybe?"

"Ha ha. You can hang it on the tree over there."

He did as he was told but then stopped and looked at me. "I'm sorry."

"For what?"

"I've done this all wrong. Do you mind if we start again?"

"Start what again?"

He shook his head and then walked out the door of my apartment, standing behind the closed door and knocking again, waiting for me to answer.

I pulled open the door. "What are you doing?"

He took one of my hands and pulled me toward him, then kissed me lightly on one cheek. "Hello."

"Hello..."

He stared at me. "You are just as beautiful as I remembered."

75

"From last night?"

"Yes."

"I was asleep last night."

"Yes."

I shook my head and tried not to smile. "Do I have to ask you about the garlic again?"

"No. Just let me wash my hands."

I pointed him in the right direction. "The bathroom is clean now."

"It wasn't dirty before."

"That's your opinion." I called over my shoulder.

He stopped in front of the door. "You haven't traveled much, have you?"

I turned to face him. "What's that supposed to mean? I know what dirty is."

"So do I. And clean is most definitely a matter of perspective."

He disappeared into the bathroom and shut the door, leaving me to wonder just how far he'd traveled. I went back to chopping. There was nothing else to do. Like I said, the apartment was spotless.

My desk looked like a picture from a Pottery Barn catalog. Anyone with half a brain could see where my priorities were. Cheap, uncomfortable couch, because really, how many hermits do you know that entertain? And right next to it, the coziest reclining leather desk chair money could buy. Hey, there were some days I spent more time in that chair than I did in my bed. Anyway, it was a 'business expense'.

Finn came out and literally walked around my place with his mouth open.

"*What?!*" I couldn't figure out if he was genuinely amazed or mocking me. Either way it was incredibly annoying.

He shrugged. "I don't know. It's just–such a transformation."

"And here I was under the impression that you'd barely noticed my apartment."

"What do you think I did while you slept?" He winked at me.

"I don't know–I meant to ask you that. You didn't sleep?"

Finn shook his head. "I may have dozed off, but no, not really."

"Why not?"

"I was memorizing your bookshelf." He grinned.

I looked over at the bookshelf, which you couldn't readily see from the couch. How long was he here after he'd put me in bed? *Did* he put me in bed? I started to get creeped out and stopped chopping, holding the knife in a tighter grip against the counter. I was cursing Kate under my breath for that X-files comment. She'd gotten me all suspicious and I was being an idiot.

He looked from the knife to my hand and back to my face and put both hands in the air. "I'm kidding. I didn't do anything of the sort. I was just laying there, I promise."

But why? Why would he just lay there? Who does that?

"Why didn't you just leave when I fell asleep?"

He looked hurt, then walked over to me and slipped the knife out of my hands, sliding his hands around my waist. "Because I like being with you." He dipped his head down and used his nose to push my hair over my shoulder, then kissed my collarbone. "My God you smell amazing..." He swallowed and stepped back. "I'd better get chopping."

He'd done it now. No one kisses my collarbone like that and gets away with it. I stepped back toward him and put my arms around his neck, popping up onto my toes to reach his mouth. He sucked in his breath as our lips met and grabbed me around the waist again, lifting me off the floor and gripping me tightly before setting me back down again.

"Maybe we'd better go out for lunch."

I smiled. "You started it."

The one side of his mouth hooked up. "I know. I apologize."

"Well stop doing that, would you?" I dropped my hands and walked back to the cutting board. He wasn't the only one that could exhibit self-control.

He took up the knife and garlic I'd laid out for him. "Stop what...kissing you?"

"Apologizing." Two could play his game. I just had to figure out his rules.

He ignored my comment and changed the subject. "So, what are we making?"

"Rice bowls. Would you like something to drink? I have coffee made."

"That'd be great. Thank you."

"So...how long were you standing out there?"

I'd tried to sound nonchalant, but he stopped to face me.

"Truly I'm not a stalker or a psycho or any other type of pervert, I promise you. I was going to just knock on your door, but I thought it'd be better to ring you first."

I pulled down a cup and got out the cream and sugar, leaving him to make the coffee to his own taste, which it turned out was a heart-stopping amount of cream and three teaspoons of sugar.

"Just living it up before the angiogram?"

"Excuse me?"

"Nothing, I just think that's ingenious and rather efficient." I peered into his cup. "That way you can have your coffee and your Danish all in one shot." I smirked.

He looked over at my cup of no-nonsense black coffee. "Oh, I see."

"You do..."

"See now, after your nearly orgasmic reaction to the chocolate last night I wouldn't have taken you for a black coffee sort of girl."

"They're separate."

"What are?"

"Coffee and dessert."

"This I have to hear. Go on."

"Coffee is meant to compliment the sweet, its acid balancing out the flavors of your dessert. If you sweeten your coffee, then there's no contrast."

He seemed satisfied, if not impressed. "That makes perfect sense, actually."

"Thank you." I turned on my heel and checked the rice cooker while he got back to peeling and chopping the garlic. "Ok, it's time to start sautéing the vegetables. How's that coming?"

He slid the chopped garlic across the cutting board in my direction. "About this much?"

"I don't know what do you like–a lot or a little?"

He tilted his head and smirked. "Garlic?"

"Yes, garlic! No wait, let me guess. A *moderate* amount..." I tried on the accent but failed miserably – and I really needed to learn to tone down the sarcasm. He was just so easy.

He leaned across the counter. "Would it surprise you if I said I wanted it all?"

Here we go. "Yes." I hoped to God we were still talking about garlic.

"And would you give it to me if I asked?"

The double entendre was killing me. "No, not at this point. My stomach can't handle that much garlic. And neither can my breath. I'll smell like a dragon."

He popped one of the peeled, whole cloves into his mouth and chewed it raw, then slid his hand behind my head and started to pull my face toward him as I struggled against the force.

"No way!" I started laughing, trying to run away from him, but he had me trapped in the kitchen and I knew it. He grabbed me around the waist and when his hips hit mine I thought I was going to faint. That gigolo comment might not have been too far off the mark. I got lightheaded and I think my eyes might have rolled back a bit.

We both realized what was happening at the same time. He backed me up against the refrigerator and locked me there. I tried to distract myself by focusing on the hilarity of the garlic and the sound of little alphabet magnets sliding around behind me as we kissed.

For a minute I thought it was over–all that talk about it being too soon. My shirt pulled away from my pants as I slipped my arms around his neck, and when his hands touched bare skin I almost lost it. I followed his lead and lifted that beautiful white linen shirt.

His skin was soft and warm, just like the rest of him, but as soon as I touched him he ripped his hands away from me and put them both on the counter, leaving me plastered against the refrigerator. "This isn't going to work very well, is it?"

I shook my head. I'd tried to tell him.

He took a deep breath in and blew it out his cheeks liked I'd done the night before. We looked at each other and laughed.

"How 'bout we go grab a sandwich and have a walk in the park?" His question was hopeful, almost pleading.

I raised both eyebrows. We were grown adults. "You're really serious about this, aren't you?"

Finn nodded, looking apologetic again. He was still leaning over the counter and gripping it, I assume trying to will his body to a halt. If this was any indication of what it'd be like once we got around to it, I was willing to wait if he was. As far as I was concerned, it just kept getting better and better.

I peeled myself away from the fridge to turn off the stove and the rice cooker. The rice would keep and we hadn't started cooking the vegetables yet. No harm, no foul.

I dipped my head toward his ear. "I do have a shower you know. You could just turn it on cold."

He kissed me lightly on the cheek. "Yes, but you'd still be here when I got out."

Talk about feeling beautiful *and* wanted. My soul was soaking up his words like it hadn't rained in years. In fact, I'm not sure it had ever rained like that, and the thought made me sad. I excused myself to use the bathroom, and when I came out he already had his coat on. I grabbed my keys and tossed them to him, going first out the door. "You mind doing the honors?"

"Not at all."

9

"Keep away from people who try to belittle your ambitions. Small people
will always do that,
but the really great make you feel that you, too,
can become great."
M.T.

I watched him fumble a bit. It wasn't like he'd memorized the
sequence, which was strangely comforting. "So, where to?" I
glanced over his shoulder, making sure he got it right.

Finn shook his head. "I haven't got a clue. You live 'round here.
What's good?"

I took him to the deli on the next block. I loved their cold cuts
and the owner was a sweet, gruff little man named Francisco. The
storefront had a few miniature tables across from the counter, so
we grabbed some food and tried sitting at one, but there really
wasn't enough room to put our collective sandwiches and drinks.
They were like those little iron tables you might see off to the side
of a garden path–accents that were never meant to be functional–

more like a decorative afterthought. We picked up our stuff and decided to walk a bit.

There was a small stretch of grass with a couple of benches on a nearby corner. It couldn't really be called a park, but it would suffice. Finn was right. Being outside walking and talking together took all that other pressure off. We laughed and ate and when we had disposed of our garbage like good little environmentally conscious citizens, he asked if he could hold my hand.

I turned toward him on the bench and picked both legs up, wrapping them under me Indian style and setting my hands in my lap. "Ok so let me ask you something."

"Sure." He didn't seem bothered by my candor, which was good, because it wasn't like I could just turn it off.

"I don't really 'get' you."

He didn't seem overly eager to assume my meaning. He just... waited, which was something else I really didn't get about him.

"How is it you can pin me up against my refrigerator one minute, kissing me until my knees go weak, and the next minute be asking permission to hold my hand? Isn't that fairly implicit, based on what's already happened between us?"

Finn's head shook ever so slightly, then he stopped abruptly, looking up at me. "Wait, your knees went weak? Really?" He broke into a smile and I pushed against his leg, pinking right up.

"Be serious!"

"I am seriously thrilled by the fact that your knees went weak. That's not a comment you hear every day, you know. It's quite an accomplishment." His smile caught my heart fast, but then his face gentled. "Listen, I don't want to assume anything. I want to treat you with honor, and respect, and I'm sorry if I've lost that at times when we've been alone."

Honor and respect? Those were words from another era – another planet maybe.

"You're not making sense. I mean, we've been intimate enough to kiss...rather passionately, I might add. We also spent at least part of the night together on my couch, but now you want my permission to hold my hand? Seems a bit backward to me."

"I know. And I've had trouble with this part before."

"Remaining chaste?" I laughed sarcastically, but I probably shouldn't have, because he looked at me in all seriousness.

"No, with women not understanding my heart. Rejecting my honor."

Finn rejected? Impossible. "Maybe it would be easier if you explained a bit more."

"You're going to think I'm old fashioned."

"I already do." I laughed. "So the worst is over."

I could tell by his hesitation that there was a lot more to the story. Maybe I wasn't the only basket case in this equation. I'd thought he was too put together to be a mess, but then I looked into the mirror of his face and saw the truth. I saw what maybe he'd seen from the first: A well put together mess can be beautiful.

My heart dissolved just a little in that moment. A few of the hard scaly parts fell off, taking fresh tissue with them. The resulting rawness was foreign and somewhat painful, the sudden feeling tingling and buzzing like a sleeping limb within me. I had forgotten how to feel.

I wasn't sure I liked it.

"I'm not a ladies' man, Truly. I used to be, but not any more."

I nudged his shoulder. "Coulda fooled me."

"I'm being serious. Please."

"Sorry." I sobered.

"I don't date much, because I don't really want to date."

I searched his eyes. "Wait. Me, or in general?"

"Both."

I swallowed, trying to grab up the pieces of scale and paste them back onto the raw parts. Where was he headed with this? I tried to do my yoga breathing, slowly releasing the pressure from my chest.

"I don't mean that I don't want to see you, because I do. I want that very much. I feel like I'm not explaining myself very well." He shifted in his seat. "What I'm trying to say is, I'm not interested in merely dating someone for the sake of having a good time."

Marriage? "So what exactly *do* you mean, because ...you're starting to freak me out."

He grabbed my hand and squeezed it. "I know, believe me. I'm sorry. Just listen."

I was trying to listen, but my head and my heart were in an all out war, and my legs wanted to run. The adrenaline was surging and I could barely control my limbs. "I mean, if you're saying what I think you're saying..."

My head was shaking and I couldn't keep my eyes focused in one place, and like a slap to the face Finn just grabbed onto my jaw and kissed me.

It worked surprisingly well. I calmed right down.

He kept his face close to mine. "What I'm saying is, I'm very attracted to you."

I nodded, trying to make sense of it. Trying to follow his logic.

"I feel something very deeply." He grabbed my hand and put it against his chest. "In here."

It was nice to know mine wasn't the only heart beating out of its chest. "I understand what you're feeling. It just... makes me nervous, talking like this. I mean, we've only known each other what, a week?" Actually it had been five days, six hours and seventeen minutes...give or take. "You can't know *anything* about a person in that short a time."

He nodded vigorously. "Which is why I don't want to rush into anything physically. Don't you understand? The more we get to know each other, the better it will be when it finally does happen."

"When what finally does happen? Sex?"

"Yes. Sex." He was laughing. "And everything else."

"Everything else?"

"I just don't think about it that way."

"What way?" This was starting to feel like a bad Vaudeville routine.

Finn shifted on the bench, as if his position in space could affect the angle at which I saw his point. He rubbed the top of my hand with his thumb. "For me at least, it can't be about just kissing or holding hands or even making love. It's got to be about deepening levels of intimacy."

When he said it like that I started to sweat.

"It's just a physical act, Finn. It doesn't mean any more or less than any other physical act - although, we do get to see each other naked." I winked, trying to laugh, but his eyes trailed me and I watched him struggle against his own thoughts. "Intimacy is just another word for naked."

He shook his head. "No. Intimacy is a whole other level of naked, and *that* kind of naked doesn't happen every day. Naked is about a lot more than sex."

My throat started to close. I felt trapped. Caged. Nailed to the bench.

He dropped his head, shaking it slowly. "Was I alone on your couch last night?"

"No, why?"

"It was like I got lost, but I didn't want to be found. It was–I don't know–otherworldly." He took my face and pulled in close, staring through to the other side of the abyss.

So he was an alien. God, what was wrong with me? I couldn't even be serious with myself! He was right though. It had been raw but beautiful, heady and sweet.

I nodded.

"Has that ever happened to you before? I mean, with another man?"

Was he really asking me to compare him to other guys? What man in his right mind even wants to know? I shook my head and he released it. "No. Never."

We sat in silence for a minute. The noise from the streets of New York faded into the background.

"And you? You're saving yourself for the right girl, are you?"

His smile was more like a smirk. "I'm not a saint, Truly. I think you've got me figured wrong."

Not likely. No man I'd ever known would pass up an opportunity to have sex with a willing woman, especially one with whom mere kisses were *otherworldly*.

He seemed to consider his next words very carefully. "Let's just say I've had more than my share of women." The admission seemed almost embarrassing for him, which caused me try to calculate just how many women might be an embarrassing number, but it was no use. There were just too many variables.

Finally, we were getting down to it. So he wasn't gay, and he wasn't a eunuch. The gigolo thing was still a question, I just wasn't sure I wanted to know the answer. I wondered briefly if there was a more politically correct term than gigolo. Male escort? He hadn't specifically mentioned what else he dabbled in.

He looked sad and distant, as if he'd survived lifetimes of pain and there wasn't enough time in the world to explain it all, so he just skipped to the end. "Eventually I realized it was all just emptiness. I promised myself that I wouldn't cross that line again unless it was with someone I truly cared for. Someone I wanted more than just sex from."

I couldn't pull my head back into the conversation. It was like a lock on my thoughts. I couldn't go where he was going. Couldn't fathom what he might be searching for.

"What exactly do you want, Finn?"

"I want to be just as comfortable holding someone as I am talking to them." He held both my hands and looked right into me. "And when I take them to bed I want it to be an extension of everything we already share."

I couldn't respond. I didn't know how. He was definitely an alien, I was sure of it now. And everyone knows aliens and humans can't procreate without making bastard super-humans who will never live a normal life.

Still, I could feel the want rising up from somewhere deep

within me. Completely unable to differentiate between the physical and emotional places he'd tapped, all I could distinguish was a deep and completely visceral want.

But this would definitely blow up my entire system.

10

"Why shouldn't truth be stranger than fiction?
Fiction, after all, has to make sense."
M.T.

I f there was a time for everything, and a season for every
purpose under heaven, then this time in my life was somehow
significant. It took me a while to figure that out, and looking back
I'm not sure why. It seems so obvious in the retelling. My therapist
agreed. He kept talking about that stupid thread.

Finn and I decided to take it slow. I let him hold my hand that
day, and as we walked through the city it felt strangely like a
second chance.

At this point I should probably mention that I lost my virginity
when I was in college–about once a week, the way some people get
saved every time they go to church, just in case it didn't take.

My roommate and I got invited to a frat party freshman year,
got more than a little drunk, and...well, the next weekend they
invited us back. It went on like that for several months. I never
drank during the week. I studied hard and was able to keep my

scholarship up, but weekends were a different story. I would go to a party, determined that I wasn't going to drink and I wasn't going to hook up with some cute guy just to have a little warmth and companionship for the night, but every weekend I'd blow my vows to smithereens and have to repent all over again. It didn't help that my roommate was tall and blond and dating the basketball team—and most of the hockey team. She made it seem almost normal.

Tall, muscular and tenacious described the first string of guys in my life, but the barrenness I felt every Sunday had me wishing I did go to church – or at least confession. Halfway through sophomore year, my roommate moved off campus and I just stopped going to parties. It was easier to quell the loneliness than to reconcile the guilt. Eventually the guilt hardened into apathy and all those memories conveniently distanced themselves from my emotions.

As Finn and I walked together I tried to recall just one of their kisses, but not one of those other guys had made any kind of a lasting impression. Most of the time it was over too fast to make a difference anyway. I thought about how Finn took his time—how his kisses warmed in my mouth and slid through me like soft butter.

When we got back to my apartment, I found myself reliving the honesty and raw heat Finn had deposited back against the refrigerator. I couldn't get it out of my head.

He squeezed my hand and smiled at me. "What are you thinking about?"

I shook my head. "You don't want to know."

We rode the elevator up in silence.

Once we were inside the apartment I plunked down on the couch. "You still want to know what I'm thinking?"

"Of course." He sat down beside me and turned to give me his full attention.

Getting him to listen was easy. Finding the right words was a little more difficult.

"Have you ever tried to diet?"

He looked down at himself, then back at me, eyebrows askew.

He was no bodybuilder, but there wasn't an ounce of fat on him. "Ok, bad example."

I could feel the color creeping up my neck. "Let me put it this way." I took a deep breath and spewed. "Ever since you told me you *don't* want to sleep with me, it's pretty much all I can think about."

He grinned at me, then looked down at his shoes. "Welcome to a man's world."

"Yeah well, laugh if you will, but this is serious."

He moved closer and slid his hands around my jaw, pulling me into his kiss until I had no doubt of his agreement. "I'm not a prude Truly. I'm a grown man. I know what it is to want, and I know what it is to have. Believe me, neither of those ideas are ever far from my mind when it comes to you."

Again we ended up horizontal on my couch, but it was harder to keep things in check this time around. When I absolutely couldn't take it any more I pulled out of his arms and rolled off the couch, standing awkwardly.

"How about some iced tea?"

He smiled weakly. "That'd be great."

"And a movie. How about a movie?"

"At the theatre I hope." He sat up, rubbing his face with both hands.

"Definitely. Why don't you fire up my computer and see what's playing?"

I walked into the kitchen, assaulted by the lingering smell of raw garlic. Heck, I could still *taste it.* I poured two glasses of iced tea and walked back to find Finn sitting in my beautiful desk chair. I held out the glass for him and he took it gratefully.

His British half was damned polite. I had a feeling it was the Irish half I met on the couch. Or maybe he was part Italian...

He took a sip of his iced tea and made a face.

"I don't put sugar in. Sorry. I should have remembered from the coffee."

"No, it's fine. I just wasn't expecting the jolt."

Jolt? Iced tea had a jolt?

"So...how long are you hoping to keep this up?"

He spun the chair toward me. "What's that?"

"I mean...what's the longest you've been able to hold out?"

His eyebrows went up. "Well, I-"

"Does this even work with other girls?" Hey, he'd asked about mine.

It was Finn's turn to blush. "At this rate, I'm hoping to make it past this evening."

I put a hand on my hip. "I have to hand it to you. It's definitely a new tactic. You get the prize for most originality. Chastity is...unexpected."

"Look, I told you, I've always been an all or nothing kind of chap. Used to be, I would have whatever I wanted all the time. No restraint." He slid his hand across the air like an umpire calling safe. "Whatsoever."

Yeah, I could see that about him, and it made a hell of a lot more sense than any of the other theories I'd been considering.

He shook his head, hesitating. "Then one day I decided to stop the madness." He took another sip of iced tea and made another face, so I brought him the sugar bowl.

"And how long ago was that–when the *madness* stopped?" I tried to imitate his accent and he chuckled at me.

He put two heaping spoonfuls of sugar into the tall, relatively thin glass and stirred to no avail. It all just kept crystallizing on the bottom. Finally he sipped anyway, then looked at me in all sincerity. "It's been three years since I've been with a woman."

Three *years*? If I was a cartoon character my jaw would have literally unhinged and hit the floor with a thud. "So what's your plan?"

"I haven't got one, really."

Great. I was falling for a non-planner. I could sense my own impending death, lingering in the room with the pungency of the raw garlic. I'd be burping it for days.

Finn was talking somewhere in the distance.

"I think if we plan activities out and spend as little time as possible in your apartment together, it would be a good start."

I scoffed. "What about your apartment?"

"Definitely off limits. For now."

"And why's that?" I asked, questions about his identity once again finding their mark. "Is it a 'den of iniquity'? A seduction palace?" I was trying to be funny, but it came out as sour grapes.

He licked his lips. "It's where I dreamed us."

"Pardon?"

He spun back around in the chair. "Our choices are wide open for the movie. We can see anything from horror to science fiction. What do you think? Action?"

"A little action sounds good to me." I grinned.

He spun toward me again, laughing. "You're going to make this as difficult as possible, aren't you?"

"Yeah, probably." I nodded enthusiastically, then tucked my face into his neck and breathed a kiss just below his ear. "I promise not to jump you at the theater, but you'd better rock my world with the goodnight kiss."

His eyes took on a mischievous sparkle. "I'll do my best."

We left my apartment a few minutes later, following the same routine as before. As he handed me back my keys I asked. "Don't you work?"

Finn's face twisted in confusion. "What kind of a question is that? Of course I work."

"Well, don't you have to be at the club? It's Friday night."

"It runs without me. No worries." His arm went around to my lower back as we got into the elevator.

"Well, don't computer geeks have to work during the day when they're not managing their nightclubs in the evening?"

"I'm going to ignore the geek comment." His answer was confident, nonchalant. "And the answer is no, not when they run the company."

I looked again at those brown Italian loafers and wondered

just how well his company must run without him–and how many other things he *dabbled* in. The gigolo theory was definitely starting to lose its steam though. A rich, successful guy didn't need women to pay him to...well, you know. And three *years* of voluntary chastity? The whole thing was a little hard to swallow.

"I see." I answered, but I didn't really. Suddenly my apartment felt tiny and drab as I imagined him in a gorgeous penthouse with a panoramic view.

Finn leaned up against the wall inside the elevator and crossed one ankle over the other. "You don't trust very many people, do you?"

He was like the male version of Kate. She never minced words either. "No. Why do you ask?"

"And you don't trust *me*." It wasn't a question, but rather a statement of fact. He was just looking for confirmation.

"I like you." I blinked a couple of times. "Granted, not quite as much at this particular point in our conversation, but I do like you." I tried to smile.

"That's not the same thing though, is it–liking and trusting?"

"Trust carries a huge time component. I barely know you."

Why should I have to defend myself? Could he really expect me to trust him after less than a week?

He nodded. "Well, we'll have to start there, won't we?"

My eyebrows went up and for some reason I held my breath, as if letting it out would bring with it some witty explosion, but all that came out was air. Typical. I was all brains and wit when I couldn't care less about a person. Put me in front of someone I found ridiculously attractive and my tongue went completely numb.

When the cab dropped us at the theater it was just like any other date. Finn paid for the tickets and we shared some popcorn and a drink. Except I insisted on paying for my own Hot Tamales because, well, no one gets between me and my Hot Tamales. Except maybe Little Debby.

Finn gave me a huge grin. "Brilliant choice. But you realize you're going to have to share those."

I popped open the box while he held the popcorn in one hand and our drink in another. "See, that's where you're wrong. Why do you think I let you buy something for each hand?"

I turned smugly and started to walk toward the ticket girl. She stared openly at Finn as he jogged after me. I felt a twinge of jealousy, then suddenly I felt the same shock she must have been feeling. How on earth was I even here with a guy like him?

"Oh I see." Finn was talking in my ear, ignoring the ticket girl completely. "You like to play dirty. Well two can play your game."

I turned toward him and popped a hot tamale in my mouth, chomping down loudly for effect.

"Oh you're going to get it later." He grinned.

"Promises, promises..." I replied, laughing. Ticket girl's eyes went wide as we walked away.

Normally I enjoy a good action flick. I really get into the chase scenes and cinematography, but as I sat in the theater with Finn, knowing much too little of his background in 'filmmaking technology', I spent most of my time watching him watch the movie. I wondered how he saw it, judged it, compared it to projects he'd done, and the journalist in me became insatiably curious about his work. I had a million questions. I wanted to interview, take notes, and cross-reference the timeline of his life to create a picture that somehow made sense. I don't remember much about the movie, but my fascination with this half-breed Irishman was starting to take over my brain.

About half-way through the box of hot tamales he leaned over. "You're really not going to share any of those, are you?"

I shook my head.

"What if I said please?"

"Depends on how you say it, I guess."

He leaned in and kissed me very gently. My hands went up to

95

his chin and I felt his strong jaw, got lost for a moment and had to remind myself that we were in a movie theater. When he pulled back he whispered. "May I please have some of your Hot Tamales?"

I nodded silently, reaching down into my lap to get the box, but it was already in his hands. He'd swiped it during the kiss without me noticing, and as I watched he poured out a whole handful and popped it into his mouth with a grin.

"I see how it is." I winked at him and he just smiled, chewing contentedly.

By the time we got back to my place it was late. He walked me to the door of my apartment and didn't ask to come in. He did, however, make good on his promise. The goodnight kiss was a thing of beauty that could have melted those refrigerator magnets into unrecognizable shapes. I'd spent much of the evening brooding about the whole 'trust' thing, but it all dissolved into thin air.

I floated inside and when I'd thrown the third lock I heard Finn chuckle on the other side of the door before his footsteps began to fade. Again he'd instinctively made sure I was safely locked in before making his exit. Who was this masked man?

When I saw him make his way onto the street I called his cell. He turned around and looked up at my window as he answered.

"What's up beautiful?"

No one ever called me that.

Oh, I'd been told I was pretty–like when Pete Jamison asked me to prom at the end of senior year. I'm fairly certain the compliment was an afterthought though, designed to convince me of his adoration and thus induce me to answer in the affirmative.

I did say yes to Pete, but not because of his afterthoughts or even his forethoughts, if indeed he had any. I just figured I was eighteen, my mom was dead, a gang-banger had recently knifed my sister to death, and I'd never really been to a dance, so why not?

It was a stupid thing to do. I wasn't a fluffy ruffle girl, and I was too busy studying my ass off for a scholarship to spend much time with friends. I knew there was no money for a dress. My dad didn't even know I was going until he got home from work that Saturday night and saw me in a dress I'd found in my mom's closet and remade with her old sewing machine.

I can see now that wasn't really fair to dad, because by the look on his face anyone would think I'd knifed him. He always said I looked just like her, and I guess in the dress the resemblance was especially striking. At that moment it didn't matter that Pete had called me pretty, because he never meant it. I looked like my mother though, and that was enough for me.

Kate always said I downplayed my looks way too much–that if I used more makeup or dressed differently I'd be knocking them over with a look. Don't get me wrong, I wasn't trying to win the prize for frump queen. I bought nice clothes that fit well, but I wasn't what you'd call an 'accentuate your assets' kind of girl either. That was never my game. I was always just me.

No nonsense. Functional.

Barely.

"I WAS WONDERING if you'd show me your office some time – the daytime one, not the one at the club. I'd love to see what you do."

"Sure. Some time." He smiled. "Goodnight, Truly."

Some time. Great. Sufficiently vague and noncommittal. "Goodnight Finn."

I watched him walk away, then plopped down into my desk chair. I spun toward my computer, trying to will my thoughts to a halt. It was no use.

I started writing. It was going to be a long night.

I DIDN'T HEAR from Finn for a couple days after that. It was strange. He didn't call, didn't come by. Nothing. Then I got a text, saying he was out of the country and would call me when he got back. It wasn't until I was having dinner with Kate that I had any idea why.

"Finn's sister in Ireland was having a baby. When he heard she'd gone into labor he booked a flight over to surprise her, but when he got to the hospital he found them all in tears, because the baby was stillborn."

"That's terrible! Was it her first baby?"

"David didn't say."

"Do you know how long he'll be gone?"

"David didn't say."

"Is she his only sibling?"

Kate shook her head. "I'm not sure, Miss New York Times. Why don't you ask him yourself?"

She was munching on a salad and chewing the croutons so loudly that the people at the next table were looking over at us. For all her style sense she did lack a few of the essentials. I thought it was cute, so I never mentioned it. Having a few reasonably distasteful quirks made her seem more real than most perfectly proportioned Barbie Dolls. Come to think of it, she was a lot like my roommate in college.

It occurred to me that I didn't know Finn well enough to pry. He was obviously keeping the painful details of his life to himself–despite the innuendo about trust. He'd call when he got back–whenever that was. And if he didn't? That was fine too. I wasn't about to let one week with a guy I barely knew waylay my plans–even if he was beautiful and sweet and soft in all the right places.

MY LIFE DIDN'T STOP. It didn't even slow down. I took an assignment upstate for a couple of days covering an enormous organizational trade show. I got a few good interviews, took tons of notes, got great ideas from samples, resource websites–all the "stuff" my writing dreams needed to finish branding my image. I gathered enough information to keep me writing for quite a while, and even began outlining a nonfiction book idea.

The interviews could be recycled into articles for women's magazines, some of which were represented at the trade show. I passed out cards, scheduled follow-up interviews, and even landed a gig writing ad copy for a startup company's new product line. They needed better advertising, and since I spent most of my time reviewing and writing about organizational products, it was practically a no-brainer.

Using my writing to both explain and plug a great new product seemed more like a cakewalk than actual work. Some writers disdain writing ad copy–they consider it beneath them. I figure if I get to string words together in a creative way and it puts groceries in my fridge, then who am I to say no? In the space of a two days I'd struck journalism gold.

I got talking to one woman whose infomercial on her product had already helped her to gross *millions* of dollars. Her name was Marilyn and she was funny and loud and her bright red lips made exaggerated enunciations as if she was talking on camera 24/7. Still, we had a great conversation, at the end of which she invited me to dinner.

The possibility of an interview was worth my time for dinner and then some. Since roughly eighty percent of all business deals happen in restaurants and on golf courses, I decided to play along, because eating required significantly less finesse.

When I showed up at the restaurant I found her sitting with two men. One of them turned out to be her date, and the other, I quickly learned, was supposed to be mine. Perhaps it hadn't been a business invitation after all.

My "date" was named Brad and he was tall and basketball-ish with big hands and a nice smile. I recognized him from one of the booths at the show. He talked nonstop about himself and his product all through dinner and bought us several rounds of drinks, which conveniently helped drown out the roar of his gargantuan ego. Still, he stood when I went to the bathroom and pulled out my chair when I came back, and before I knew it he was in my hotel room.

He laid me down on the bed and started undressing me and I thought about how nice it would've been if Finn were there. I was just drunk enough to let him kiss me, but not too drunk to notice that I didn't feel anything when he did. It had nothing to do with my level of intoxication. Brad didn't kiss like Finn, and he didn't move like Finn. He moved like a man who wanted something from a woman he barely knew. It felt cheap and robotic and I grabbed Brad's hand at the last button.

"Look, I'm sorry I dragged you all the way up here, but I really can't do this."

Unfortunately, a man who's had a few drinks is harder to stop than a freight train. He wiggled out of my grasp and leaned harder into me, kissing down my neck and whispering lewd urgencies. I pushed my way out from under him and went for the door, holding my blouse together with one hand and opening a view of the hallway with the other.

"I said no. Please leave."

Brad sat up, stunned. He blinked a couple of times, obviously not used to being told no. Truth was, I wasn't used to saying it, but it felt right somehow–empowering, in a way. He stumbled toward the door and gave me his room number, just in case I changed my mind. I threw the deadbolt behind him and the slider lock as well.

Then I sat down on that stupid, ugly bedspread and cried. After a few minutes of self-indulgent wallowing, I opened my laptop and tried to write, but nothing would flow. Then, as if on cue, a text came in from Finn. I picked up my phone and stared at it.

Sorry–I know it's late there, but I was thinking of you and wanted to let you know. Visiting with mum. Should be back some time next week. Can I call when I get back?

I crawled up under the covers and hugged the extra pillow.

Finn's text snuck inside me and warmed all those places I'd thought maybe a guy like Brad could reach, only Finn did it from across the ocean.

I'd like that. I replied. *See you soon.*

11

―――――

"Never try to teach a pig to sing.
You waste your time, and you annoy the pig."
M.T.

My dad's birthday was on Sunday so I headed over there on Saturday–my usual routine–to clean the house and make dinner for the two of us. We always celebrated birthday dinners the night before the person's actual birthday. I don't remember why but it was always that way, for as long as I could remember.

Like I said before, birthdays were a little dicey for me personally, but for dad's sake I tried not to let the day go by without at least doing something nice. I usually visited on weekends, so dad's birthday falling on a Sunday was like a bonus, because on Saturday nights I stayed over anyway. Dad never worked Sundays, so I'd make breakfast and we'd sit silently at the kitchen table and trade sections of the paper over a pot of too strong coffee.

Besides, going over on Saturday gave me a chance to really see how things were going. I timed my arrival for an hour or so before he got home from work. I would bring a couple bags of fresh groceries that I would load into his fridge, then check the garbage for empties and try to determine what exactly he'd been eating and how much he'd been drinking.

The house was surprisingly neat when I walked in, and I scared some woman half to death who was standing in dad's kitchen. She had a hand over her chest and her scream subsided once she realized I had my own key. Surely the arms loaded with paper grocery bags placed me at a threat level somewhere between green and blue, but hers was yet to be determined.

She was blonde and a little too thin and had big, bowling alley hair all poufed up toward the back. I silently wondered if she teased it or used one of those bump-it things to give it that characteristic sixties shape.

"Can I help you?" I asked suspiciously. After all, I was the one with the keys.

"Oh honey, you must be Trulane! Your father's told me all about you!" She stuck out a leathery hand with too many rings and a bad acrylic job.

Well, now this was interesting. I set my groceries on the kitchen table and gave her my hand. "Please. Call me Truly."

She smiled and I waited for her to find her manners. They must have been on the next train, but when it finally blew into the station she put her hand back over her heart, this time embarrassed. "Oh my! I'm so sorry, I'm Gigi."

"Gigi? Really?"

Hey–she was a stranger standing in my father's kitchen. I had a right to a least a small dose of sarcasm. Unfortunately it was lost on her.

"Oh it's short for Georgia–my family still calls me that, but my friends call me Gigi."

I wasn't sure I wanted to be in either category. "Is...my dad here?"

"Oh no honey, not yet, but he should be home soon. He usually works 'till about four on Saturdays."

As if I didn't know this? I had no idea what to even say to that. I turned toward my groceries and began unloading, then turned and faced her again. "I'm sorry, but...who are you? I mean, my dad didn't mention he was–"

"Dating?" She grabbed one of my hands and put it between both of hers. "Oh sweetie it's all right. I understand this must be a bit of a shock to you."

What was shocking was the accent, the hair, the skin-tight jeans. Not the fact that my dad might be shacking up, but the fact that it was with someone so completely unlike my mother I had to keep from laughing out loud.

I pulled my hand out from between hers, trying to be nonchalant. "Are you...living here?"

"Oh no!" She waved her hand at me. "I live in Jersey!" Unfortunately for her, the southern drawl mixed with Jersey just made her sound trashy. "I just come over on the weekends sometimes. We both work all week so it'd be pointless to do it any other way."

I turned back toward my groceries and resumed the process of unloading, trying to take mental stock of all I'd bought and wondering if there'd be enough of the chicken to serve three–not that Gigi looked like she ate all that much. Then I spied an open beer on the counter and glanced at the clock. It was after three–respectable, but still slightly suspicious.

"So what is it you do? For work I mean?" Small talk was even harder in a small room with a small amount of common ground.

Gigi puffed up her goldilocks. "I own a hair salon."

The bump-it was starting to make sense now. I opened the fridge to put stuff away and found it had already been stocked–with beer. So, they were drinking buddies. And I was pretty sure I didn't want to know what else.

Gigi peeked into the bag still left on the table. "Oh you brought food! How wonderful! Your dad tells me you're a great cook."

Now I was sure they were drinking buddies.

"Well, I was thinking of chicken for dinner in honor of his birthday tomorrow. Will you be staying? Or did you guys already have plans?"

"It's his birthday?"

I was somehow both amused and relieved that she had no idea.

"Well I just need to run out to the store then. She looked through the bags one more time. Should I get us some dessert? What does he like?"

Privacy. Routine. To be left alone. No wonder he hadn't mentioned his birthday.

"Um. Anything is fine. There's a bakery about three blocks down on the corner. They make great wedding cookies."

"Weddin' cookies? Why would I want to get those? We're not gettin' *married* sugar!"

God I hoped not. I might have to rip her squeaky southern voice box out and replace it with a real one.

"They're a type of Italian cookie. He likes them. Just get an assorted box of those."

"If you say so!"

She hooked her purse over her forearm and put on her sunglasses, though why she needed them was beyond me. It was forty-five and cloudy.

I was surprised I'd forgotten dessert, being birthday weekend and all. Then again, providence did prevail. With Gigi gone I'd have a chance to do some investigative reporting.

I found everything normal except Gigi's overnight bag was sitting next to dad's bed. It didn't look like she kept any clothes there–not even a toothbrush, and that seemed to jive with dad's personality just about right. His trash looked pretty normal and he didn't seem to be drinking any more or any less than usual, so I checked his desk for unpaid bills and found a few things that needed attention, but nothing that would send him to collections. Come to think of it the lawn didn't look bad at all. I wondered which one of them was doing the mowing.

I'd just stuck the chicken in the oven when I heard dad's characteristic screen bang. "Tru? Is that you?"

I walked out of the kitchen, kissed his cheek and he gave me a standard two-pat hug. He looked around like a cornered dog, so I decided to put him out of his misery.

"She's not here."

His eyes widened a bit. "You've met?"

"Dad. I'm twenty-five years old. I get it."

He nodded, then licked his lips. It was time for number one. He went to the fridge and grabbed a beer, noting the open one still on the counter. "You having one?"

I started cutting broccoli. "No, that one belongs to princess Gigi."

He frowned. "Be nice."

I stopped cutting and turned to him. "I mean, I get it dad. Mom's been dead a long time, but how in the world did you end up with someone like *her*?"

He took a long drink off number one, and number two was being called up on deck. "I'm not *ending up* with anybody ok? We're just friends."

"With benefits."

"If that's what you want to call it, then yes." He took another long drink and dropped the can in the garbage. I saved him the trouble and tossed him another, since I was closer to the fridge.

He nodded his thanks. "Why are you here this weekend anyway? You usually come on the third week."

Impressive that he knew my schedule. Even more impressive that he seemed to have been scheduling his time with Gigi *around* my visits.

"I thought I'd make you a nice birthday dinner. So sue me." I turned back toward the cutting board and chopped with a vengeance. "Unless you'd like me to leave. Because I can totally do that."

"Don't be ridiculous Truly. Of course I want you to stay." He popped the second beer and took a smaller drink. The preloading was over and it was time to start pacing. "I just...forgot it was my birthday, honestly."

I looked at his grease-smeared blue shirt and worked-hardened hands. He'd been busting his hump longer than I'd been alive. He deserved a little happy.

"Why don't you go take a shower? We can talk later."

He nodded. "Where'd Gigi go anyway?"

I tried not to smirk. "Wedding cookies."

"You didn't!"

I ducked my head and nodded, going back to my chopping.

"Aw Jesus. This should be good."

I laughed as dad left. He knew exactly what he was doing–and who he was doing it with. I'd long suspected our clocks were wound alike. Now I was sure of it. In fact, the older I got, the more I understood how he ticked.

12

"Do something every day that you don't want to do;
this is the golden rule for acquiring the habit of doing your duty without
pain."
M.T.

Dad's shower didn't take long and he emerged in a clean button-down and some decent looking jeans about the same time Gigi came sauntering back in the door. Her purse was hooked over one arm and under the other was a thin white cardboard box tied together with string. Leave it to the Italians to make everything a party–even a box of cookies.

She put her hands against dad's chest and peered up at his freshly shaven face, then took a big exaggerated whiff and planted a kiss right on his cheek. "Mmm! You smell almost as good as these cookies!"

Dad shot me a look that said 'laugh and I will beat you senseless' so I decided to set the table. I pulled down three plates and all of a sudden there was Jenny, taking up all the space in my mind's eye, obstructing the view. Jenny's laughter, Jenny's stomping temper tantrums, Jenny's smile turning dad to butter. I hadn't set for three of us since then. It was hard to even remember four.

Our round, Formica-covered table was a holdover from the sixties, like Gigi's hair. My grandmother gave it to my parents when they bought this house. My mother said since she grew up eating at it, there was no reason we shouldn't. It had a few chips and scratches, but Mom was practical like that. Good enough was good enough.

I couldn't give Gigi mom's place, so I settled for Jenny's, but that wasn't any easier. We only had the four chairs so there weren't many options. How hard could it be to share your table with another woman?

I suddenly wished Finn was there. He would know how to be gracious, even if it was incredibly awkward. I usually had no desire to be nice, but I'd seen dad smile when she kissed him, and for him, I could be just about anything–as long as it didn't involve being in that house longer than twenty-four hours in a row.

We sat down to basic baked chicken, white rice and steamed broccoli. You'd have thought dad was at a five star restaurant. He kept talking about how good it tasted, but the really strange part was that he was talking at all. He asked about my work and Gigi thought it was so interesting that I wrote for the newspaper. I wasn't sure she'd ever read one. I eyed dad and he shook his head, trying not to laugh with me.

This was not the same man who'd sat closed-mouthed at this very table for the last ten years. It was quite an educating experi- ence. Was this what he used to be like? Before mom got sick?

"So how did you two meet?" I asked.

Dad started to open his mouth but Gigi opened hers first. I wanted to stuff it with chicken.

"Oh, well it's a funny story really. I was here for a hair dressin' convention down at the Ramada Inn and my car started makin' funny noises so the clerk down there–"

Dad and I looked at each other and both said "Harold" at the same time.

"Yes! Harold! What a sweet little man! Anyway, Harold said I should take it to the best mechanic in town, so there I was at your dad's shop." She stopped then and looked at dad with an admiration I wasn't sure he returned. "He came over to the Ramada that night after work and we had a couple of drinks together and–well, you know how these things go."

Gigi forked the rice around her plate in the awkward silence that followed.

"What about you?"

I looked up at the sound of dad's voice. "Me?"

"Yes, you." He smiled again. That had to have been three smiles already. "Anyone special in your life?"

I wanted to be sarcastic and ask him when the last time was that I brought anyone home to meet him, because of course he would have to answer never. Christopher wasn't interested in anything but himself, and Pete Jamison just sat in the driveway and honked. But I couldn't answer. I just sat there with a mouthful of chicken and marbles.

Finally I swallowed, rolling my fork around in circles, trying to pull the attention away from my face. "I've had a few dates lately. I'll let you know if there's anyone worth meeting."

Gigi waved her hand at me again. "Oh I'll bet you've brought lots of nice fellas home to meet your dad here."

Dad's eyebrows went up.

I looked over at the stove. "Who wants more chicken?"

By the time we cleaned up from dinner and had coffee and cookies, I'd had so much conversation with dad and Gigi I think it filled a couple months' worth of quota. Turns out keeping a straight face is exhausting, so I excused myself and went up to bed.

Laying there in what used to be my tiny bedroom at the top of the stairs I could hear Gigi giggling. I tried putting the pillow over my head but in the end the iPod seemed a better choice, so I floated away on the strains of Horse Feathers and Iron and Wine.

In the morning I found dad at the table with the coffee and newspaper but no Gigi. When I asked about it he just shrugged.

"She left early to go back to Jersey–some baby shower or something. Said to say goodbye."

I thought about Finn's sister and the baby clothes that would never be worn and sadness washed over me–the same sadness that tended to trap me there in that house. I only had a few hours left. Surely I could make it a few more hours.

"I brought bacon." I announced.

Dad's eyes lit up. "I brought my appetite."

"Eggs?"

"You bet."

We settled into our routine, quietly trading sections of The Sunday Times and occasionally commenting about gas prices and terrorism or a new movie that was grossing billions at the box office. Dad didn't know books or economics and we never talked about religion, so we ate our eggs and bacon and sipped coffee in stained old mugs that had seen my mother's lipstick prints.

No mom. No Jenny. No Gigi. Just us.

We didn't talk any more about Gigi. He did, however, ask me about Finn.

"So, what's his name?"

I looked up from my bacon and stopped chewing. "Who's name?"

"The guy you don't want to talk about."

"What makes you think there's a guy I don't want to talk about?"

He hit me with a deadpan stare. "It may *seem* like I've been in a coma for the past several years, but I'm actually fairly observant, and you're not yourself this weekend. Something's different, and I know you haven't changed jobs or apartments recently." He set his fork down and took up a southern drawl that would have made Gigi proud. "I ain't a smart man, but I ain't dumb neither." Then he winked at me.

Now, I couldn't remember the last time my dad and I made eye contact, much less held it. And to my knowledge he had never, *ever* winked at me.

"Touché."

"What's that mean?"

"It means right back at ya."

He put both hands up. "Hey, you've already seen mine. There's nothin else to tell."

"Nothing I want to hear, anyway."

His arms went up on the table, waiting. I tried to keep eating but he just kept staring at me. It was no use.

I sipped my too strong coffee and made a face. I couldn't help smiling. "His name is Finn."

"Fin? Like a dolphin?"

"No, Finn. Like Finian's Rainbow. Only it's Finnegan. I think. He's from Ireland. And England. Both."

Wow. Some writer. Couldn't even get a sentence out, and Dad was plenty amused.

"So he's a ginger?"

"Not really. His skin is fair but he has dark curls and these gorgeous deep blue eyes–"

"Gorgeous, huh?" I wasn't one to use words like that to describe guys. I knew I sounded dorky. Dad started chuckling.

"I've known him like a week or two. Don't worry, you'll probably never have to meet him."

"And why's that?"

I stopped eating and looked dad right in the eye. "Because he's not even on this *continent* right now. Anyway, I'm trying to build my career. I'm not exactly looking for a relationship."

He just ignored me and kept right on chewing and talking. "And how did you two meet?" He was still smiling. A charming, infuriating smile. Like Finn's.

I pushed my plate away and gave up. "He dumped a coke down the front of my shirt at the Yankees game."

"You were at a game?" His eyes got huge and he looked like a kid again. As far as I knew, he hadn't been to a game at Yankee Stadium since he was a teenager, but he never missed them on TV.

"Yeah." I felt the color creeping up into my face again. When my editor at The Times offered me a couple of comp seats I never even thought of calling him up. I suddenly felt guilty that I'd given Kate my other ticket, but dad wasn't pulling the guilt card. He was genuinely excited that I got to see the game in person.

"Was it an accident or on purpose?"

"The fact that I was at the game?"

He shook his head, exasperated. "The coke! What happened?"

"I punched him in the nose."

"And that's why he dumped the coke on you?"

"The coke was an accident. It was mobbed, getting out of there. I didn't punch him for dumping it on me. I punched him for trying to wipe it off."

"Atta girl!" Dad sat back and crossed his arms over his chest, proud as can be.

"So he apologized and asked me for a drink and I was with Kate and he had a friend with him...so we all went to his club afterward."

"*His* club?"

"He and his dad own it together."

Dad's eyebrows went up. "And?"

I went back to my bacon. "And nothing. We've had a couple of dates and he's in Ireland visiting his family for a while."

Dad waited for a while but I didn't say anything, then he just mumbled. "Hmm."

"What *hmm*?"

"He got to you. That's good." He looked up at me from over the edge of the newspaper. "It's about time."

"What? What's that supposed to mean?"

"I knew *someone* would be able to crack the code, but he'd have to be good. Real good."

I narrowed my eyes. "Thanks a lot."

"Like Fort Knox in there." Dad ruffled my hair and pushed back from the table. "But oh what a treasure inside." He rinsed his plate and left it in the sink, leaving me to clean the kitchen and put things back in order for him.

I left dad with a couple of easy meals he could stick in the oven and a few frozen dinners. Shopping wasn't his strong suit, unless you counted beer, which I was willing to hand over if I happened to be closest to the fridge, but I refused to buy. In hindsight I guess it didn't matter all that much, but we had an understanding, and he knew it just as well as I did.

I went through the usual motions with a stunned sort of numbness. Apparently dad had an entirely differently opinion of me than I thought, suggesting that maybe–just maybe, he hadn't been in a beer-induced coma the *entire* time. It felt good to think of his unobtrusive little place in the recliner as half cave, half crow's nest.

Maybe I hadn't been the only one looking out for us all these years.

13

"Don't wait. The time will never be just right."
M.T.

By the time I got back home Sunday night it was late. The machine was blinking at me and I was surprisingly nervous about pushing the button. There were only three missed calls, but I figured one of them had to be Finn, until I realized I'd never given him that number. I checked my cell–nothing there either. The messages turned out to be from Kate, dad, and The Times. I don't know why I was surprised. They were the only people who ever called me anyway.

I was leaning all the way back in my desk chair, trying to rub the tension out of my temples when a voice started talking to me. It was the mysterious foreigner from my novel. He started out speaking in his normal voice and ended up, of course, with an Irish brogue and some very dry humor. We talked all night long, this character and I – in what turned out to be a complete departure from the storyline. My character (I renamed him Ian) refused all my attempts to learn his tells, however. It was a frustrating sort of back and forth that ended in my finally telling him off, so he hopped on a plane and headed back to Galway.

About four a.m. I stumbled to the bathroom and then fell headlong into bed. At five my cell phone rang. I propped opened bleary eyes and tried to focus on the numbers but I couldn't recognize the pattern. It was all strange and jumbled. There were three numbers like an area code followed by a group of two, then another sequence of three, then four. I blinked several times trying to make sense of it all.

Finally I realized what was happening. I sat up, pushed the hair out of my eyes and slapped my cheeks.

"Hello?" I tried to sound chipper.

"Hi there."

No need for coffee. My heart jump-started immediately. "Finn?"

"Did I wake you?"

I thought about coming back with something flippant, but his voice was quiet, almost shy. "It's ok. It's...good to hear from you. How are you?"

There was a long pause on the other side of the phone.

"Finn? Are you all right?"

"Yeah, yeah. I'm fine." Another pause. "No, not really so fine."

I'd already guessed as much. The question was just a formality. He knew what time it was. So why the call? Why now?

"What's going on? Where are you?"

"I'm in Ireland." *Galway, perhaps?*

"Kate told me." Silence. "...uh, well–David told her and... and it had been a while since I'd heard from you so she just-"

"I know. I should have called sooner. Did David tell you that my sister lost her baby?"

"Well, technically Kate told me. I'm so sorry Finn. How is she?"

"She's good. Holding up fairly well I'd say... all things considered. Her recovery hasn't been an easy one though. She's had an infection and she's still in hospital. I've brought my mum up from London to stay with her."

That fit, actually. I imagined him as the rock. The glue holding his fractured family together. "And how are you holding up?"

Another pause followed by a sigh. It wasn't the weather we were discussing– it was death and grief. Suddenly the idea of making small talk seemed out of place. I didn't even know his sister's name, and yet, there we were, tiptoeing around delicate details and trying not to stumble over our discomfort.

"It's not easy."

"Is your dad there?"

"He's coming this next weekend."

I nodded dumbly, as if he could see my face. I honestly didn't know what to say. I had often wondered how other families dealt with their grief. Images flooded my mind of my mother's silent funeral, of Jenny's slow destruction, and the tomb that our house became.

Relationships died in the wake of mortality. Unhurried, yet deliberate.

"I miss you." His words landed with a thud and brought me back to the conversation.

Neil Young once said that it's better to burn out than to fade away. I wanted so much to feel the burn, but my heart didn't know what to make of it. I'd made a point of staying as far away from the flame as humanly possible without actually freezing to death.

"I know that sounds silly, missing you. I mean, seeing as we haven't known each other very long, but I've been thinking about you–nonstop, as it turns out." His laugh was warm. "And I can't wait to come back. Truth is, I don't usually miss The States when I'm gone. This is home, you know? But this time it's different."

I was the difference? To my knowledge I'd never made a blip on anyone's radar, much less a *difference* in their lives. That couldn't have been what he meant.

Looking back, I'd have to say one of the great moments of truth happened in my life just then. There, at five in the morning, I was laying in my bed talking to a man half a world away who had called simply because he missed me. *Me.*

And yet, I had no idea how to support him. I wasn't exactly skilled at reassurance, but he wasn't calling because he needed a therapist. His humanity simply needed to touch someone else's. To know he was cared for. Understood. It was basic—almost primal.

I knew it in theory, but that's about it. I probably needed the same thing once upon a time - twice upon a time, but there wasn't anyone around. I wasn't sure I was capable of being that for someone else, but my own need that had kept itself hidden away all those years came screaming forward, demanding attention. My thirst for it overwhelmed my emotions and I began to cry. What a stupid thing to do.

"I miss you too." I managed. "And I'm so sorry for your loss."

The tears really made no sense at all. I couldn't be crying for him. It must have been triggered by the whole death-thing. Mom, Jenny...It had been a long time since I'd been confronted with personal loss. Like I said, I'd kept as far away from emotionally broken people as I could manage.

I felt like a traitor.

He was probably feeling flattered, thinking I was crying for him, but really I was just a mess. A big, bawling, one-hour-of-sleep mess. He was there, in the mix, of course, but I didn't know how to give him a place in my heart. It was too crowded. Too many areas taped off in yellow and black. Too many detours.

"I shouldn't have called like this. I'm so sorry."

I wiped my nose. "No! Please, don't be sorry. I'm glad you called. Really." I pushed up and settled against the pillows, looking up at the ceiling for the teleprompter that would translate my tangled thoughts into some sort of comprehensible sentence. *Just say it Truly. Just be honest with him.*

"Finn, I don't know what to make of all this either, believe me, but I miss you like crazy, and I'd half convinced myself you weren't going to call—that maybe you weren't even coming back, and—" The words were tumbling out and I was tumbling with them. Flipping over on myself and losing my center. What was I doing? But Finn interrupted.

"Have dinner with me?"

The thought temporarily stopped my momentum. "In Ireland?"

He laughed softly. "Well someday, yes." My stomach dropped. "For now, how about Thursday in New York? My flight lands early Thursday morning."

"A redeye? Really? I took you more for a first-class sort of 'chap'."

Finn laughed again. "I am in first-class. It was just the first plane I could get after the funeral."

When he said the word 'funeral' my world started to go black. Images flashed in and out of my vision without warning and my eyes filled with tears again. I tried desperately to hold it together and not let my voice quiver. "What's the rush? Is the film industry dying without you or do you have to take over for your dad at the club?"

"Neither." He let the word hang in mid air. "But I do have a date on Thursday and I really don't want to miss it."

I smiled through my tears. "I guess I'll see you then."

"By the way? I'm making reservations, so dress accordingly."

"Ooh! A *real* date?" I teased. "No hot dog vendors or walks in the park?"

"Hot dogs are fine for every day. I want to take you someplace special."

"What's the occasion?"

"There has to be an occasion?"

I don't think I'd ever put a dress on just for the hell of it, but still, he had a point. "I might have a little black dress somewhere in the back of my closet." *In the back for good reason!* Kate might even make me *wax!*

Finn sighed audibly. "How little? You may have to hire a bodyguard."

I chuckled at the thought. "Maybe I could borrow Adonis from the club?"

"I'll give you his number."

"Oh yeah?" I teased.

"–On second thought! Maybe I'll just behave myself."

"Have it your way."

Finn laughed again. "It's good to hear your voice. I feel better already. I'll see you soon."

I HUNG up the phone and dialed my emergency number. I realize it was a very girly thing to do, but I couldn't help it. Kate picked up on the first ring, in a panic.

"What! What's wrong?" I imagined her with bed head and the covers in a huge heap, until I heard David's voice in the background too, saying "What is it? Is someone dead?"

"Kate it's me. It's ok. No one is dead."

"No one is dead." She repeated.

"I just said that."

"I was talking to David."

"Oh."

There was a long pause, followed by a heavy sigh.

"Kate don't go back to sleep. I have a fashion emergency."

I could hear her voice moving farther away and coming closer, like a trombone. "At five-fifteen?"

"Not right this minute, no, but I do need you." I heard a door close somewhere in the distance. "What was that?"

"Ok David's in the bathroom–what's going on?"

"I'm really sorry I woke you up."

"It's ok I was about to get up anyway. Now hurry up and tell me. Is it Finn or someone else?"

"Of course it's Finn! Don't be silly!" I hadn't told her about the near miss with Brad. "He just called to say he's flying in Thursday morning and asked me to dinner–somewhere that needs reservations. So I told him I had a little black dress hiding in my closet but you know better than anyone how bleak the back of my closet looks. The only black dress I've got is the one I wore–" I stopped mid-sentence. "Anyway, I need to go shopping."

Kate's voice perked up. "Baby I am so there! I've got a break from two to five this afternoon. I'll meet you at Barney's."

"Barney's? Kate I don't have a Madison Avenue budget. Starving freelance writer, remember?"

"I know that! We're just going to look–try on some high end designs, see what kind of dress fits you and your style then once I know what you really want I'll find it for you in a knock off version. Trust me–I do this all the time!"

"Why not just go straight for the cheap stores?"

"Every cheap store has its own flavor. I don't want to run all over town trying to figure out yours. The high-end stores have every style imaginable, all under one roof. Their sales clerks are trained to take one look at you and fit you into a great dress that will flatter you unmercifully. Saves us both time and I've got a rehearsal tonight."

"*Then* we go to the cheap stores?" I bit my lip.

"Yes. Don't worry. It'll be fun!"

"If you say so..."

"Meet me there at two and dress nice."

"Why?"

"Because you get better service if you look like you're really going to buy a dress from them."

Something was inherently wrong with that statement. "If I already had something that nice I wouldn't be going there."

"Don't be ridiculous. That is so not true. Just wear those black wool slacks of yours and a pair of heels. Oh! And the white crepe blouse with the black lace cami underneath it."

It was disconcerting that Kate knew my wardrobe better than I did. "I can't shop in heels! I can barely walk in heels!"

"Then you need all the practice you can get." She was starting to sound like my third grade teacher. "Don't bullshit me Truly. I've seen you in some stunning outfits. Quit being a coward!"

She was right, of course. I knew how to dress, I just didn't favor the girly thing. But I could wear the outfit she suggested. It spoke business elegance rather than frills.

"Ok. I'll be there."

"Did he mention where he's taking you? Like which restaurant?"

"No, he just said reservations–and that he wanted to take me someplace special."

"So he's flying back from Ireland to take you to dinner?"

I could hear David in the background again. "Finn? I thought he wasn't coming home till the weekend."

"As far as I know that's the plan."

"Fancy!"

"I know, right?" I smiled in spite of myself. "Thanks for your help."

"I haven't done anything yet."

"I know, but..."

"Ok. Love you too. Bye."

"Bye Kate."

14

"Give every day the chance to become the most beautiful of your life."
M.T.

After Finn's call, I was only able to sleep for three more hours before I sat bolt upright in bed, drenched in sweat. I'd been dreaming, I guess, but whatever it was that had scared the crap out of me vanished into the blinding light that entered my eyeballs.

I got up and took a shower, then decided to go through my closet and just see what was there. I was right. The only black dress I had I'd worn to Jenny's funeral. I don't know why I'd kept it. Even if I had another funeral to go to I wouldn't be able to put that dress on ever again, so I threw it away.

That left me with two skirts and three very casual summer dresses that I wore when Kate and I went to Cape Cod the summer before last. Not a lot to work with, and the one pair of black heels I had were super uncomfortable. If I was going to try to look like I knew how to walk in heels I'd have to have a pair that fit me better, but I could go shoe shopping without Kate, once we had the dress picked.

Next I balanced my checkbook and paid the rent. Even with the check I'd received from a recent magazine article, it was too tight for Barney's. I decided to do something I never do and slipped my credit card out of its holder in the file drawer and into my wallet. Just in case.

By the time I finished a quick sandwich and got dressed it was time to go. I took the subway uptown and walked the avenue a bit before heading into Barney's. Some of the stores were already decorated for the holidays, and it put me in a happy place, which was rare considering it reminded me of my mom. She loved Thanksgiving and and always made a big deal about Christmas when we were kids. On Christmas morning she'd get up early and bake cinnamon buns. Jenny and I would wake up to the whole house smelling like warmth and nutmeg and caramelized sugar.

I found myself staring at my own reflection in a storefront window. Baggy coat, hat pulled down over my eyes, hands stuffed in my pockets. What the hell was wrong with me? I imagined Finn in a tailored suit coming to pick me up and realized I needed to step up my game. Kate was absolutely right.

The inside of Barney's was bright and vibrant and it somehow matched my mood, which I realized was also rare. I found the evening dresses and started thumbing through the racks. All the styles seemed way too short and clingy and low cut. I thought about the girls at Finn's club and how they advertised for exactly what they got. I didn't want to be that girl. I wanted to look sexy but still retain some class–if that was even possible.

As if on cue, a well-dressed older woman showed up at my elbow. "Hello. My name is Marion. Can I help you find something?"

"My friend is coming to help me. I'm afraid I'm not very good at this."

"Good at what, dear?"

"Shopping."

"Well, let's start with the occasion. Where will you be going?"

"Dinner."

"That shouldn't be too difficult. What kind of restaurant?"

I bit my lip. "The kind that requires reservations?"

Marion tossed her head back and laughed at this.

"I'm sorry but he didn't say. He just said he wanted to take me someplace special."

She opened my coat and looked me over, which I found somewhat invasive and yet comforting at the same time.

"Size six?"

I looked at her, incredulous. "Yes, but how did you–"

She shook her head. "It's my job to know dear. Now what's your budget for this dinner dress?"

Kate hadn't prepared me for this part, but Marion could see my hesitation. I stumbled a bit "Well, I'm not sure. It depends."

Her smile wasn't condescending, but more like a mother. "Don't worry dear. We'll try to find something that won't break your piggy bank." I swear the woman could read my mind along with my dress size.

She wrapped her arm around my shoulders and walked me toward the dressing rooms. She asked how Finn and I met and I told her how I punched him in the nose but he turned out to be the nicest guy I'd ever known and how he owns several businesses and is flying back from Ireland to take me to dinner. She got kind of misty-eyed and nodded in all the right places, then sat me in a large mirrored room on a big, round upholstered couch kind of a thing. A few minutes later Kate showed up.

"Sorry I'm late! I got caught up with an irate parent who wanted to know why her daughter wasn't on Broadway already." She plopped down next to me. "Why are you sitting in here?"

"I'm waiting for Marion."

"Who's Ma–"

Just then Marion showed up with five or six choices of varying lengths and cuts, introduced herself to Kate and promptly sent us into the dressing room to have me try them on.

"So why isn't she?"

"Why isn't who? What?"

"The girl. Is she ready for Broadway?"

"Oh. Well, not with a bun in the oven she's not." Kate slipped the first dress off its hangar. "Wow. This fabric is amazing!"

"Bummer. I take it her mom didn't know?"

"She does now."

I winced. I could just imagine the look on the mom's face.

"Yeah. She had potential too." We were silent for a minute as Kate slipped me into the dress and finished fastening the clips in the back.

"I'm so self conscious Kate. I never wear anything form fitting."

I turned around and we both looked in the mirror at the same time. It was incredible.

I was zipped into a deep navy blue shift with shimmering stripes of a lighter tone that hung perfectly to my mid-thigh and hugged my hips just enough to drape softly at the waist. The slight flair at the bottom was fun but not too flirty, and a sweetheart neckline dipped down to reveal a small amount of cleavage that was suggestive without being revealing. The wide-set shoulder straps accentuated my collarbones in a way that looked almost supermodel-ish. It was...

"Stunning." Kate breathed out all at once.

Marion knocked lightly. "How'd we do?"

When Kate opened the door, Marion was holding a pair of strappy silver heels in one hand and a matching clutch in the other. "Come on out into the open room. There are more mirrors out here. You'll be able to see yourself from a different angle."

If only...

I slipped my feet into the shoes—which also fit me perfectly, by the way, and Kate spun me around until I was dizzy.

I looked at Marion through disbelieving eyes. "How did you know what size shoe I wear? I mean, is there a pumpkin waiting outside to take me to dinner too?"

Marion smiled a strange sort of knowing smile.

I searched the folds of the dress. "I'm afraid to ask where the price tag is, but I have to know..." Kate shot me a look, but she didn't know that Marion and I already had an understanding.

"I can guarantee you it's within your budget."

"You already discussed budget?" Kate asked.

"Not exactly." I bit my lip.

"Don't you want to try on anything else?" Kate asked insistently. I knew she wanted to go to the thrift stores, and we'd probably even find something great, but this dress–it really was like a Cinderella transformation.

"I'll give you the benefit of my discount, so you don't have to go searching all over Manhattan for the same look at a better price." Marion smiled when she saw my jaw drop.

Kate looked like she'd been shot by a stun gun.

I stared at Marion. "But why? Why would you do that?"

Marion shook her head. "I'm a sucker for a great romance."

Was that what this was? A great romance? Had I somehow become the leading lady in my own story? I studied myself in the mirror, then looked at all the other dresses hanging there. I'd never felt more beautiful in my life. This dress somehow defined me and although I couldn't put my finger on it, I knew I had to have it, even if I spent the next three months subsisting on ramen just to pay off the credit card bill.

I spun from side to side. "No. This is the one. I could try on a million other dresses and never feel as beautiful as I do in this."

"You do look pretty amazing." Kate was hesitant but smiling. "Besides, I don't know that I've ever heard you admit that you're beautiful."

"I didn't say I *was* beautiful, only that the dress makes me *feel* beautiful."

"Well, if you ask me they're both true." Marion added.

I felt confident and sexy but not the least bit trashy. I wasn't even self-conscious about my shape, which was a miracle in itself. I'd always hated the sensation of being ogled by men, and tried to steer clear of clingy fabrics and tight sweaters because of it.

Somehow none of that mattered. All I could think about was

Finn. Being on his arm, and the protection I knew he offered, unspoken. It didn't matter what other men thought, because I wasn't dressing to please them. The difference was subtle, but oh so important. It hit me like a cold breeze and I shuddered.

"So, I'd be ok in the car and in the restaurant, but what about in between? It's November!" The bust was slightly padded so that was great, but still, we're talking sleeveless and drafty!

Kate sighed and spun me around again. She could see I was a goner. "You've got that cute black coat that goes down just past your hips. You'll answer the door with your coat already on and buttoned up. Don't take it off until you're already inside the restaurant. Let *that* be the first time he sees you in it."

By this time Marion was grinning from ear to ear. Kate stood up and started pulling my hair off my shoulders. I've got a great necklace with matching earrings to compliment this neckline. I'll let you borrow them. Oh, and your hair needs to be up."

"Up?" I looked in the mirror. My only attempt at an up-do had been on prom night, but I pulled the pins at the last minute when I heard the car horn. I just couldn't do it.

"I'll come over after rehearsal on Thursday and help you."

It's a good thing one of us thought that would work out. "The most I ever accomplish is a pony tail. I don't even have the right stuff to put my hair up. What do I need?"

"I've done a million of these for dance performances over the years–just trust me, I'll bring everything we need."

I nodded silently at my reflection in the mirror and realized that it didn't really matter what my hair looked like. Either way, it was going to be a lovely night.

15

"Never argue with a fool.
Onlookers may not be able to tell the difference."
M.T

It was a good thing I had three days to get ready, because it took that long to convince myself this Cinderella date was really happening. I looked up every beauty tip the Internet girly mags had to offer. I plucked. I waxed. I lotioned. I trimmed my hair and deep conditioned my split ends. I soaked and exfoliated my feet. I even went and got a real manicure.

On Thursday I spent an hour lying on my back with cucumber slices over my eyes. Supposedly that was the old school way to reduce puffiness and dark circles, and since I'd barely slept, I figured it couldn't hurt. I followed that up with some type of concoction that was supposed to tighten my pores. By the time Kate showed up I must have looked like a different person, because she took me by the shoulders and moved me around at different angles to look at me.

"Oh you've got to be kidding me."

"What?" I asked. "What is it? Did I do something wrong?"

"Oh this is bad."

"Crap! I knew I should've bought a book or something."

She picked up a few strands of my hair and noticed the trim. "You did all this since I saw you on Monday?" She even rubbed the hair between her fingers and smelled it.

"Yeah...?"

A smile broke all the way across her face. "I've never seen you like this. You're like...a girl!"

I pushed her away from me. "I just want to make a good impression! So sue me!"

She picked up my hand and studied it. "A French manicure? With nail polish and everything?"

"Look, are you here to help me or not?"

She opened her bag. "Absolutely! I just–came prepared for a fight, but I can see that won't be necessary. In fact, a quick little up-do and some makeup and I'm outta here!"

"Yeah well, I don't want to look like a hooker. I just want to look natural – well, a little better than natural, obviously."

"Don't worry I'm not planning on creating a monster. I just want to accentuate what you've already got, but first the hair." Kate started unpacking her bag and the first thing she pulled out was a bottle of Cachaça.

"I already put mayonnaise in my hair. You want me to soak it in Cachaça now?"

Next she brought out two shot glasses. "No, silly, it's not for your split ends. It's for your split personality."

"Ha ha. Very funny."

Kate poured us each a shot and handed one to me. "It's for good luck." She smiled sympathetically. "And to calm your nerves."

It really was very kind of her. My nerves were shot, and as the sweet rum slid down my throat it seemed to burn off all the frayed ends. I took a deep breath and opened my eyes.

Kate was grinning at me. "Ok, ready?"

"Have at it, maestro."

"Speaking of which!" Kate reached back into her bag and pulled out a CD.

My eyebrows went up. "You made me a mix CD? What are we in high school?"

"It's to get you in the mood!" She went over and popped it into the sound system.

"In the mood for what? Cheerleading practice?"

Kate put her hands on her hips. "Would you mind just working with me a little here? Now listen, it's designed to take you from start to finish, as you get ready. It starts out with upbeat, fun 'getting ready for a date' music, then starts to slow down and there are a few ballads at the end to get you feeling nice and romantic. By the time he gets here you'll be perfect."

"That's gonna have to be *some* music selection!"

"Ha ha."

As usual though, Kate was right. The music began to fill my apartment with energy, and by the time she was halfway done with my hair, I was bopping along. I couldn't help myself.

"This is a fantastic idea! Why haven't you ever told me about this music thing before?"

"Well, that's easy." Kate lodged a bobby pin between her teeth and studied my hair, trying to decide where to put it. "When was the last time you asked me to come over and help you get ready for an important date?"

"Good point."

"Mmmhmm."

She let my natural curls do their thing and left a few strands to hang around my shoulders, but otherwise it was a beautiful, understated lift that made my jaw line and cheekbones look like they were chiseled onto my face. By the second song she was adding foundation and some mineral makeup that was so light it felt like my natural skin, but the glow was beautiful.

I picked up some of the round containers and funny looking

brushes. One of them looked like something you'd stencil paint onto a wall with. "Where do you even get this stuff?"

Kate smiled. "I'm glad you like it."

"I do!"

"Now for the eyes." She started with navy blue eyeliner, and finished with a light combination of baby blue and silver shadows that perfectly matched my dress. I rarely wore eye shadow but Kate used a light enough hand that I didn't feel uncomfortable. In fact, I'd never seen my eyes look that way. She finished with some deep black mascara and a light pink lip-gloss.

I looked in the mirror and had trouble believing what I was seeing. It was like I was my own avatar. It was me, but...not. I started to sweat. Good thing I wasn't zipped into that dress yet.

"I don't know if I can do this."

"What? What do you mean?"

I got up and started to pace. "This isn't really me, Kate. I'm not this girl. What was I thinking? I can't do this."

"Yes you can."

I started shaking my head.

Kate looked at her watch. It was five forty-five and Finn was due at six thirty. She poured me another shot. I downed it gratefully, but immediately felt it go to my head.

"Now let's get you a piece of bread and a big glass of water." Kate led me over to the kitchen and sat me down. "Listen to me. You are still the same girl you were an hour ago. You're just getting dressed and going out on a date. No big deal."

"No big deal." I repeated, taking a big gulp of water.

"C'mon now. Man up. Let's get you into that dress."

She was absolutely right. It was just a date.

A date to some unknown special place that required reservations, in a dress I'd spent a small fortune on.

"What if I don't know the right fork?"

Kate zipped me up and pulled out a beautiful diamond and sapphire pendant. It hung at just the right length to accentuate the neckline of the dress.

"Oh my god! You were right about this necklace! It's perfect!"

The matching earrings had just a bit of a drop design so with my hair up they dangled and shimmered in the light. She put one in for me and handed me the other.

"Forks are easy. Just start on the outside and work your way in and use common sense. You'll be fine."

"If you say so."

"Now the shoes."

"Why? It's only six. Why do I have to be dressed so early?"

"So you can get used to wearing the dress and the shoes and the whole combination."

"You mean like a *dress* rehearsal?" I started laughing at my own joke. Kate was not amused. She was serious.

"Exactly like a dress rehearsal." She pointed at me. "I want you to walk around the apartment after I leave. Sit, stand, dance, move all around into and out of different positions and feel the dress around you. Let it become a part of you and then you won't feel self conscious in it. By the time Finn gets here you won't even remember you have it on. You'll move with confidence as if you dress like this all the time, because that, my friend, is what class is all about."

I thought back to all the times I'd watched Kate in a dress and heels. She did make it look effortless. I wondered if half an hour would be enough time for me to look like anything but a stumbling fool.

She grabbed her purse and picked up her coat.

"You're leaving?"

"I told you, I've got rehearsal. Besides, you look like a princess. My work here is done!" Kate waved her hand in a regal flourish and bowed to me. Then she picked up the silver clutch and held it out to me. "Some lip gloss, a small mirror, your driver's license and bank card, a little cash and some tissues." I took it from her, trying to make a mental list of the things she'd just said. "Nothing more, and nothing less. Got it?"

"I got it." I answered, wondering if she believed me.

Kate grabbed me by the shoulders and kissed my cheek. "I'm so proud of you! You can totally do this. Now don't you doubt yourself, not for one second, you hear me?"

I stood there watching her leave, trying my best to feel beautiful.

Kate kissed me on the cheek and stood in my doorway for a couple more seconds. "You're going to be great. Truly."

"Thanks. I'll call you."

"I know." She smiled and walked out the door.

AFTER KATE LEFT I closed the blinds and turned up the music. I swayed and turned and tried a few of the old dance moves I remembered. I felt ridiculous, of course, but that could hardly be helped. I was, after all, dancing around my apartment to romantic music. Alone.

Kate left her bag full of goodies along with the bottle, but any more Cachaça and Finn might have to kiss his chastity plan good-bye. As I twirled past my reflection in the mirror, the room spun momentarily out of control and I suddenly remembered a piece from that dream—the one that woke me up in a sweat.

In the dream I was standing, looking into that very mirror, when a silhouetted figure came up behind me and tried to choke me. I couldn't make out a face or a voice or any other indicator except his hands looked enormous against my tiny throat. My heart started hammering as I strained to remember any other significant details, and when I heard the pounding on the door, for a split second I couldn't distinguish what was real from the memory struggling to find its way into the clearing.

Then I heard it again. Someone pounding on the door.

I looked back at the bag Kate had left. She'd been on her way to rehearsal. She must have forgotten to grab it.

I pulled open the door with a flourish and put on a sexy voice. "Did you forget something?"

But when I opened my eyes my heart stopped and I swallowed down a scream.

It was Christopher.

And he was drunk.

"Hey baby!" He pushed his way into the room before I could stop him and closed the door. He looked me over hungrily and threw one of the locks, fingering the other two. "Nice work. Afraid the big bad wolf's coming to blow your house down?"

I was panicking but I tried to steady my words. "Something like that. What are you doing here?"

He came over to me and wrapped his hands around my waist just tight enough to remind me how much bigger and stronger he was. "Aw, now is that any way to greet an old friend?"

"You're drunk."

"Occupational hazard."

I took his hands and peeled them off my dress. It made me sick to think he'd touched me in it. "Last time I looked, we were hardly friends."

His finger traced my clavicles and he leaned in to kiss my neck. My body responded without my permission and I backed away.

"Yeah, well. That wasn't exactly my choice." He started toward me again. "The not being friends part. Where you goin' anyway? You look..." He swallowed, searching for the words, genuinely amazed. "Incredible."

Without warning his expression stung and the poison began to spread. "What, no snide comments? No suggestions for improvement? Come on...surely you can find something you almost love about me."

He smiled at me then. His Christopher smile. I took at good look at the man standing before me. A man whose whispered lies had made me doubt my convictions and whose touch melted my resistance until I was nothing but liquid that formed to the shape of his container, with no form or substance left to call my own. My heart broke all over again. And he saw. And he knew.

I cursed myself and stuck my chin out. "I have a date. In fact, he'll be here any minute, so please leave."

"Must be a pretty fancy date." Christopher slurred. "You never dressed like this for me." He fingered the material of the dress.

I looked him straight in the eye. "You never asked."

It was true in more ways than one. He had never asked me for anything– he only took what he wanted and left. Again and again. So what the hell was I doing? Fishing? Some pathetically desperate attempt to obtain closure on a seeping wound? This man had systematically ripped my self-confidence to shreds, but not before he played his games that left me bruised inside and sometimes even out.

I used to tell myself he didn't know his own strength. That in the throws of passion he just grabbed too hard. He did have a tender side, and when he was tender his touch was like angels' kisses. I had craved him in ways that didn't make sense, and needed him more than food, which, it turns out, was not a wise decision on my part. When he stopped calling I spiraled into a cycle of obsessive exercise and stress puking that finally landed me in the hospital, which is where I met my therapist.

For about a nanosecond I thought I might have wounded him, and it somehow gave me a burst of courage. In a move of unrehearsed brilliance, I sidestepped him at the exact moment he reached for me. I managed to get around him and over to the door before he could recover his balance. I threw the lock and willed my heart to a slow gallop, then pulled the door open. I could hear my neighbors talking in the hallway and thanked God for witnesses.

I said, purposely loud and insistent enough for them to hear. "You're not welcome here. Please leave!"

The murmuring stopped and the couple from next apartment over appeared in the open doorway. "Is there a problem here Truly?"

I looked at Christopher and said, with all the confidence my wilting heart could muster. "Not as long as he leaves there isn't."

Rich Beaufort was ex-marine. He wasn't especially tall but what he lacked in stature he made up for in biceps. Christopher looked at Rich and then at me and he knew he'd been beat.

He sniffed and straightened, then put his hands up in front of him. "No problem here. There's nothing in this apartment worth my time. I was just leaving anyway."

Rich stepped into the room, pulling his wife Kristie in with him. "Sure you were. And we were just coming over for a visit."

Christopher stalked out and hit the button for the elevator with enough force that it echoed down the hall. Rich closed the door behind him and that left the three of us standing awkwardly in my apartment. I knew their names and the basic sketch of their story, but that was about it. Mostly we just exchanged sociable waves and nods in passing.

When I heard the elevator doors close I started hyperventilating.

Kristie was staring at me. "Are you ok? Do want us to call someone? The police maybe?"

I shook my head. "I should've never opened the door. I thought it was my friend Kate. She...left something behind." I nodded in the direction of the bag as I steadied myself on the wall.

"Why don't you sit down?" Kristie took my arm and led me to the couch. "Ex-boyfriend?"

I nodded, staring dumbly into space. The heaving came out of nowhere and I sprinted for the bathroom. Up came the cachaça and the bread and the water until all that was left was the putrid bile Christopher's presence inspired. I brushed my teeth tried to pat my face dry so as not to smudge Kate's beautiful makeup job.

Thankfully the dress came out relatively unscathed. My heart was another matter entirely. It kept spinning in circles, even after the room had stopped.

Rich and Kristie were still there when I came out.

"I think I'll be ok now. Thanks so much for stepping in when you did. I don't know what I would have done."

Rich shook his head. "Don't mention it. Anytime you need anything—"

Kristie handed me a slip of paper with their phone number on it. Who said New Yorkers were hard and unfeeling? "You can call anytime."

"Thanks."

Kristie managed a smile. "Going out tonight?"

I nodded.

"But not with him?" Rich added hopefully.

I shook my head. "No. Not with him. Never again with him." I hoped I sounded convincing, because I didn't trust my heart enough to know what I might have done if he had stayed.

Kristie smiled sympathetically. "Well...have a good night."

They let themselves out but not before Rich reminded me to lock the door behind them—as if I could help it.

I'd let myself get lazy. I knew better than to rip a door open like that without looking to see who it was. I was slipping, and it just wasn't like me.

My thoughts went back to the dream. The choking thing behind me, threatening what I could see of myself. It absolutely freaked me out that I'd remembered that piece of the dream just seconds before Christopher knocked on my door. Was it some kind of premonition? And if so...why?

I sat down on the couch and began to rock back and forth. I thought about calling my therapist but I couldn't untangle my thoughts. Where would I even begin? I wanted to call Kate, but I was so ashamed of my weakness.

Just then another knock came at the door. My heart sped up and I tiptoed over to the peephole.

Finn.

16

"Do the thing you fear most and the death of fear is certain."
M.T.

F inn looked exactly the way I'd pictured him in my mind. His deep navy blue suit was perfectly tailored and had a slight sheen that complimented the shimmering silver stripes in my dress. Although, how he could have possibly known that completely baffles me, even to this day.

I turned each lock slowly, trying to give myself time to compose an opening line, but when I finally got the door open all I had for him were eyes rimmed with tears. The concern on his face bordered on pain, and I couldn't understand it for a moment, until I remembered what he'd just been through with his family. Poor guy. He'd flown from tragedy to basket case. What a great catch I was turning out to be.

Still, he closed the door behind himself and immediately drew me into his arms. I let myself fall into the sweet smell of his chest and just tried to breathe. It wasn't easy. I felt the choking around my throat as if the dream and the reality had somehow combined, blocking my airway and sending me into a panic. I started to shake but his arms held me fast.

He didn't say anything for a few minutes. He just let me breathe, and soon the rhythm of my breath matched his, strong and slow and steady. I let go of his suit and took a step back, re-locking the door with shaking hands. Finn watched this and the concern on his face turned to alarm.

"Truly what's happened?"

I moved silently toward the couch and he followed. When we'd both sat down, I took a deep breath, trying to form the right words in my mind. I had to tell him about Christopher, but how?

There was guilt and shame mixed in with the fear, and alto-gether it was just an ugly combination. Talk about a downer on date night...But it was already too late. Somehow I had to explain.

I stared up at the locks on the door and remembered an earlier conversation we'd had. Finn already knew why the locks were there, if only in vague generalizations.

His eyes followed mine. "Was he here?!"

I nodded dumbly and Finn started gently squeezing both sides of me from my shoulders all the way down my arms.

"Did he hurt you?"

I shook my head. *Not physically, anyway.*

He grasped my hands. "Are you all right, then? You didn't let him in, did you?"

I could see Finn going through the image he had of me and my triple locked door. Of course he would assume my diligence–that I wouldn't have been stupid enough to open the door without looking first.

But I did. I did and now I was paying for it. And so was Finn.

Tears that had only threatened before now spilled over in earnest. I put my head in my hands and let them come. Let them wet my dress. The night was already a mess.

"I thought it was Kate. She'd left here only minutes before he showed up. I thought maybe she was coming back for a bag she'd left." It was still sitting on the counter and I pointed over to it as proof.

Finn was nodding. "So you opened the door."

I nodded back, shame washing my face red through the streaks of tears. Finn pulled a handkerchief out of his breast pocket and tried to dab my eyes. A hankie? Really? Who the hell carried hankies anymore?

I snatched it out of his hand in frustration and got up, trying to somehow dry my face without obliterating the makeup that must be completely ruined by now.

"How long ago was this Truly? Is he still hanging around somewhere?" Finn got up and went to the window, searching already darkened streets for a man he'd never seen.

"Don't be ridiculous Finn. Come away from there. Do you really think he's hanging around watching my apartment?"

As soon as I said the words the possibility became real and my whole world constricted.

"Do you really think he's *not*?"

I'm sure he didn't mean to make it sound as ominous and threatening as it did, but with his hand still parting the curtains I tasted bile and ran for the bathroom again. Great. Now he was listening to me heave. I thought about making him leave, but the last thing I wanted was to be alone that night.

My hair came out of its pins and fell down around my face as the next wave hit, but somewhere in the midst of it Finn was there, jacket off and sleeves rolled up, crouched down beside me. He gently gathered up my hair and held it out of the way. He smelled like a million bucks and I was absolutely mortified.

"I don't remember asking for help." I managed between heaves.

"You shouldn't have to ask." He said softly.

"There's nothing left in me anyway." I sat back against my thighs and tried to breathe through the shaking, which had returned with a vengeance.

Finn let go of my hair and stood up. He took a washcloth off the shelf, got it wet, and tucked it in against the skin on the back of my neck. It felt surprisingly good. Why didn't I know this trick?

Of course, when you own a bar, watching people throw up is probably an occupational hazard. Kind of like Christopher being drunk.

Christopher was a few years older than me, and he'd been bar tending since he was eighteen. Not legally, of course, but his family owned a restaurant and he'd been feeding the cops free pitchers of beer on game days since he was in junior high probably.

Like every good bartender he was extremely observant. He was also funny and good-looking and sharply sarcastic. He told me once that he'd been drunk on every possible kind of alcohol. I used to think that was cool, but now I just think it's sad.

That man could make a mean drink. Unfortunately, he also made a mean drunk.

He was the one who made me that first Caipirinha. He was also the first person who ever made me wish I was dead. I'd always thought rejection was the deadliest form of torture. As it turns out, being inconsequential is worse. Truly worse.

Finn was just standing there, looking at me, wondering what to do next. The wave passed and I stood on trembling legs. "Would you mind getting me that bag that Kate left? It's on the counter."

"Not at all." He was back with the bag in about a nanosecond. Granted, it was a small apartment and he did have fairly long legs.

God, he looked good, even in rolled up shirtsleeves. I was crazy about him, and it scared me to death. I couldn't afford crazy. Not again.

"How late are we for the reservation?"

Finn blinked at me. "You're worried about a reservation? That doesn't matter."

Doesn't matter? Of course it mattered! I'd spent a month's worth of money I didn't really have on that outfit, but he didn't know that. Or maybe he'd figured as much.

At that point I was having trouble making sense of anything. I just closed the bathroom door and left him standing in my living room. There was no way Christopher was going to make me a prisoner in my own apartment. I was going out on that date and I hoped with everything in me that Christopher *was* watching.

Unfortunately, I knew better. He'd already moved on to the next best thing on his list.

I hadn't paid attention much to what Kate was doing, but I knew how to put on makeup, so I reapplied a little foundation and some blush. Thankfully, even through the tears the eyes had stayed mostly good. I could never accomplish the hairdo, so I just arranged it loose around my shoulders and brushed my teeth for what felt like the twenty-seventh time that day.

In the bottom of Kate's bag was a small bottle of perfume that perhaps she'd thought better of earlier, but I sniffed it and realized it was the perfect mask for puke and tears. I walked through a light cloud of it and decided that was the best I could do.

When I emerged Finn was standing by the window again, looking out.

"If you're trying to look menacing, don't bother." I said.

Finn raised an eyebrow at me.

"But if you're trying to look wildly handsome you're doing a great job!"

His smile was like a warm breeze. "Are you sure you still want to go? We could order in, you know."

"Are you kidding me?" I twirled around. "I'm already fancy!" I joined him by the window. "What are you looking at over here anyway?"

He slipped his arm around my waist and turned me away, leading me toward the door. "Never you mind."

I looked back over my shoulder. "Listen if he is out there, I want nothing more than for him to see me with you."

Finn chuckled. "Me too. Now do you have a coat?"

The coat! I was supposed to be wearing the coat when he got there! I sighed loudly and my shoulders slumped.

"What's wrong?"

"Nothing."

Finn turned me around to face him. "I don't feel right about this Truly. Do you want to talk about it? Please, tell me what happened."

"Can I tell you over dinner? I'm starving and I really don't want to be here anymore."

He placed a kiss on my forehead and slipped into his jacket. "Of course."

I walked over to the tree and reached for the black coat Kate had suggested, but Finn's hand got there ahead of mine.

"Please. Allow me."

He helped me into my coat and gently lifted my hair out of the back of the collar for me, then kissed my neck before he laid it down again. "You have gorgeous hair. It looks so beautiful when it's down 'round your shoulders."

If he was trying to make me feel better about losing Kate's hairdo it was working. The warmth spread down my neck and through my back until I shuddered. He smiled down at me. "Now you know how I feel."

"Pardon me?"

"I was standing by the window wondering how I'd get through dinner looking at you."

"Well, watching someone throw up is enough to make anyone lose their appetite." I winked.

"That's not what I mean. I mean the whole of you. Your *fancy* dress." He tried to imitate my twirly exuberance. "Your hair. Your eyes."

"You're joking."

He put my face in both of his hands and shook his head. "I'm not."

I stared at him. Christopher was handsome too, and he always knew just what to say. Of course, he was just trying to get me into bed, which, to be honest, wasn't all that difficult.

But Finn wasn't, and for the life of me I couldn't figure out his angle.

He kissed me softly and I blinked back more tears. "Can we just go?"

"Sure."

When we got down to the street level I realized what Finn had been looking at. Double parked in front of my building was a black stretch limo. Oh, how I wish Christopher had been there to see that.

I looked around on the street but there was no sign of him, not that he would have been standing out in the open, taunting me or anything. That wasn't his style. Still, I tried to look confident and happy as an older man in a black suit got out and opened my door. When we were safely inside the tinted-windowed land yacht, I let myself relax a little. It probably wasn't bulletproof, but it sure felt that way. I'd never been inside a limousine before and I tried to forget Christopher and just revel in the luxury of it all.

Finn, on the other hand, looked fairly comfortable sitting there with his jacket unbuttoned. He put his arm around me, and motioned to a chilled glass sitting next to me.

"I took the liberty of pouring us a glass of white wine. I hope that's all right?"

I picked it up and took a sip. "That's great. Thank you." The first taste was terrible after having just brushed my teeth, but once I got past that, it wasn't bad. It was a relief not to be drinking Cachaça. After throwing it up so many times I wasn't sure I'd ever drink it again.

I turned toward him, crossing one leg over the other. The dress was a lot shorter than I was used to wearing, but I was determined to at least *try* to act like a lady. I reached up and put my hand against his chest. It was warm against my chilled fingers and I kissed him on the cheek. "Well, thanks in advance, for tonight... And for everything before too."

"It's my pleasure, really." He threaded his fingers through mine.

"So, where are you taking me?"

"Hartford."

I sat up. "*Connecticut?*"

"Yes."

"What? There were no good restaurants in New York?" I regretted the comment as soon as it came out of my mouth. You could dress me up, but you couldn't take me out.

He narrowed his eyes. "Have you ever been to Connecticut?"

"Not for dinner, no."

"Then why don't you reserve your judgment for later, like after dessert."

"Fair enough." The wine started to smooth over my frayed nerve endings and my body relaxed a bit. With so little in my stomach all day I'd have to be careful not to completely lose my cool. He sat quietly, just watching me drink. Then it dawned on me. He was waiting for me to talk some more.

"I'm really sorry about all that, back at the apartment."

"You don't need to apologize. You didn't do anything wrong."

"Except ruining your beautiful plans."

"You didn't ruin anything."

"I was a basket case when you came to pick me up, I've been in tears, you've watched me throw up, and now we're extremely late for where ever it is we're going. It's just - I would totally understand if didn't want to–"

I pulled away ever so slightly and shook my head at him, whispering. "You think you want me, but you don't. Not really."

He leaned his forehead back into mine. "How do you know what I want?"

"I'm broken, Finn. My heart doesn't know how to do this the right way." It was the most honest I'd ever been with myself, and I could hardly believe I'd actually said those words to another person.

"We're all broken."

"Yes, well...some of us irreparably so."

"Nothing is beyond repair. Trust me."

"I don't know how."

Finn put my face back in his hands. "What's his name?"

"Who?"

"Your ex-boyfriend. The one who inspired all the locks."

I tried to shake my head but it was difficult with him holding it like that. "It's not just him Finn. I was broken way before he came along. Just ask my therapist." Another admission. Only Kate knew I'd been seeing someone. I'd never even told my dad. Sure, dad knew I had the eating disorder, but he never knew why. At least, he never asked. I guess he assumed it was mom or Jenny or maybe even him. Come to think of it, I was so busy exploring my own emotional landscape, I never even stopped to wonder about his.

Finn went to put his arm up on the back of the seat. I coiled back involuntarily, and I caught myself, but not before Finn saw what I was doing. He blinked, incredulous. I hadn't meant to respond like that. I didn't think of him that way, it was just...reflex.

"Christopher." I said plainly. "His name is Christopher, and I'd be happy to bring you to his apartment. Feel free to hunt him down." I waved my hand and smirked. "Duel at dawn, pistols at thirty paces. Whatever it takes. Be my guest."

He grinned at the reference and that broke the ice a bit, which was a relief, since my desire to jump from a moving vehicle was ill-advised in a cocktail dress and heels. I reached for the bottle and refilled my glass. Finn tipped his up to me for a refill as well.

I started to explain the events of the evening. How Christopher had been drunk when he showed up–how he'd reached for me, and how my neighbor and his wife had pretty much rescued me.

Finn laughed when I told him how I'd taken advantage of Christopher's drunkenness and thrown him off balance enough to get to the door ahead of him.

"You're quick. I like that in a woman. I guess I'll have to stay on my toes."

We'd finished another glass of wine and my body was warm from the tip of my head to my four-inch heels. I knew if I didn't eat something soon I'd be in trouble. I looked at him in all serious-ness. "Somehow I don't think you're going to have to worry about that. I've never once considered dodging your advances."

Finn's eyes almost blinked and he swallowed with a shallow breath. "You." He leaned in and kissed my cheek. "Are the most lovely woman I have ever laid eyes on."

I smiled up at him, but I couldn't seem to maintain eye contact.

"One of these days you're going to have to learn how to take a compliment."

"You know your dad told me something similar a couple of weeks ago?"

He laughed. "Now *that* doesn't surprise me. He's quite taken with you."

"With me?" My chin tucked in as I shook my head. "Why?"

Finn just smiled and pointed. "Because of that right there."

I looked over my shoulder. "What?"

"Because you don't even realize how beautiful you are. Most women who come into the club are so full of their own virtue it's a bit sickening after a while. You don't even realize what you're like and it's...enchanting."

If the Brits had ever made the cultural leap into the twenty-first century there was certainly no sign of it from Finn's mouth. He made me laugh.

He also made me want to cry.

I'd never in my life felt so valued as I did in this man's presence, and it was frightening. Simply frightening.

17

"Don't part with your illusions.
When they are gone, you may still exist, but you have ceased to live."
M.T.

J ust about the time I thought I couldn't drink any more of that wine Finn pulled out the appetizers–a small plate of cheeses and meats, chilled shrimp, a few crackers and some grapes. It was just what my rebellious stomach needed.

We ate slowly and began to talk about his sister and his family. The date wasn't going to begin once we got to the restaurant, it had already begun. The limo ride gave us a good long time to talk face to face, with no crowds to impress and no traffic to stress over. There was a black privacy shield up between us and the driver, enclosing us in our own little moving room. It didn't matter how long it took to get to Hartford. I had Finn all to myself.

The baby's death had affected him more than I realized.

"Eiran was the baby of our family. We all doted on her. She's very petite, like you."

"*Petite?* Is that a nice way of saying I'm short?"

Finn smiled. "Yes, but also very cute."

"Nice recovery!" I teased, nudging him in the ribs.

His intensity was a little overwhelming at times. If we didn't break the ice here and there I might end up trapped beneath it.

Finn was quiet for a moment. "She never wanted anything more than to be a mother. She loves children, and children love her. She wants a big Irish family, and this loss has been devastating. They had to do some surgery, and aren't sure now if she'll ever be able to have children, which has shaken her entire world, you know?"

I just nodded, staring with what I'm sure was a really stupid look on my face. I didn't know if I even wanted kids, so I couldn't really relate to someone who wanted a truckload of them. Still, I could relate to loss, even if it was at a sort of distance.

Then the distance started closing in.

"It wasn't like I knew this baby, but it was a part of Eiran, and now it's gone and a part of *her* is gone, you know? She'll never be the same person I knew growing up, all bubbly and fun and carefree. She's been changed by this, and you can't – change back."

I just kept nodding. I didn't know what would come out of my mouth if I tried to open it so I just kept it shut.

"Do you feel like a different person now, having lost your mother?"

No real person had ever asked me that point blank, except maybe my therapist, but I don't consider him a real person. I was completely unprepared to answer, so I just sat there, sweating.

"Will you tell me about her?"

My mother? Could I talk about my mother?

He didn't seem fazed by my inner hysteria, or maybe he couldn't see it. I opened my mouth and words began to exit through the hole.

"I was fourteen when my mother died. It shaped my whole life after that – or maybe distorted would be more accurate."

Finn focused in on my face as I spoke.

"I don't think I really understood how it affected me, because I was so young."

It was Finn's turn to nod.

"Not that I felt young at the time. I felt ancient at fourteen."

"Why ancient?"

"Because mom had been sick for over a year when she died, and it was me and Jenny, trying to take care of her and dad." When I spoke Jenny's name my eyes teared without my permission.

"Is Jenny your sister then?"

"She was."

He looked puzzled. "Where is she now?"

I lost it then. I made the mistake of blinking and huge tears rolled down my cheeks. "She's dead too."

"I'm so sorry." Finn pulled me into his arms and I began to rock. I didn't mean to. It was just something I did when I was sad. He rocked right along with me, stroking the hair back from my face as I cried.

"Great. Now I've ruined your suit *and* my dress."

"I don't care about suits and dresses." He whispered gently. "How did she die, Truly?"

"She was stabbed." I managed. My voice got stronger, fueled by anger and injustice. "By her boyfriend's rival gang leader." I had to laugh at myself. "Kind of like a bad movie, isn't it?"

He was shaking his head while kissing the top of mine. "Some lives have more than their share of grief."

I looked up at him and caught the faintest sense of regret, but I couldn't figure out where it was coming from.

He shook his head. "How long after your mother died was your sister murdered?"

Murdered. Wow, I never really used that term, even in my own head, but it was true, wasn't it?

"Did the person who did it go to jail at least?"

My voice took on that monotone, disconnected sound. I could hear myself telling the story somewhere in the distance, but it wasn't close enough to feel anymore, which was comforting, if not completely senseless.

"No, he's dead too. There was a big fight after it happened. A lot of them died that night. Jenny's boyfriend too. It was just as well. I didn't want a bunch of gang-bangers at her funeral and they were too busy burying their own to come to hers."

Finn's arms went somewhat slack, as if he'd spent every last ounce of energy he had listening to me. I knew how he felt, but for me it was replaced by need–the need to feel something on a different level. I stared up at him, trying to somehow convey the emptiness I needed filled.

He seemed to understand and I watched him struggle with the want. He reached up and stroked my face with the back of his hand. He was human, after all, and he'd been here before, I could see it.

Then he kissed me, tentatively at first, but the fire we'd sparked a couple of times before flashed immediately into flame, and there was no escape in a moving vehicle. He pulled me onto his lap and I don't even think a fire hose would have done us much good, but within moments the car stopped and a voice came over the intercom, telling us we'd arrived at our destination.

We had just enough time to right ourselves when the driver opened my door. I shook my hair out and blinked a couple of times, laughing. "You sure you want dinner?"

Finn was breathing hard, trying to reverse his engines. "I'm not sure of anything right now!"

He looked up at me like a helpless little boy and my heart about exploded, but I turned toward the open door and caught my first glimpse of our destination.

"Oh my God." I looked back at Finn. "Oh my God!"

He was grinning. "What do you think? Was it worth the drive?"

"Is this for real? I mean...it's so late! Are they even open for tours?"

"We're not here for a tour, although you can have one if you want. This is where we're having dinner." Finn was still grinning. He knew he had me. I was flabbergasted.

He followed me out of the car and we stood there in front of 351 Farmington Avenue, the beautiful and architecturally unique Mark Twain house.

The chill caught me off guard. I'd walked out of the car without my coat. Finn retrieved it and wrapped it around my shoulders.

"How did you know?"

"That you were cold? I saw you shivering."

I looked up at him through raised eyebrows.

"Oh *that*! You mean this?" He spread his arm out to indicate the house, which was impeccably decorated with white lights strung through the trees and a candle in every window, just like a Victorian fairy tale.

"Umhmm."

"Well, you practically have a shrine dedicated to him on your bookshelf, so I figured it was a safe bet." He was still grinning.

"So you were studying my bookshelf that night!"

Finn put his hand behind my back. "Shall we?"

"Is anyone even here at this hour?" Even as I said the words, the door opened and some staff dressed in period clothing greeted us. They took our coats and led us into a room warmed by a roaring fire, where an older man offered us some tea and began to tell us the history of the place. Most of it I already knew. I'd written my thesis on Mark Twain when I was at NYU, and although I'd never physically been here, I felt like all the rooms knew me somehow.

He told us about the family's life, the ghost stories associated with the house, and asked if we wanted a tour. My stomach was growling, but there was no way I was passing up this opportunity!

I walked through the rooms with my mouth open, like a kid at Christmas. The tour ended for us in the stunning conservatory, where a small table was set for two. "*This* is where we're having dinner? Off the library in Mark Twain's house..."

"Yes."

"How?"

Finn smiled warmly. He seemed genuinely thrilled that I was so happy. "One of my friends in NY knows the chef at the café here. I hope you like Japanese food?"

The white wine and shrimp were beginning to make sense now. "I love it! Bring on the tempura!"

A cart came rolling out with a selection of sushi and appetizers like calamari and edamame. After that, we feasted on an amazing udon noodle soup and finished it off with Tempura Twinkies.

"I know it's not chocolate heaven, but it is unique, and lovely in its own way."

I had to give him that. It was one of the more interesting meals I'd ever eaten. "Everything has been fabulous, and who would've thought of deep frying a twinkie? I mean, this is genius!" I held up the last bite of my dessert before popping it into my mouth, then forced myself to wait until I'd finished swallowing. "That is amazing right there!"

Finn's face flushed. "I'm so glad you liked it."

I stared at him for a minute. We both knew what was coming, and even more wine with dinner hadn't helped any. "You know, it's going to be a long car ride home. Maybe we should take separate limos."

He made an overly exaggerated gesture and patted his stomach contentedly. "I've been well fortified. I think I can control myself now."

I smiled back. Oh, how I wished he wouldn't...

18

"I do not fear death.
I had been dead for billions and billions of years before I was born,
and had not suffered the slightest inconvenience from it."
M.T.

I t was strange, being back in the limo after dinner, like a dream sequence had just ended and I was waking up in that weird, twilight sort of state. At the same time I felt drowsy and fuzzy-headed, probably from all the wine. As we settled in for the long ride back to New York, Finn took off his jacket and pulled me into his chest, where I promptly fell asleep.

I dreamt about my mother and Jenny. Horrible images went in and out of focus. There was blood everywhere. And pain. Tangible pain—as if I were bleeding to death instead of them. Then there was the vague, rhythmic flashing of the ambulance lights and the driver's voice inside my head, yet somewhere in the distance. I could hear them on the radio, alerting the trauma team. I was reliving Jenny's death piece by piece, scene by scene, and I wanted desperately to wake up, but I couldn't.

In the dream I was screaming for them to leave us alone. I just wanted to hold Jenny in my arms for a few more minutes before she slipped away, but the voice got louder and louder, pulling me to the surface of the pain until I just couldn't take it anymore.

I opened my eyes and saw the lights flashing in the background. A man was standing over me, trying to get me to tell him my name. I reached for my purse and realized I was wrapped in blankets and strapped to a board. And I was cold. Really cold. My dress felt wet and sticky against my skin. Beyond the man's face was a canopy of trees. Where was I? My head and chin were strapped to the board as well and I began to panic.

My eyes scanned toward the right and that's when I saw it. Black metal, disfigured and burning. *Burning? Finn!* My throat was parched and there was smoke and some other putrid smell making its way in around the mask I was wearing. *Oxygen?* My head was still fuzzy from the dream. Or maybe this was another dream? I couldn't quite tell, but I felt myself being lifted into the air and when I was set back down the pain that shot through my right thigh was so intense and nauseating that the world went black again.

Next I woke up in a clean white room with bright lights. There was someone standing over me again, but this time he was wearing a blue face mask and telling me to count backward from a hundred. It felt like he was asking me to recite sixteen digits of Pi. I had so many questions. I didn't want to count. His smile was kind, as if he understood, and I fell back asleep before I could say ninety-nine.

Loss of consciousness is a tricky thing. If your lights go out all of a sudden, they certainly seem to turn back on one at a time. At first I thought I was in my apartment. Then I heard an unfamiliar voice talking to me and opened my eyes to find clean white sheets wrapped around me, so I knew I couldn't be in my apartment. I hate white sheets. They remind me too much of hospitals. *Hospitals!*

I looked around, and sure enough, there was an IV hooked up

to my arm and some oxygen blowing up my nose. At least the mask was gone. My right leg felt incredibly heavy, as if it was pinned to the bed by a piano or something. I was too weak to actually lift my head up so I inched my hand down the sheet until I felt hard plaster–or whatever material they make casts out of these days. It hurt to breathe on the left side of my chest, and my middle felt swollen, like the skin was pulled too tight. I crept my hand up to my stomach and realized there was gauze and tape covering over it. My mouth felt dry. Too dry to speak, even though I wanted desperately to ask someone where the hell I was.

It wasn't long before I got my wish. By some miracle I was still awake when a nurse came in to check on me. The room was dark and the drapes were drawn.

"Where am I?" I managed.

A cute young blond in blue scrubs smiled down at me. "Well! Look who's awake!" She was way too perky for...well, whatever time it was.

"Where am I?" I repeated.

"New Haven."

"New Haven?"

She set my chart down next to the bed and pushed a few buttons on the IV pump before smoothing her hand across the covers. "Yes. You're at Yale-New Haven Hospital."

Ok. So I was still in Connecticut, but..."Why?"

Blondie sat on the edge of my bed and looked at me. Her name tag read 'Becky' and she was weighing her words carefully. "What do you remember?"

This couldn't be good. What was wrong? And why was I alone? What day was it? "I... I don't remember much." After all, this was only the third time I'd been awake since...Finn!

"What happened to Finn!" I tried to sit up. "Where is he?!" Becky tried to calm me down, but I was beginning to panic. She held my shoulders and tried to ease me back down toward the pillow. Pain shot up from my gut, then my leg, and my head began to throb. A sudden wave of nausea beat me and I dropped back against the pillow, a line sweat breaking out across my forehead.

"Ok just lay back. I'll answer your questions, but you have to rest."

I let my breath out slowly, trying to control the shaking from the pain. "Why do I hurt so much?" I looked at her. "What's wrong with me?"

"You were in a car accident. Do you remember? A limousine."

I nodded as understanding dawned. Jenny's dream was my dream. At least, partially.

"I just remember falling asleep on Finn's chest. Then I woke up here." It wasn't exactly true. I remembered part of the ambulance ride, and a possible trip to the operating room, but I wanted to see what Becky had to say about it. For all I knew, those were part of the dream too.

"You weren't the only one who fell asleep. The driver hadn't been drinking, but the tracks suggested a slow drift toward the shoulder of the road. The limousine rolled several times down an embankment and hit a tree."

I strained to remember details, but nothing was clicking.

"Is he ok?"

Becky averted her eyes. "When it hit the tree the car burst into flames. We think he died instantly, even before the fire."

I remembered then. The black twisted metal. The terrible taste of smoke and that smell! That putrid smell! It was flesh burning...

My heart began to sink. I knew what was coming. It was "THE END." The end of my fairy tale. I swallowed and closed my eyes. It was, of course, too good to be true, and I'd known as much, hadn't I? I was just holding on for the ride. The long, breathtaking fall over that cliff had been so intoxicating and yet, I knew. I knew it would end. Just like everything and everyone else in my life, Finn had been ripped away from me. I didn't want to know what was wrong with my body. I was obviously broken but alive and it didn't really matter. Not without Finn.

The darkness closed over my heart and I turned my head away.

"Have you called my father?" The one person in my life who was still alive. Still warm.

"Sweetie? We don't know your name..."

I looked at Becky. "Excuse me?"

"All your personal effects were destroyed in the fire."

"You mean my purse?"

"Yes."

I glanced at the spine of the chart she'd set on the bedside table. Sure enough, it read: Doe, Jane. I could hardly believe what she was telling me. "Truly."

"Yes, truly. I wouldn't joke about something like this."

I shook my head. "No. My name. It's Truly. Well – actually it's Trulane."

She picked up my chart and started scribbling the information as I gave it to her. "Are you sure?"

I raised my eyebrows. "That I know who I am? Yes. I'm sure. Would you like to know my social security number?"

"Absolutely! Whatever information you can give me will help us get started, Trulane."

I put my hand on Becky's arm. "Call me Truly. Please. I beg you."

"Fair enough." When I smiled Becky's face melted into some combination of relief and camaraderie.

"Thanks." I gave her my dad's number, and Kate's number too. She took them both and started to walk out of the room. "Becky?"

She turned and smiled. "Yes?"

"You said the driver was dead."

She came back and sat on the edge of the bed. My heart was beating faster than my breathing could account for, but I had to know.

"Yes."

"And I've got some pretty serious injuries, right?"

She nodded. "As you've probably figured out by now, you're right leg was broken in several places. You've also got a couple of cracked ribs on the left, which caused some internal injuries. You had surgery a couple of days ago to fix the leg and to repair a tear in your spleen."

"A couple of... *days* ago? What day is it today?"

"It's Sunday evening."

"I know this is going to sound silly, but...is this the first time I've been awake?"

Becky sighed. "Awake and coherent? Yes."

"What was I before?"

She pursed her lips, trying to figure out what to call it. "Delirious." She decided. "Although with good reason. We've had you on a considerable amount of pain medication."

"Well I prefer to have my wits about me, so if you wouldn't mind waiting until I ask for it next time?"

Becky only managed half a smile. "Well, you've been moaning a lot. And crying out."

"I have?" My face got hot. "What have I been saying?"

"Listen, why don't you just rest now? We can talk more later."

I grabbed onto her hand. Why wasn't she telling me what happened? "What else was destroyed in the fire?"

She looked at me with steel blue eyes. "Are you asking about Finn?"

I swallowed. "How do you know his name and yet you didn't even know mine? Was I calling out for him?"

She weighed her words carefully. "His wallet was in his pocket."

I could barely breathe but somehow my mouth formed the words. "Is he dead too?"

She hesitated just long enough to give me hope. "No. He's in a special Intensive Care Unit."

I wrinkled my brow. "How bad is it?"

"We're not sure. He hasn't woken up yet."

"You mean like a coma?"

Becky nodded. "Something like that."

I swallowed again. Or tried to. My mouth was unbelievably dry. "Can I get something to drink?"

She reached for a little pink sponge and dipped it in some water. "Not yet, no. But you can swish this around your tongue and teeth. It should help a little." Becky helped me clean my mouth. "He saved you, Truly."

I looked up at her. "What?"

"He saved you."

"I thought you said he was in a coma."

"We're keeping him very sedated. So it's not a coma like you're thinking. This one is on purpose."

I tried to digest that information. Why would they chemically *induce* a coma in an otherwise healthy person? Unless they weren't healthy...otherwise.

Becky just kept talking. "But they've done a thorough investigation at the scene over the last couple of days. The police say that his body was thrown from the vehicle during the rollover. Then it looks like he crawled back to the limo while it was burning and – well, he pulled you out."

"He went in after me?" I was incredulous.

"You were so lucky, Truly. All you lost was your hair."

"My hair?" I tried to lift my hand to my head but I couldn't. It was tethered to the bed by the IV tubing. Or maybe it was just caught. "What's going on? Why can't I lift my hand?"

"Hold on." Becky reached over and freed the tubing.

I reached up to my head and sure enough, I had about four inches of hair and then nothing but frazzled ends. "Oh my God."

Becky laid her hand over mine. "That's enough for today. Let me go make these phone calls for you."

"No!" I insisted. "You can't just drop that on me and leave! Tell me the rest – please!" I grabbed her hand. "I have to know."

She glanced at my left hand. "Are you and Finn married?"

"No! Of course not!"

"Well, if you're not related I really can't give you infor–"

"I'm in love with him!" I blurted. I couldn't believe I'd said that out loud. It was preposterous, of course, but it felt true enough.

"And he saved my life, for God's sake! Who saves the life of someone they barely know?"

Her demeanor softened, and she looked over her shoulder as if she was breaking the law or something. "He's in the burn unit."

My eyes filled with tears as I imagined Finn crawling toward a burning vehicle. On purpose. But not just on purpose. To save me.

JUST THEN I heard a man's voice coming from over Becky's shoulder.

"Hey there beautiful!"

As Becky turned toward the voice, Finn's father came into view. I thought of my hair, all frazzled and burnt. Beautiful, indeed. But how good I must look compared to...

"What are you doing here? I thought you were in Ireland?"

"I was. I've just come back." Finn's father extended his hand toward Becky. "Colin McCarthy. I'm Finn's da."

"They won't tell me anything."

Becky smiled and shook his hand, then looked at me. "I'm sorry. I was just trying to follow the rules. The privacy laws are very strict."

Colin looked at her. "Well, put her on the approved list, will you?"

I started to cry. After all Finn had been through, why was he being so kind to me?

He came over and sat down next to the bed, taking my hand between his. "There, there. It's all right now."

Becky nodded. "I'll give you two some time."

Colin nodded back. "Tanks."

"How about some pain meds, Truly?" Becky offered.

I shook my head, grimacing through my tears. The pain was substantial, but I needed my wits about me. "I'll let you know."

Becky looked back and forth between the two of us. "I'll have it ready when you call. Just put your light on and I'll know to bring it."

"Thanks." After Becky left I looked at Finn's father and let the tears spill over. "Up until just now I didn't even know your first name."

"Well, there you go then. Now you know." He grinned.

I squeezed onto Colin's hand. "Tell me how he is. Please."

"I've just come from sitting with him. He's not awake yet."

I nodded toward the door. "They said he's in the burn unit."

"Aye. He is at that."

I blinked and tears ran down both cheeks. "Becky said he went in after me. Into the limo while it was burning." Color crept up my neck. I was so embarrassed to still be alive, and so ashamed that I'd caused Finn pain.

"Aye." He brushed my hair back and then wiped one of my cheeks clean with his thumb. Such a tender gesture from a man I barely knew. He was watching me and I could tell he was calculating the odds of giving me the whole truth.

"Please. You have to give it to me straight. Is he going to live?"

"Of course he is darlin'! He's just got a wee bit o' swelling in his brain right now."

"Swelling? From what?"

"Hit his head somewhere along the way, maybe when he got thrown from the car, they aren't sure."

"And yet he had the wherewithal to crawl back and somehow free me from a burning vehicle? It doesn't make sense." Unless he was somehow out of his mind already when he decided to go back for me.

"Near as they can figure he was awake for a few minutes after the accident. Had enough of his wits still about him to get the two of you pulled to safety before he lost consciousness."

"How bad are the burns?"

"Could have been a lot worse. Mostly on his back, where he took the heat trying to untangle you from the car, and a good-sized gash on his head, but they've stitched that up now."

I nodded, silently breathing a sigh of relief. I'd imagined him blackened from head to toe, somehow unrecognizable. This was better. Much better.

"Other than that a broken ankle is the worst of it. Put some pins in to stabilize the bones, but it should heal up just fine." He smiled at me again. "Might make airport security a bit of a problem from now on though."

Colin winked then, as if the thought of Finn being frisked and scanned brought him some type of guilty pleasure, and I had to giggle.

"The nurse made it sound like he was dying."

"Well, we're not going to think like that, are we now?"

I watched Colin's face. So determined, yet concern was etched into his features.

I swallowed. "Could you hand me one of those pink swabs?"

He pulled one out of the water and gave it to me. My body was using up liquid way faster than they were dripping it into my arm, and my mouth felt like I'd been chewing cotton balls. As I lifted my hand to use the swab my whole left side knotted into a thick wad of tight pain and I cried out unintentionally.

"Are you all right? Let me call for the nurse."

I shook my head but before I could protest too much he'd pushed the call button. I knew I had a limited amount of time to get the answers I needed. Once that pain shot hit I'd be lost in the haze again.

"But why, Colin? Why would he do that?"

"Do what darlin'?"

"Save me?"

"Well now, if you haven't figured that out yet, I'm not gonna be the one to tell you."

Becky came in and inserted a syringe into one of the ports on my IV tubing. I didn't argue with her. I wanted to float away. I needed to float away. I didn't know what to think, or even how to respond. I just laid there and watched a tiny air bubble ascend the tubing up into my arm.

"Will you come back and visit me again after I sleep a bit?" I was already starting to feel the effects of the drug. "There's so much more I want to talk to you about..."

Colin's face was kind as he nodded. "I'll be around, darlin'."

In my mind I was saying 'thank you' but in reality I'm not sure what happened exactly, because suddenly his face, and all my questions, faded into black.

19

"It is curious–curious that physical courage should be so common in the world,
and moral courage so rare."
M.T.

It wasn't long – or at least, it didn't seem that long, before I woke up to find my dad sitting next to me, holding my hand. He looked a bit ragged, and older than I remembered him.

It occurred to me that he'd been aging all along and I'd just missed it, as if at twenty-five too much of my life had gone by without me noticing. The realization was painful, but not as painful as the throbbing in my leg. A push of the button would send me straight back into dreamland, but I needed to talk to dad first.

"Hey peanut." He smiled tenderly, giving my hand a gentle squeeze. Dad hadn't called me peanut since I was about six. I was really small for my age and dad found this annoyingly cute. I, on the other hand, had always hated feeling small.

"When did you get here?" I tried in vain to reposition. The

twisting movement sent shards of glass up through the left side of my abdomen. I grunted with the exertion, and began sweating again, trying to breathe through the pain.

Dad got up to retrieve a cool washcloth from the sink. He placed it on my forehead and took my hand again. So natural, as if he'd done it a thousand times. How many nights he must have sat by mom's bed, trying to provide some small comfort, knowing full well that no amount of kindness would stay the tide of loss that crept steadily toward our shore.

I hardly ever saw him with her in the hospital, because we mostly took turns. I was there when he was at work and he was there when I was asleep or doing homework or laundry or grocery shopping or any number of other things I did to try to pick up the slack in our lives.

I stared up at him. After Jenny died, dad was all I had left, but I guess I'd never realized that I was all he had left too, and for some reason, today, it scared him. I could see it like a ticker tape across his face; the fear running in circles around his head.

Was I worse off than Becky had let on? Or was he still in shock from being summoned to a hospital in New Haven not knowing what he'd find on arrival? He'd been summoned the night Jenny died, and mom too. I'd been with each of them when it happened, but he'd missed it both times, being called in only after the fact.

"I just got here. Maybe a half hour ago." He managed.

"Is it still Sunday?"

"Yeah, peanut. It's Sunday. Barely though. It's about 11:30."

"What about work? You'll never get enough sleep to drive back in time."

"I'm not going to work tomorrow."

I took a minute to digest that information. It made sense, but dad making sacrifices for me seemed like a juxtaposition. "Where will you sleep?"

"Nurse says that chair in the corner folds out to a twin-sized bed. She brought me some blankets. I'll be just fine. Don't you worry about me."

I glanced over at the chair. Sure enough it was piled high with pillows, sheets and blankets.

Just then Kate came running into the room, obviously out of breath. "Oh my God, Truly! Are you ok?" She slid to a stop when she saw the huge cast on my thigh. Then she just started staring at my head. "Oh, sweetie..." She crossed to the other side of the bed and stood fingering my hair. "What the hell happened?"

Dad's eyebrows went up. "Yeah, I'd like to know that too. They wouldn't tell me a whole lot."

My eyes went wide. "What? But you're my *father!*"

"I know, but you're not a child anymore. You're an adult, and apparently you get to say whether or not they can talk to me about your medical condition."

Although I continued to act surprised, the thought was somehow comforting, knowing that some things were still within my control.

"Finn and I were coming back from our date when the accident happened."

"Finn? The one from the Yankees game?" Dad was nearly grinning remembering the story.

Kate was shaking her head. "Wait. Your date was in *New Haven?*" She decided she'd better take a seat for this story.

"Actually the date was in Hartford."

She folded her arms. "What, there weren't any good restaurants in Manhattan?"

You had to love Kate. She and I were so similar.

"That's what I thought at first. But this restaurant was one of a kind. He took me to the Mark Twain house."

"Mark...Twain? As in the writer?" Kate was obviously perplexed.

"Yes."

Dad was just sitting there with his eyebrows still up. "The one whose books you've read a million times? Isn't he dead?"

I looked at him. "Yes, of course he's dead. But his house is a museum now and it has this awesome Japanese restaurant in it and–"

"Wait a minute." Kate put her hand up to interrupt. "*That's* what we got you all gussied up for? The Mark Twain house?"

I nodded, trying to keep the smile from my lips, but it was no use. Kate could see I was smitten, and she laughed out loud, then looked at my hair again and stopped short. "I'm sorry. This isn't funny. Not at all. We can talk about the other stuff later. Please – go on."

"What other stuff?" Dad wanted to know.

I looked over at his puzzled face. "Girl stuff. Don't worry about it." I grimaced. All this talking and moving my head from side to side was exhausting.

Kate looked me over. "Honey, just get to the part about the accident. What happened after the date?"

"I don't really know. We were in the limo, and–"

"*Limo?*" Dad ran his fingers through his hair as if he'd have to meet Finn any minute and was somehow afraid he wouldn't measure up. I thought of his blue shirts with the stains and the constant grease under his nails and his couple of beers to make it all go away. A hole opened up in the deepest pit of my stomach, and the pain I felt had nothing to do with broken legs or stitched up spleens.

"–The driver fell asleep at the wheel."

Kate's face fell. "Oh no…"

"I'd fallen asleep as well, so when I woke up I was strapped to a backboard." Dad's hand squeezed mine even tighter. "I only know what they've told me though. I don't remember any of it. Apparently the car rolled down an embankment and hit a tree."

Kate's hand went to her mouth. "Oh my God." She looked pointedly at my hair. "And it caught fire."

I nodded.

Kate's eyes filled with tears.

"The driver's dead, Kate."

"No…" She started shaking her head. "Finn?"

"He's alive. But he's in the burn unit."

I watched dad's head hit his chest. Tears were running freely down Kate's cheeks but I was surprisingly calm, despite the excruciating pain in my leg and ribs. It took everything I had just to keep from pushing that call bell and slipping back into oblivion.

I jiggled dad's hand until he looked up at me again. "He saved my life, dad. He pulled me out."

I watched dad's face as understanding dawned. He looked back over his shoulder as if he needed to go see Finn. To thank him for saving me. When he looked back at me his eyes were glassy and damp. "I think I'd like to meet this Finn."

"I'd like that too, but he hasn't woken up yet."

Kate looked at me. "What's wrong with him?"

"He has swelling in his brain, and a shattered ankle, and burns on his back."

"Swelling from what?" Kate asked.

"I don't know. They think he hit his head when he was thrown from the car."

"Then how did he manage to pull you out?" Dad wondered.

I shook my head. "I don't really know. He must have been awake at first."

Dad rubbed his hand across his stubbled face. "And now he's in a coma?"

"The nurse said they're keeping him sedated on purpose, because of the swelling in his brain. I don't understand that part, and I don't know anything else."

Kate leaned back and closed her eyes.

"You must be exhausted, Kate. Unfortunately dad's taking the only bed in the room, but I don't really think you'll be missing much."

"Oh don't worry about me. I'm staying with a friend."

"Who?"

"Someone I went to school with. It's only about three blocks from here."

I looked at her. "You shouldn't walk the streets this late."

"I'll be fine."

Dad sat up a little straighter. "I'll walk with you and then just come back here."

"Thank you, really, but I'll be–"

"You don't get to argue on this one." Something in dad's tone left no room for discussion. Maybe it was Finn's heroics or Jenny's getting jumped in the dark or the near miss of losing me. Whatever it was, the conversation was over and Kate sensed it.

"Ok. Thank you."

Dad nodded with some satisfaction.

Kate fingered my hair again. "We're going to do something about this. Don't you worry."

I shook my head, thinking about Finn. My frazzled hair would be cut and then grow again. No one would ever have to know I almost went bald in a fire. Finn, on the other hand, if he survived, would carry scars on his back for the rest of his life. A debt I could never repay, and neither could my father.

The thought caused me to shudder and the shudder caused me to cry out in pain as a tight band of spasms gripped my abdomen. I could deal with the leg pain by limiting my movements, but the side was another story entirely.

"I really need to just lay here and be still. I might even ask for some more pain medication."

Kate kissed me on the forehead. "It's ok. I'm going to Jo's place to get some sleep. I'll be back first thing in the morning, ok?"

"Sure. Thanks Kate."

She waved me off. "Are you kidding me? What are friends for?"

After they left I wondered about that–about what friends are for. They were for hospitals and makeup and picking out dresses. But they weren't for pulling you out of a burning vehicle. No, that was another class entirely.

20

"Don't go around saying the world owes you a living.
The world owes you nothing.
It was here first."
M.T.

S ome time in the middle of the night I woke up. There was
light in the room but it was dim and down low, like running
lights along the aisle on a redeye. I had no idea what time it was,
but for the first time since I'd woken up on that backboard I felt
awake and relatively calm.

In the quiet of the night, with dad snoring just a few feet away,
I could finally think a bit. I tried – really tried – to remember the
events of that night, but it was gone. All I could picture was Finn
crawling toward the fire. Finn lying in a bed a lot like mine somewhere else in that hospital.

My joints felt stiff and heavy, but I knew better than to try to
move. If I laid perfectly still, I could just concentrate on breathing
and thinking and it worked out pretty well. For a while, anyway.

It wasn't long before a nurse showed up. Then a phlebotomist to draw my blood. Then a guy toting a portable x-ray machine. I almost hit the ceiling when they had to sit me up and move me enough to put that cold hard plate behind my back. The pain was excruciating. By five the nurse was back with a pain shot, but not before all the commotion had woken up dad. He was used to being up early, but he looked as if he hadn't slept in days.

"Dad?"

He rubbed his face a few times. "Yeah."

"You look a lot more tired than just a bad night's sleep in a hospital room. Are you ok?"

"Are you saying I'm getting old?"

"I'm saying I'm worried about you."

"Yeah well, look who's talking" was his only reply.

He was right. My frazzled hair was damp with perspiration from the combination of sleep and pain and exertion.

Another round of vital signs and assessments, then suddenly the room filled with about twenty people – doctors, nurses, interns, residents and God knows who else. They all reiterated my condition as if I were an item on a menu. "Today we've got Truly. She's got a broken drumstick with a side of freshly cracked ribs, slightly charred and glazed with sweat."

They all seemed to know a lot more about my case than I did though, so I listened carefully. They expected me to be in the hospital for at least a week, maybe two depending on blood counts and infection. Dad sat in the corner and listened as well. He seemed relieved to hear from a group of bona fide medical professionals that I wasn't dying.

I heard one of the medical students tell the girl standing next to her that my boyfriend was still critical in the burn unit ICU. They shook their heads and made that girly "aww" face like we were some tragic story that belonged on the big screen. They also said I wouldn't likely be able to stay by myself with that enormous cast on my leg. The thought was perplexing, but we'd have to cross that bridge later.

The day shift nurse showed up shortly thereafter and tried to interest me in some breakfast. A lovely selection of juices, teas and jello were on the menu for my dining pleasure. I told her to leave the tray and I'd work on it. God, I hated jello.

"You want some help with that?" Dad offered, after the nurse left.

"If you could just get the tray over to where I can reach everything."

As I mentioned before, dad was surprisingly adept at all things hospital. He even knew how to raise and lower the bedside table and roll it under the bed just right so it didn't bang into the frame. He had me set up in no time.

"I'm gonna grab a shower and some real breakfast."

"Thanks a lot." Nothing at all on that tray looked even mildly appetizing.

"Besides, yesterday was Sunday and I missed our eggs and bacon."

I looked up. "But this isn't a week I would have usually come."

"I know that." He paused in the doorway. "But I miss it every Sunday that you're not there."

When dad left the room I pushed the tray back away from my chest. Any appetite I had was gone. I felt sick all over. And disgusting. I pushed the call button and the aide came in carrying an armful of towels, washcloths and sheets.

Her name was Nita, and she was a big, thick woman who looked like she could pick me up with her two pinkies and do pushups with me over her head. She closed the door and pulled the curtain and got to work with some warm soapy water. Her hands were strong but surprisingly gentle. When she was finished I felt so much better. Except for one thing.

"Now, what are we gonna do with this hair?" Nita mused.

"Can you at least try washing it? Please?"

Nita smiled gently. "Of course I can do that. I was thinking more along the lines of a cut and style."

"Know any hairdressers who make house calls?"

Nita shook her head. "Honey, I wish I did."

I was glad she didn't try to patronize me. I knew how awful it looked, I just had no way of changing the situation.

While she still had my head tipped back over the end of the bed I heard Kate's voice at the door behind the curtain.

"Hello! Can we come in?"

I was fully covered in a fresh gown and blankets and all, but... who was 'we'?

Nita looked at me and I nodded. "Come on in!" She said. "We're just washing her hair."

Kate pulled back the curtain. "Great! Good morning sunshine!" Kate had always been a little too perky in the mornings. "How ya feelin'?"

I tried to tip my chin down so I could see her but Nita was still rinsing the soap out of my hair. "I've had better days, thanks."

When my hair was in a towel Nita slowly raised the bed back up. Standing next to Kate was a woman I'd never met. "Truly? This is Jo. The one I told you about. We went to PA together."

Not that it mattered but for some reason when she mentioned she was staying with a friend from PA named Jo, I assumed it was a guy.

"I'm so sorry about your accident." Jo offered.

"Thanks." There was an awkward pause as she looked at my head in the towel. Kate must have told her about my hair. "So, you're a dancer?"

"Dancing didn't really work out for me. I broke my ankle and it never healed enough for me to dance on it like I used to. I had to change careers."

"Which is why she's here!" Kate gushed. She put her hands on my one good foot at the end of the bed. It was strange to think that because of my injuries, I couldn't run away from someone, even if I wanted to, and for some reason the thought made me extremely nervous.

"Excuse me?"

"Jo is going to cut your hair!"

"Well, God be praised!" Nita said as she started cleaning up the mess we'd made with the bath.

"Her career change–it was beauty school! She works at a salon nearby and doesn't have to be in until ten today so I asked if she'd come over here and cut your hair for you! It'll make you feel so much better, I promise!"

I couldn't figure out who was going to benefit the most, me or Kate, but it was probably a combination of the two. After all, they were the ones who had to look at me.

"Thanks so much for coming."

Jo addressed Nita. "Can you leave that headboard piece off for a little while?" Nita agreed and they got right to work, Jo cutting and Kate holding my head up so I didn't have to.

I was already exhausted from the morning's activities, but she worked surprisingly fast, cutting off all the burnt parts and fashioning what was left into a short, sassy, Halle Berry-style supermodel cut. When they lifted the mirror to my face I was shocked, but so relieved. It looked cute, sort of. I thought about Finn's comments on my hair and realized there was nothing left to *hang down 'round my shoulders* now. It couldn't be helped of course, but I began to mourn the loss of the one feature I knew he liked about me.

Jo left for work and Kate managed to get the headboard back on, then took a seat next to my bed.

"Kate. There's something I need to tell you before my dad comes back."

She leaned forward. "What? What is it?"

"Can you lower my head down? It really hurts sitting all the way up like this."

"Sure honey." She did as I asked then sat back down.

"The night Finn and I went on our date."

"Yeah?"

"Christopher showed up."

"What! When?"

"After you left but before Finn got there. When I heard the knock I thought it was you, coming back for your bag."

Kate was staring at me in disbelief.

"So I opened the door."

Her eyes went wide. "You did not!"

I nodded, embarrassed. "I don't know what I was thinking."

Kate was shaking her head. "And?"

"And he was drunk. And I was all...dressed up in that beautiful dress. So he kept coming at me."

"Jesus, what did you do?"

"I got around him and opened the door to the hallway and yelled at him to get out. My neighbor and his wife heard the commotion and came over to see if I needed any help."

"Oh thank God!"

"You're telling me." I sighed. "When Finn got there I was still shaking. And I threw up in the bathroom and he came in and held my hair."

"What did he say?"

"He just let me cry. He even offered to cancel the date and order takeout. He was so great about everything, but I still wanted to go. I mean, that dress cost a fortune and we'd spent all that time getting me ready and I didn't want to waste it. Now I wish we'd stayed in. I wish to God I could take it all back."

"Don't say that! You weren't the one driving that limo! This is not your fault!"

"Well, it sure feels like my fault."

"You can't blame yourself Truly."

"Can't I?" I started to cry again. I swear to God I'd cried more since I met Finn than I had my entire life. "Finn is in an ICU somewhere with burns because of me! Why couldn't he have just let me die in the fire!"

Kate was horrified. She stood up and towered over me. "Are you *kidding* me right now? You need to snap out of this Little Debbie funk before I kick the shit out of you! You're *alive* because of that man, and you'd better be damn thankful for it. Don't turn it around like it's something you did wrong. Someone *else* fell asleep on the job and he died for it and it nearly cost both of you your lives as well. It was an accident Truly! Repeat after me: *ac-ci-dent!*"

I stared up at her. I was so mad I wanted to storm out of the room and slam the door, but I was stuck. Stuck in that stupid bed with a thousand pound weight strapped to my leg.

"Yeah, well that's easy for you to say isn't it? You're not laying here wondering what just happened to your entire life! You know the first three days I was here they didn't even know my name? My purse is gone, my identity is gone, my leg is shattered–I can't even live by myself for who knows how long – and Finn could *die* because of me! Do you even get that?"

By then I was yelling and if felt like my ribs were going to rip a hole in my chest. I was clutching my side as the nurse came in to see what was going on. "Hey, let's just take it easy, Truly. You need to stay calm. Let me get you some pain medication."

Kate looked at me. She looked at the nurse. "I gotta take a walk."

I FELT like throwing up again. There was nothing in my stomach, but I asked the nurse for the basin anyway. I was breathing heavy as she held a cool washcloth to my head.

"I'll be right back."

She left me with the basin under my chin, and before she could come back dad showed up. I had to admit, he did look rather fresh and kind of handsome. He'd obviously found a razor in his travels, and I'd always loved his face clean-shaven. For some reason I adored the smell of cheap aftershave, and was hoping he would lean down and kiss my cheek so I could remember what it smelled like. The fact that I was craving a man-smell at all should have been my first clue.

When dad saw me laying there with a puke bucket he got concerned. "Hey peanut. What's wrong? Breakfast not agreeing with you?"

"I didn't eat breakfast." I couldn't tell him about Christopher so I just gave him half the truth. "Kate and I got in a fight."

He just nodded. I guess living in a house with three women taught him to stay out of it.

"What happened to your hair? It looks really..." He searched for the right word. "Feisty."

Feisty? Ok dad, you stick to fixing cars, I'll stick to fixing sentences.

"Kate's friend cut it for me. I don't look like a boy?"

Dad studied me honestly. "No. Of course not. You look beautiful." He leaned down, kissed my cheek and there it was–that aftershave I loved so much. I took a slow, deep, purposeful breath in.

"Dad?"

"Yeah."

"What kind of aftershave do you wear?"

He laughed. "Aqua Velva, why?"

"I like it."

"Five bucks a bottle and it lasts a guy like me a good long time. I only wear it when I've got a hot date."

A guy like him? What was that supposed to mean?

"And your hot date today is with...?"

"You, peanut!"

I squinted in disbelief and stared him down. "It wouldn't have anything to do with a hospital full of nice-looking nurses?"

I think he might have actually blushed. "What, so it's a crime to put on aftershave *after* you *shave*?"

"All right, all right. Fair enough. Whatever. It's not like my heart would be broken if you dated someone other than Gigi."

Dad smirked and sat back in the chair just as a different nurse walked in. She was small, like me, and my God if she didn't remind me of my mother. She didn't look like her exactly, but there was something about her, and I felt it right away when she came in the room. It was strange. I watched dad's face register the same reaction and we both looked at each other.

"Hi there. I'm Celia. Your nurse had an emergency with

another patient. She said you needed your pain medicine though."
Celia's smile was warm and genuine.

"I'm Truly, and this is my dad."

Dad stood up and the chair scraped back loudly. He stuck out
his hand before I could even finish. "Bob Wright."

Celia looked at dad as if she really saw him, as a person, not
just the dad of one of her patients. Dad noticed too, and held onto
her hand until she let go. She was pretty, but not in a flashy kind of
way, and definitely not in a big hair, bowling alley sort of way. She
wasn't wearing a lick of makeup, and yet her eyes were sparkly and
her lips were naturally full and moist.

She was very professional, but personable as well. "It's nice to
meet you both." She asked me for my name and birth date,
checked it against my wristband and got right to work inserting
the syringe full of sweet relief into my IV. As she stood there slowly
pushing the medicine into me she smiled at dad again, then
chuckled softly.

"What's so funny?" Dad asked. His voice was smooth and
strange, and I wondered if maybe I should move to a stool down at
the other end of the bar.

She shook her head. "I bet you catch a lot of flack for that."

Dad's head tilted. He was genuinely confused. "I'm sorry?"

Celia looked down at me. "If that doesn't help enough, you put
your light on again, ok?"

I nodded and watched her gather her supplies. She purposely
avoided dad's eyes until she was ready to leave, then she looked
right at him and smiled again.

"Well, it's not every day you walk into a patient's room and just
happen to meet Mr. Wright."

Celia turned on her heel and walked out. It was a perfectly
executed line and I shook my head in admiration. Dad practically
fell back down into the chair. Her arrow had hit its mark–smack
dab in the middle of his chest. I'd just witnessed pure genius and it
made me laugh out loud.

Dad looked over at me, embarrassed.

"Well, that Aqua Velva sure did its job, now didn't it?" I teased.

He shook his head. "She was somethin', wasn't she?"

"Like I said—"

Dad put his hand up to stop me from talking, which was fine, because I felt like I was starting to slur my words. Whatever Celia put in that IV was working fast. "Hey dad? I think I'm going to take a nap."

He held my hand. "You go right ahead."

21

_"Wisdom is the reward you get for a lifetime of listening when you
would rather have talked."_
_M.T._

At first I thought I was dreaming again. That weird, narcotic-
induced twilight phase is a strange thing to try to come out
of. I had to run through all the things my semiconscious mind
thought might be true and pit them up against what I remembered as real.

Two men were talking in the distance. I remembered I was in
the hospital, and thought perhaps two doctors were in my room,
discussing my care, and if that were the case I'd better wake myself
up so I wouldn't miss anything.

When I opened my eyes my dad was still sitting next to the bed
but so was Finn's father. I blinked a couple of times to make sure
he was real.

"Colin?"

His smile was wide and jovial. "Well, now there's our little imp.
How are ya, beautiful?"

I blinked a few more times. Who was he calling beautiful?

"I see you've met my dad."

"Aye." Colin nodded. "We've been having a little visit, waitin' for you."

"Well, here I am." I tried not to sound confused, but I was still coming out of a strange sort of dream-state. "How's Finn?"

Colin's smile softened a bit. "Fightin' like a good soldier. Don't you worry."

What the hell was that supposed to mean? I couldn't help but panic at the thought that someone wasn't telling me everything I needed to know. "Is he still sedated?"

"They're turning the medicine off slowly, but he hasn't woken up yet, no."

My heart started pounding in my ears. I couldn't bear the thought of losing him. Not now. Not like this. "I want to see him. Please. Can I see him?"

"Oh, well it's fine by me, darlin' – it's the nurses have to let you out of this bed here."

Dad sat up and interjected. "Let's concentrate on getting you better first, shall we?"

About then Celia walked back into the room. "Hi Truly! Glad you're awake. How's that pain level?"

Just the person I needed to see. "Much better, thanks. Listen, when do you think I could go see Finn? Could I go in a wheelchair if you prop my leg up?"

She walked over and took my hand. So it was a no, then.

Her voice was firm, but kind. "Right now you have to stay on bed rest. As you heal up we'll get you used to sitting in the chair, and when you can tolerate that we'll talk about rides in a wheelchair. Trust me, you're not ready for a road trip just yet."

I hated being told no, but she was right. I could barely sit upright for the chest x-ray.

"Finn's in excellent hands, ok? We'll take good, good care of him for you."

I nodded, trying to stave the tears forming in the corners of my eyes. Every time I even thought about him I wanted to cry. If I saw him face to face I just might lose it altogether.

Celia turned and addressed Colin, extending her hand. "I'm Celia, the charge nurse on this floor. Truly's nurse got tied up with another patient so I'm taking over for her the rest of today."

Dad smiled and she smiled back, but she was still shaking Colin's hand.

Colin seemed rather amused by that, and looked back and forth between the two of them. "Well I'm Colin McCarthy, Finn's da."

Celia flipped through some pages and made a couple of notations. "And what part of Ireland are you from Mr. McCarthy?"

"I've lived a bit of everywhere, but my mother's from Galway and me da's from County Cork."

"Hmm. The rebellious part." Celia teased, closing the chart. She hooked her thumb over one shoulder in an exaggerated motion and winked at me. "You let me know if he gives you any trouble."

I couldn't help but laugh. "Ok, I will."

She turned and addressed dad. "Can I see you out at the nurses' station Mr. Wright? I have a few questions about that maybe you could help with."

"Sure thing." Dad got right up and followed her out. "You know, you could call me Bob..."

I thought it was cute that dad was embarrassed to be called "Mr. Wright". Why shouldn't he be someone's Mr. Wright? He was a good man. A solid man. A lonely man...

I turned my attention to Colin, who was still sitting there, looking at me. "I'm so glad you came back."

"Me too darlin'. Finn would want someone keeping an eye on you. I'm glad you're da's here."

"Me too. You know they didn't know who I was at first?"

Colin smiled indulgently. Had we had this conversation before?

"I like your hair. How did you get it cut like that? Did the hair faeries come and visit you in the night?"

I liked Colin. He was funny. "Sort of. Kate brought one of her friends over this morning. She cut it right here in the bed for me! I feel a lot better now that the burnt parts are gone." Even saying the word 'burnt' brought terrible images of Finn to mind. I struggled to keep my focus on the conversation.

"Kate. Is she the pretty blond that's been with David at the club?"

"Yeah, that's her." Of course he would have noticed Kate. Everyone noticed Kate.

"Where is she now?"

"We got into a fight."

"Already?" Colin chuckled, as if that was the most normal thing in the world, friends fighting. If it was, why was I feeling so out of control?

I nodded, tears threatening again. I hated myself for being so emotional. I couldn't understand it, and started to wonder if the rollover had somehow turned my heart upside down.

He patted my hand. "Tell old Colin about it. Get it off you're chest."

I'd forgotten he was a bartender–used to blubbering, drugged-up losers pouring their hearts out. How could I say what I was really thinking? I didn't want to be placated or patronized. I wanted *someone* to acknowledge the fact that one man was dead and another was in a coma, and that my life had hit that tree and exploded along with the limo.

I was pretty sure I was falling in love with Finn, and yet we were just getting to know each other. This sacrifice he'd made was just too big–too disproportionate for this stage in our relationship.

Colin looked me in the eye. "Shall I take a stab at it?"

I swallowed. "Ok."

"I'll bet right about now you're wondering why you didn't die in that fire." His voice was so gentle. I nodded, wide-eyed. "And you're feeling just a wee bit guilty that Finn got hurt."

The tears started to free flow.

"And you're frightened." He waited while I wiped my eyes. "And that's ok, love. It's ok."

I put my hand up to my mouth and just let the tears come. It did feel good to release all that pent up tension. After a few minutes he handed me some tissues and I blew my nose, letting my breath ease into a regular rhythm.

He and Finn had the same calming presence. I guess I shouldn't have been surprised. The apple doesn't usually fall far from the tree.

"How is it you know exactly what I'm feeling?"

"I know because that's how Finn felt, when he came home from the war."

The war? What war? Which war?

I dropped the tissue into my lap. "The what?"

Colin smiled. "Well I know he doesn't look all that big and tough, but me boyo there's a decorated war hero."

I tried to process that information. "Afghanistan?"

Colin nodded. "Only one tour, but it nearly killed him."

I rested my head back on the pillows, realizing with some finality just how little I knew about this man who'd recently risked his life for me. The look on my face must have made it obvious.

"He spent four months in an army hospital in Birmingham recovering from a bomb blast that blew him full of shrapnel."

"Birmingham. Alabama?"

"England."

Such a stupid question. What was I thinking? "He fought for the Brits then?"

"Aye."

Army, huh? Interesting. No wonder he was quiet about his life.

"He survived that bomb blast, but..." Colin was searching for the words. "Some of his closest friends were killed. It wasn't easy for him to get over that."

My chin dropped to my chest. Of course! *That's* why he tried to save me. At least it made sense.

Just then Kate walked back in. "Ok, this is stupid. I didn't come all the way to Connecticut to sit in the waiting room and sulk." She was talking as she walked through the door and didn't notice Colin was sitting right there. "Oh. Hi!"

Kate smiled at him and I watched Colin's eyes register the sight. She really was breathtakingly beautiful sometimes. Today of course, had to be one of those times, when I was a pathetic, sweaty mess. I sighed.

"You're right. I'm sorry. I shouldn't feel sorry for myself."

She seemed satisfied with that.

"It's just–"

"Ah da ta ta ta." She put her hand up. "Let's not ruin a perfectly good apology, ok?"

God I hated it when she was right. Since when did I become a sniveling, whiny idiot?

"Kate you remember Finn's dad?"

He stood and extended his hand to her. "It's Colin."

"Nice to officially meet you." Kate smiled. She took the seat my dad had vacated. "I brought you something."

I stared at her. "Please tell me it's my laptop."

She reached into her enormous silver purse and pulled out a small yellow carton, held it up in front of her face and started laughing. "Truce?"

"Nutty Bars?" It hurt to laugh but I couldn't help it. "You're hilarious, you know that?" I clutched my side, starting for the box, but she pulled it momentarily out of my reach.

"Ok, so here's the deal."

My eyebrows went up. I knew it was too good to be true.

"You are allowed a pity party once a day, for as long as it takes you to eat one of these packages of nutty bars. After you're done, you snap out of it and do the work necessary to get your ass out of that bed and get back home. You keep doing the work, I'll keep replenishing your supply. It's that easy."

"For you, maybe." I laughed. "I'm not sure I can have any just yet. I haven't even choked down the jello."

"Ew. You poor thing." She made a sour face. The jello thing we had in common.

"I know, right?"

She set the box in my hands and kissed me on the cheek. "Well, consider it a reward then. You can work up to it. You can do this, you know."

I swallowed down the lump in my throat. I know it seems silly, but that one small token of kindness meant more to me than anything. It turned my whole day around, as if suddenly everything was going to be ok.

"You're one of the good ones Kate."

Kate winked at me while Colin just sat back in his chair, grinning.

"Would you like to try one?" I offered.

He shook his head. "I've already had my pity party for today, thanks."

The room stilled as my heart returned to an image of Finn, unconscious. I did have a long road ahead of me, but Finn's was even longer. If I was going to be strong enough to help him through his recovery I'd have to get through mine first.

Dad came back in and stood awkwardly at the foot of the bed, and I felt like an attraction at the zoo. I knew dad couldn't stay, and honestly I wasn't sure I wanted him to.

"You look better." His head tilted slightly as he studied me. "What happened?"

I looked down at the box in my lap. "Little Debbie happened."

Dad smiled, shaking his head. "You still eat those things?"

I nodded in earnest.

"Oh my God, I haven't seen a box of those since...well, in a long time anyway."

I knew what he was going to say. The last time he'd seen a box of those was when he found me hiding in the quiet room at the funeral home, stuffing my face with them after my mom died. Little did he know I puked them all back up just as fast as they went down. At Jenny's funeral I was too busy being in charge to feel sorry for myself.

"I've decided to get better." I announced.

"Well, that's a relief." Dad looked at me, puzzled. "It took was Little Debbie to convince you?"

"Yes." I faked being mildly indignant. "Is this a problem?"

"No. Nor is it unusual for my daughter."

"What's that supposed to mean?"

"It means, my dear, that you are, and have always been, an all-or-nothing kind of girl."

I heard Colin snicker and raised one eyebrow at him. Dad glanced down at his watch. It was getting on in the afternoon and I figured he needed to get back. With me in good spirits and obviously on the mend he might just be able to justify it with the right kind of push.

"Dad?"

"Yeah peanut."

"Would you do me an enormous favor?"

"Sure thing. What do you need?"

"Could you go to my apartment and get my laptop, then bring it to me when you come back this weekend?"

His eyes narrowed. Too bad he wasn't fooled. "This weekend."

"Yes."

"And what makes you think I'm going anywhere?"

I started to fold my arms across my middle before deciding that was a really painful idea.

"Well, I don't expect you to sit around here and stare at me all day. That would drive both of us crazy. Maybe you could take Saturday off and come up Friday night?"

He thought about that for a minute. "Yeah, I guess I could do that."

"Thanks. You know where the spare keys are to my apartment?" As soon as I said it I realized it was a silly question. Of course he didn't know where they were.

"You have spare keys?"

"They're in the bottom drawer of mom's dresser–at the house." The one place he'd be sure not to look. There were still clothes in there and he'd never been willing to go through them.

"My house?"

I leaned my head forward. "Yes, your house. Did you think I would keep a set of spare keys *in* my apartment?"

Dad smirked. "You mean all this time I could've been spying on you, breaking and entering, that sort of thing?"

"Not if you didn't know the keys existed you couldn't."

"Hmph. Good point."

I turned my attention to Kate. "What about you?"

"What *about* me?"

She looked offended, but I just stared back at her. I knew she couldn't afford to miss more than one day of work. Besides, the high school was in full production for their rendition of Footloose and she was the main choreographer. "You can't stay here. I know you can't. What will Ren and Ariel do without you?"

Kate blinked a few times. "There's a train leaving at four, but I won't go if you need me."

"I don't. I mean, of course I *do*. Just not this minute. I'll be fine for a few days. Maybe you could come out with dad after work on Friday?"

Dad piped in. "Sure. That would be fine with me. You don't have to take the train, Kate. I'll drive you back."

"Really?" She looked from me to my dad. "Ok, thanks!"

It was all shaping up nicely.

Dad seemed suddenly uneasy. "Are you sure, peanut?"

"Of course I'm sure."

It was terribly awkward for a few more minutes. "Jesus, would you guys just go already? You're making me uncomfortable!" Like I said, about twenty-four hours was all I could take of intensely close contact with my dad, and Kate and I weren't exactly used to spending every waking moment together either. I was used to living alone, and I had enough to process to keep me holed up in that room for quite some time.

Dad shrugged his shoulders. "Well, ok then." He shook Colin's hand and gave me another hug. "I'll be calling to check up on you."

"Calling Celia, no doubt." I winked at him.

Kate followed his hug with her own. "If you need anything. *Anything.* You call me."

"I will."

22

"War talk by men who have been in war is always interesting;
whereas moon talk by a poet who has not been in the moon
is likely to be dull."
M.T.

As they walked out the door I suddenly realized I had nothing of my old world left. My purse was gone, my cell phone was gone, and my laptop was in New York. If I was going to survive recovery I'd have to learn a different way to function that didn't involve constant text messages and email. I had deadlines to take care of, but I sure didn't feel like writing. It was kind of nice, having an excuse. The Times would survive for a couple of weeks without me. A break might not be so bad. Besides, the hospital had cable!

Unbelievable exhaustion settled over me. Right after dad and Kate left I put away the mask and let my face fall back along my skull bones, resting my head against the pillows for just a moment.

I looked over at Colin through the side of my left eye. "How'd I do?"

He was shaking his head, amused but perplexed. "You did fine, darlin', but are you sure you don't want their company? Friends and family are important in times like these."

"Most of the time I'm more comfortable dealing with things on my own."

"Tell that to the tearful little sprite who was laying in that bed earlier."

My eyes closed as I steeled myself against the emotions of it. "That was a momentary lapse. Nothing more."

Colin's eyes hit the floor as his head bobbed gently up and down. "Aye, and I'm thinking you could use a few more of those."

"Don't worry. I've been through worse than this. I can handle myself."

Colin kept looking at the floor. He didn't seem convinced of my strength and truth be told, I hadn't sounded very strong when I said it.

"Tell me more about the war. About Finn. What else don't I know about him?"

"A whole lifetime darlin'. I wouldn't know where to begin."

"Start anywhere." I tried to adjust my position but the pain stopped me short. "I've got nothing but time."

Before Colin could say any more, Celia came in and put her hand on his shoulder. "Mr. McCarthy?"

He whipped his head around, ready for anything. The fact that he went to full alert in the space of a breath caught my attention.

"They need you in the ICU."

He stood right up and started to walk, then stopped, presumably for my benefit. "Is everything all right?" he asked Celia.

"Yes." She smiled up at him. "Finn's awake."

Colin looked back at me and smiled. "You see? I told you he was a good soldier!"

"Tell him..."

Tell him what exactly? The words were all jumbled up in my throat, and nothing would come out. Maybe I needed that laptop more than I realized.

Colin nodded once, as if he understood completely. "Don't worry. I'll tell him."

Later that evening a light knock sounded at the door and a smiling Colin stuck his head in. "Mind if I come in?"

"Are you kidding?" I grinned. "Of course you can!"

Celia and I had been talking. More like, I'd been spilling my guts and she'd listened.

"I'll get out of your way." Celia said. "I've got to finish up some paperwork before I leave for the night."

"Maybe I could sing her a wee Irish lullaby." Colin grinned.

"You might have to sing fast. I just gave her a hefty dose of pain medication." Celia laughed. She stood up and stretched briefly then made her way to the door. "Good night you two!"

"Good night."

Colin pulled up a chair. "You don't *really* want me to sing, do you?"

"Not unless you want to." I smiled over at him. "How is he?" I asked.

"Smiled soon as he saw me."

"So he recognized you? Is he talking?" I think I'd convinced myself that the swelling in his brain would cause some weird case of amnesia.

"First thing he did was ask about you."

"What?" I tried to swallow, but all the moisture had left my mouth.

"Said to tell you he was sorry."

"Sorry for *what*? What does *he* have to be sorry about?"

Colin shook his head. "According to Finn, if it wasn't for him and his hair-brained idea to take you to the Mark Twain house, you wouldn't be in hospital right now."

"That's ridiculous! You know that right? I mean, if he hadn't tried to save me he would have walked away from the accident! I owe him my *life*! He owes me nothing..."

"He thought you might not believe me." He pulled a phone out of his pocket. "Made me take a video for you."

I shook my head. The swelling must have been worse than we thought. He'd just woken up from an induced coma and his first thought was to take a video of himself? For me?

Colin pushed a few buttons and handed me the phone. I held it with trembling hands. There was Finn, except he seemed to be looking at me through a donut hole.

My face must have registered the confusion because Colin whispered "He's in a special bed so his back can be open to the air. For a while they had it tipped up high to keep the pressures down in his head, but that seems to be stabilizing."

"So you put the camera under the bed?"

Colin nodded. "Finn's idea."

Of course it was. I shook my head and pushed play. The sound of his voice about crushed me.

"Truly..." He looked like he was in pain, and his face was bruised and swollen. "I'm so sorry."

I put a hand to my mouth and started to cry.

"I feel like this is all my fault. Please forgive me."

He started breathing heavily and I could hear Colin's voice in the background. "That's enough son. You need to rest."

"No." Finn insisted. "There's one more thing."

He took a deep breath and looked into the camera. "I know you're scared. I'm scared too, but in case anything happens, I need you to know this: I'd do it again. And again. And again." He swallowed and closed his eyes, then opened them slowly, forming a weak smile. "I'm in love with you. And I wanted to tell you that in person, but I don't know when we'll be able to see each other again." His breathing was heavy and labored. "And I don't want any regrets."

His eyes got all scrunched up and the pain was so obvious. "If anything happens to you" Finn's words started to get all jumbled and slurred. "I don't know...I don't know..."

I'm not sure what happened then, but Colin's hand came over the top of the camera and Finn was gone. I looked up in horror. "Is he ok?"

Colin patted my hand. "He just passed out is all. He shouldn't 'a tried to talk so much, but he's stubborn, that one."

I was confused. "That was it? You just left him like that? Did he wake back up?"

Colin shook his head, but seemed completely calm. "The nurse said he just got too excited. Tried to do too much talking too soon. That's Finn for you though - all or nothing. Sound familiar?"

"No." I pouted.

"He'll be fine darlin'. Don't be worrying."

How could he be so sure? I mean what if–what if those were his last words? No regrets? Who says that unless...I tried to shake away the chill that ran down my arms.

"Thank you. For showing this to me. I–I don't know what to say." I started to give the phone to Colin but he pushed my hand back and closed my fingers around the metal.

"Why don't you tell him yourself."

"I'm not going to keep your phone."

"It's not mine–it's Finn's, and he won't be needing it tonight."

My guts felt all twisted and achy but the pain medicine was already starting to take the edge off. I held tight to the phone. I did want to watch it again–in private. *And again. And again...*I closed my eyes and tried to just breathe. "Will you tell me about Finn now? About the war?"

"Aye."

I reached out with my free hand and he grabbed on. His grip was strong and sure.

"It may not be easy for you to hear though. Are you sure?"

"Nothing in my life is easy right now." Nor had it ever been, really. Why should this be any different? "It's ok. I'm a big girl."

"Well, I beg to differ with you there. You're no bigger than a sprite." He gave me a smile and a wink.

"And now with the hair I look even more like Tinker Belle."

"Aye, that you do." He gave my hand a squeeze. "And you're beautiful no matter what your hair looks like."

The spasm in my gut seemed to have subsided. It felt so good having Colin in one hand and Finn's phone in the other. I was about as connected to him as I could possibly be at that moment. My whole body relaxed and I forced myself to stay awake. There'd be time to sleep later, after Colin was gone.

"It wasn't easy–the things Finn went through over there. War... does things to a man."

I was suddenly worried. What kind of things?

"That's why Eiran's loss hit him so hard."

His sister? "Excuse me?"

Colin shook his head as he spoke. "He doesn't like to talk about it much. He probably didn't tell you about his wife then?"

My head came up off the pillow. "*Wife?* Uh. No. No he didn't." I was starting to put two and two together. Or so I thought. "Where is she?"

"She died, darlin'. In the war. In the same bomb blast that landed Finn in hospital."

I was dumbstruck, and it took several minutes to register the information. It wasn't that he couldn't have been married before. I guess I'd just never thought of him that way.

"What was her name?"

"Kathleen." Finn's father smiled. "She was a spitfire, that one. Shot a gun just as good as old Finn and was pretty to boot. Or so I've heard."

I thought about my frazzled hair turned pageboy. I'd never shot a gun or done anything remotely interesting. "Was she in the army too? Is that where they met?"

"That's right. Only I don't think he'd planned on marrying her. Finn was never really the marrying type."

He winked at me again and if Finn had been there I got the feeling Colin would have given him a pat on the back.

"The baby changed that though."

"*Baby?*"

If I hadn't been lying down already I probably would've passed out. This was too much to process all at once, and my world was already getting fuzzy. My gut twisted into a knot that shot pain all through my body. I heaved with the intensity of it and Colin put his hand on my forehead.

"Are you all right, love? Would you like me to get the nurse?"

I clutched his hand desperately and willed back the desire to heave-ho the small amount of broth in my stomach.

"No! Please, I need to finish this conversation!"

Colin smirked at me. "I see Finn's met his match in the stubborn department."

How could he be joking at a time like this?

I tried to line it up in my brain. "Let me get this straight. Finn, the *former playboy*, joined the army, accidentally got a girl pregnant, married her, but then she *and the baby* were killed in some kind of explosion?"

Colin's face turned serious. "They'd only been married a few days–took a weekend furlough and made it official. She hadn't told her commanding officers about the baby yet or they probably wouldn't have let her near the fighting, but it was an ambush anyway, so there was nothing they could do."

"Oh my God." And I thought my life was full of drama. I couldn't make this shit up if I tried. "How long ago was that?"

Colin took a moment to calculate the time. "About three years I'd guess."

It's been three years since I've been with a woman. I sighed. "So many things make so much more sense now."

"He'll tell you the rest in his own good time." Colin smiled.

The rest?

"He's a good man, Finn is, but he's careful now. A little too careful sometimes."

"So then when Eiran lost the baby it brought it all back for him?"

"Aye."

"And that's why he tried to save me. Because of her." It wasn't a question, really. I was just solidifying the truth in my own mind.

Colin's face softened and he squeezed my hand. "Didn't you

hear him, darlin'? The boy's in love with you. This wasn't about Kathleen."

Tears were running sideways down my face as I laid there looking up at him. I wanted to believe him, but now? Now I might never be sure.

23

"We all do no end of feeling, and we mistake it for thinking."
M.T.

That night after Colin left I watched Finn's message over and over, the look on his face burning itself into my memory as he said the words "I'm in love with you." *Was he?*

Somewhere around three a.m. I was awake again. I flipped on the light and decided to push record. My message to Finn wouldn't be much, but at least it'd be honest.

"Hey Finn. I can't believe we're in the same hospital and yet we're reduced to video chatting, but I guess this will have to do, for now."

I pushed the stop button. The beauty of technology meant you could stop your thoughts from coming out of your mouth. I hadn't stopped thinking about my conversation with Colin all night. It didn't matter to me that Finn had been married. She wasn't a wife, really, just some girl he'd gotten pregnant and tried to do the right thing by. I'd known countless girls who'd gotten pregnant in high school and college by guys who never even stuck around.

Even though I felt small and insignificant in the big scheme of things, it actually made my feelings for Finn that much stronger. I ached for his pain in losing them both–especially the baby he would never know. Colin was right. He was a better man than I'd ever known.

I pushed record again. "Ok, so here's the deal. You need to get better, and I don't want you worrying about me."

His face and his words ran in circles around my head until I was dizzy with it. *I'm in love with you...And I don't want any regrets.*

"I'm going to come and see you just as soon as they let me out of this bed. But I don't want you to be sorry. Believe me, I've spent a lot of my life being angry about things I had no control over. We just have to start from here."

My words hung in the air for a few seconds. "I was thinking that maybe we could start dating, kind of...*long distance.*" I smiled into the camera. "You in the burn unit and me..." I looked around the room. "Wherever it is I am now." I laughed even though it made my side burn with pain.

"It's the middle of the night for me, but I'll get this to you as soon as I can, and when you feel up to it you can send me a message back."

I pushed stop and let all the air out of my lungs. God that sucked. Finn was right. Talking in person is much better than talking over a video, but if it was all we had, it would have to do.

The next morning I had an excruciating session with a physical therapist and asked if he would deliver the phone to the burn unit ICU. He smiled at me when I told him Finn's name, which I thought was odd, but he seemed happy to do it.

I fed myself lunch and took it extra slow so the nausea wouldn't make me lose it again, then I reached into the tray table and found a comb. Since I had very little hair left anyway, it wouldn't take long to comb it. My movements felt thick and slow. Like pushing through molasses. I probably looked like an eighty year-old with Parkinson's the way my limbs trembled with the effort. Celia was right. Even the smallest movements were exhausting.

When I woke up again the room was dusky. I must have missed dinner completely. My tray table was empty except for Finn's phone.

I reached for it hungrily and switched it on. The clock said nine-thirty. How could I have slept the entire day away? Celia hadn't been there at all. Must have been her day off.

This message was more upbeat. He even tried to be funny. "You'll be happy to know they've given me a room with a view. I've got a mirror under the bed and a controller up near my hand so I can tilt the mirror to see different parts of the room. It all seems a bit backwards to me though." He smiled at his own joke. God he was adorable.

"I wanted to thank you for your message and to let you know that I would love to date you." He smiled. "And I like your hair, by the way. It was beautiful long, but this way I can see all of your face, which is good, you see, since I happen to like your face."

He looked away for a moment, like he was finding his bearings in the room.

"If I were alone right now, I'd be telling you about some of the other things I like about you." He winked at me then and it made me laugh out loud. He was a charmer, I had to give him that. "Until we meet again then." He smiled and Colin's hand closed over the phone, signaling the end of the message.

I'd never been so tired. That PT must have taken more out of me than I thought. I felt hot all over and pushed the blankets off.

The real Finn was in there still. His coma hadn't taken him away and left him there, present in body but distant in mind. He was strong enough. He would overcome. Relief covered me like a warm blanket and I drifted back to sleep.

UNFORTUNATELY, my sleep was anything but peaceful. I dreamt I'd been captured by terrorists in Afghanistan and they were torturing me. They had my laptop and they were reading all my private journals out loud. Then they put clamps around my broken leg and started crushing the bones, telling me I had to admit that I loved Finn or they'd keep crushing. I kept yelling that I loved him and I'd already said it. I begged them to stop but the sun was beating down on me and I was so hot and so thirsty I could barely scream.

I hate those dreams. You know, the ones where you need to run away but your limbs move in slow motion or you're trying to scream but nothing's coming out of your mouth? I had other dreams too. It must have been a long night. Either that or the meds were finally scrambling my brain.

A couple of times I even knew I was dreaming and I kept trying to wake myself up. I imagined Celia's face, then Colin's face, then Finn's face. I locked onto Finn's face and I kept telling him *I love you. I love you. Please make them stop.* He was dressed like a soldier with a gun and I wanted desperately for him to use it. To kill the people that were doing this to me.

It wouldn't have been so bad if I didn't feel so hot all the time. With as much force as I could whisper I just kept saying *I love you Finn. I am in love with you. I am.*

Noises came and went, and people came and went, and I didn't have the energy to even look at them. I wondered about Finn - talked to him in my sleep. It was all so bizarre I thought maybe we'd both actually died in the car crash and I was living in an episode of *Lost.*

One day I saw his face just as clear as anything and I smiled and he smiled back. And then he kissed me and the warmth of his lips was so different from the cold, sterile environment I'd been living in I came awake with a start.

"Hi there."

I blinked hard. Twice. "Finn?" I whispered.

He reached up slowly, painfully and grabbed my hand. I kept blinking, trying to make sense of things. Was he real? Or was I dreaming again? When my vision started to focus I saw Colin there too, behind Finn's wheelchair. *Wheelchair?* Then I remembered his burns. His broken ankle. How was he out of bed?

He spoke again, squeezing my hand. The electricity was still there. That much I knew had to be real.

He winked at me and leaned forward, but his face contorted and I heard a nurse say. "Ok lover boy, that's enough for today. This field trip is over."

Colin was smiling down at me. His tiny nod told me everything I needed to know. He carefully turned the wheelchair and I felt Finn's grip drop from my hand.

"Bye" I managed.

Finn left my room slumped forward in the chair. He couldn't possibly sit back against those burns. I could hardly believe he was there at all.

Turns out not all of it had been a dream. I know this because Colin came back and told me the story. At least, I think I've got the timeline right. I wished once again for my laptop and hoped that someone was keeping track of all this so I could put the pieces back together later. Apparently I got some sort of infection and they had to open up my leg and they moved me to the ICU. Ironic, I know.

"Just so you know, your da's comin' back again this weekend." Colin explained. "Kate was here with him, and so was David. They sat by your bed and fretted and worried and you had no idea they were even here."

That wasn't exactly true, because I sort of remembered my dad and Celia, talking about surgeries. And I saw Kate's face somehow. But the weekend? What day was it now? I couldn't form the words so I just listened.

"Last week you developed a fever. Infection of some kind, and with your spleen just tryin' to heal it took hold pretty good. Then you started screaming about your leg."

*Screaming? How embarrassing...*It was time that was the problem. My brain was too fuzzy. I couldn't put it all in order in my head. I'd lost another entire week? More surgeries? How was I going to pay for all of this on bare bones insurance? And what about my apartment? My savings would be blown in a heartbeat.

I started to hyperventilate and the machines started beeping. A nurse came hurrying in. "Mr. McCarthy I'm going to have to ask you to step out."

"Aye." He squeezed my hand. "One step at a time darlin'."

He patted my hand and he was gone. One step at a time. Who was he kidding? I didn't know where to even begin sorting things out. Luckily I didn't have to spend much time worrying about it. The nurse put something in my IV and I was gone.

24

"When you fish for love,
bait with your heart, not your brain."
M.T.

Recovery was painful and slow, but eventually I could sit up and use my laptop, so I started sending video messages to Finn. Colin had brought him his computer too, and that's when the real fun began.

I was trying to type an email to my boss at The Times when the alert sounded. A call was coming in – from Finn!

I clicked 'answer' and suddenly we were talking–real time–and he looked amazing!

"Hi there." He smiled.

"Well, hi!"

"Fancy meeting you here."

I laughed. "Well, I don't know why we should be surprised. Our entire history up to this point has been one strange chance meeting after another, starting with Yankee Stadium."

"Ah yes." He nodded thoughtfully. "The night you punched me in the nose."

I sighed. I was never gonna live that one down. "Well, if I hadn't punched you we probably would never have met." His eyes drew me all the way in. I think I could have stared at him all day. "So tell me, how is it you charmed the nurses into wheeling you over here that first time? You were hardly up for travel and you look incredible now compared to–whenever that was. All the time is running together lately."

He wiggled his eyebrows a little. "You think I look incredible? How 'bout this scar? It's a real turn-on, isn't it?"

I know he meant it to be funny, but all I could think about was the multitude of scars he would have all over his body by the time this was all said and done. We'd both have scars–inside and out, and it wasn't funny. Not really at all.

"Hey now." He interrupted my pouting. "Look at me. None of that. You said it yourself, remember? We're just going to start from here. No dwelling on the past, no blaming, no pity parties. It is what it is." He let those words work their way in until I nodded. "Ok?"

"Ok."

He was like an anchor in the storm, tethering our story to a rock that was solid and somehow immovable, and I was so thankful for his strength.

He smiled as if he had a delicious secret. "You'd be amazed if you knew how many people are on our side."

"Our side?"

"Oh yes. Our story is famous in the hospital. All the staff know who we are and what's happened with the accident, and about you calling out for me all the time in your sleep and–"

"Wait, what?"

"Our story–it's famous!"

"No no! The part about me calling out for you. That was real? I thought for sure I was dreaming that."

He smiled sheepishly and I blushed.

"Oh God, I'm just gonna go *die* now!" Finn was just about the cutest guy I'd ever known, much less kissed, and now he knew I'd been calling out for him in my delirium. I covered my face with one hand. If all the things I remembered dreaming had been said out loud they might have heard way more than they bargained for.

"Anyway, all the nurses think its exceptionally adorable and romantic and all that." His voice got extra quiet. "So they pretty much give me whatever I want when it comes to you."

I had to laugh at that.

He shook his head, chuckling. "We're almost celebrities. Any moment now I expect to be signing autographs. I'm surprised Da didn't tell you about it. Some of the staff are taking bets about who will play us in the movie version."

Colin hadn't mentioned that part, but the stuff he had told me would have made a pretty intense movie as well. Finn's dead wife. A lost child. I'd wanted to talk to him about it, and then all this happened.

Finn must have noticed the change in my face because he got serious all of a sudden. "What is it? What's wrong?"

I shook my head. "We can talk about it some other time."

"We've got nothing *but* time. Why don't you tell me what's wrong?"

I stared back at him. "Your dad, he..." I licked my lips and tried to form the words. "Told me about Kathleen."

His eyes registered the shock of that, but behind the shock I watched a lingering pain flare up at the mention of her name.

"And the baby too?" He asked.

I nodded.

He took a deep breath in and watched my face. "And?"

"And...I don't want you to confuse the two of us."

There. I'd said it. Bluntly, and possibly hurtfully, but there wasn't really a nice way to say something like that. He flinched, physically, as if I'd punched him in the gut.

"It's ok." I looked down at my lap, because I couldn't look at his face if I was going to get this next part out. "And when I say it's ok what I mean is, I'm not upset that you were married before, or that you didn't tell me about such a deeply personal thing. I mean, it's your life and we haven't known each other for that long and I feel awful for your loss, it's just..."

I took a deep breath and continued. "Well, you didn't have to save me, and if you think somehow that saving me makes up for losing them, I don't want to be caught under that kind of pressure, you know? I can't live up to that. I'm not...strong enough to be that for you."

When I finally looked up at the screen Finn's face was in his hand and he was wiping his eyes. "That's not what this is."

I wanted to believe him, but it was tricky. Of course he would say that.

"When I told you it had been three years since I'd been with a woman, I wasn't kidding. All that time I didn't trust myself to be with anyone, but I would never have pursued you if I wasn't ready." He straightened somewhat and looked straight into the camera. "I never really wanted to get married. Didn't work out so well for my parents, and I doubt it would have worked out for Kathleen and I. We knew we weren't in love, even after she told me about the baby, but I couldn't leave a child in this world without a father, so I had to try. Now, God seemed to have other plans and I don't understand that, but losing them changed something in me. The consequences were just too real. Sleeping with beautiful women was no longer my life's goal."

"So *not* sleeping with beautiful women became your life's goal?" Hey, it was a valid question.

"No, changing the way I saw myself and my relationships became my life's goal, but you have to understand. That didn't start with Kathleen. It started with my best friend, who spent a lot of years trying to convince me there was a better way, long before I ever joined the army. I just wasn't a very good listener."

Kate was a friend like that. She saw my pain but didn't allow me to wallow. She was there through all of the Christopher stuff, all of the hospital stuff. Even though I hadn't told her every detail, she was the closest thing I had to a confidante. I could definitely see where a good friend could make a huge difference.

"After the explosion, something in me snapped. A lot of other things happened–things I can't explain right here and right now, but the night you and I met, I ended up at Yankee Stadium because David won those tickets on a bet. I wasn't even going to go."

"Me neither. My boss gave me those tickets at the last minute, and Kate pretty much made me go."

"As soon as I met you, I knew without a doubt that you were meant to be in my life, no matter what. When I gave you my card that night, it was all I could do to put you in that cab and walk away, knowing you might never use it."

Love at first sight? Preposterous.

I shook my head. "I didn't need the card to find the club."

"True. But I wanted you to have more to go on than an address at a bar. I wanted you to be able to reach me. I wanted you to know that it wasn't a chance meeting."

"But it was a chance meeting. It was an accident. You said it yourself. Someone pushed you and your Coke went flying."

"Sometimes accidents happen on purpose."

"You're not making sense. That's an oxymoron. Are you talking about fate?"

"Look, I care about you and I want to have a relationship with you, but not because I'm living for what's past. I want to leave behind the man that I was and build a new future with someone I care about. And that someone is you!"

He'd raised his voice and I could somehow hear it echoing off the walls, or maybe I was hearing it because he wasn't that far away and our respective computers were magnifying the volume. In either case, the next thing I heard was applause. The staff had overheard our conversation, and they were applauding!

Finn wasn't kidding. My life had become its own reality TV show! I was mortified, but regardless of who was listening, or what my thoughts were on the likelihood of love at first sight, he wanted to build a future. With me. His words hadn't escaped my notice. They made me feel humbled and small.

"I'm sorry. I shouldn't have brought up Kathleen. I know it's in the past."

"You had every right to bring it up, because it affects us, but we still have to move forward." He drew these next words out slowly and very intentionally. He even lowered his voice as if to say *this isn't for show – this is just for you*. "I. Am. In love. With you. Do you understand that? I have never said those words to another woman before. I have never felt these feelings before. And I'm scared too, so don't shut me out. Please."

My heart melted. Watching his face as he said those things made all the difference. He wasn't giving me a line, he was opening his heart and offering it to me. Two tiny tears dropped from my eyelids. "Ok. I won't."

"Do you think they'd let me come over?"

I shook my head in disbelief. "I think they'd let you do just about anything you want."

I watched Finn look up from the screen and call out loudly. "Can a guy get a kiss around here?" I could hear some loud laughter and a ruckus in the hallway. Finn's screen went black and the call ended, but I'll be damned if about five minutes later Finn didn't show up in a wheelchair. They slid me over to the edge of the bed and got his chair as close as they could, then pulled the curtain and shut the door to give us some privacy.

My heart was pounding in my chest just to look at him. He leaned forward as far as he could and I did the same. Our lips met at the edge of the bed and his mouth felt like coming home. I reached up and held his face in my hand. The electricity passing through every nerve ending felt like the waking of a sleeping giant. I'd begun to crave his touch, because it fed some unnamed hunger, and I followed him willingly, deep into his kiss until I completely lost track of time and space. It was magical.

It was also on camera. When I looked up into the corner of the room I saw a small surveillance camera, for practical purposes I'm sure. A nurse can't be in a patient's room every second of every day and night, but still.

Finn turned slowly in the direction of my gaze. "What are you looking at?"

"Smile! You're on camera!" I waved at the corner.

Finn put the back of his head between their view and my face. "Let them look. I don't care." He kissed me one more time and whispered. "This is the way I wanted to say it–with my lips right next to your face. I love you Truly. Truly." He grinned.

I looked into the eyes of this man that had completely captured my heart and it all fell away. All the fear. All the pain. All the insecurity. "I love you too."

"That's what I thought, but I had to be really sure." He smiled softly, pain still visible underneath it all.

"You need to go back to bed."

"I know." He nodded. The fact that he admitted it without hesitation was telling. I pushed my call light and within seconds two people were there, spinning his chair around.

"Ok, lover boy. Time to go."

Finn nodded once and gritted his teeth against the pain as they wheeled him out. It had taken an enormous amount of effort for him to come in there and act like everything was ok, when clearly it wasn't. All I had to do was lay there.

25

"Too much of anything is bad,
but too much of good whiskey is barely enough."
M.T.

When the weekend rolled around again, dad came by and Celia was with him, and by with him I mean...*with* him. Like, they walked in hand-in-hand and Celia was dressed in a pair of jeans and a light sweater. Her hair was hanging loose instead of being pulled back like it normally was, and she had just a little makeup on. She looked natural and very pretty. Dad looked–I don't even know. Relaxed? It was different from the Gigi look. They looked comfortable together. Like they fit. It was weird, but nice.

It had been ten years since my mom died, and although I wasn't interested in a mother figure, I could see Celia and I being–I don't know, friends, sort of. She walked over to me like it was the most natural thing in the world, gently brushed my hair back and kissed my forehead. "How are you honey?"

Honey? How many hours *had* she spent sitting by my bedside the past couple weeks? It wasn't that I wanted her to go away. It was just strange to think that she had somehow entered my inner circle while I slept.

Dad looked a little uneasy, watching the two of us, like he was waiting for something to happen.

"I'm ok." I looked over at dad. "Day off?"

He and Celia smiled at each other. "Yeah."

I looked at Celia. "You too?"

She smiled at me and nodded. The look in her eyes said it all.

"So, you two are doing the *long distance* thing?"

"Sort of." Dad cleared his throat and chuckled. "She lives in Stamford, which is just about half way between here and the city." He turned toward Celia "I told you she says exactly what she thinks."

"Well, I happen to like that about her." Celia winked at me.

"Me too." Dad ruffled my hair.

"No Kate this weekend? It feels like its been ages since I've seen her."

"I think she's coming on the bus tomorrow. Said something about dress rehearsals and a show tonight."

Footloose! I couldn't believe I was missing it. I'd promised her I'd be there. Not that there was anything I could do about it, but still. I couldn't help feeling like my whole life was going by without me.

Celia spent a few minutes answering my questions, but then looked at me knowingly. "I hear Finn's been on a couple of field trips."

I blushed. "Oh, you heard about that, did you?"

Dad's eyes narrowed a bit. "You know, I still want to meet this *Finn* person. I'm beginning to think he's a figment of everyone's imagination!"

Apparently Colin walked in right behind that comment. "Looks like I've come at just the right time." He shook my dad's hand and they exchanged greetings. They'd obviously gotten to know each other a bit while I was out of it.

Dad was quick to qualify. "I didn't mean right now. It can wait, believe me."

"Nonsense!" Colin practically pulled dad out of the room. "He's awake and would love the company! He's just over there." Colin pointed and I tried to crane my neck to catch a glimpse of his room. How close was it?

Celia looked at me, wide eyed.

"Well, go on with them! You might as well!" I shoed her out with a laugh.

She grinned back at me and hurried out behind them. I assumed she could go anywhere she liked, see any patients she liked, but the fact that she seemed to have kept her distance physically in spite of the obvious gossip spoke volumes about her character.

I'm not sure how long they were gone. I must have dozed off a few times while I waited, but when they came back in they were laughing, like they'd all shared some great joke and I'd missed it somehow. Being helpless was no fun. I wasn't used to asking anyone for anything. Now I couldn't even turn over in bed by myself.

"So? Does he make the approved list?"

Dad smirked at me. We both knew there'd never been one of those. "He seems like a really good guy."

Not that I needed his approval, but still, it was nice to hear.

Celia touched my shoulder and winked at me, mouthing the words 'he's really cute!' so dad couldn't see her.

When I giggled, he looked between the two of us, shaking his head. "I'm not even going to ask."

"Probably best." Colin added.

"How is he?" I asked.

"Worried about you." Celia replied, pulling a chair over to sit next to me. She took her place as a matter of fact, as if it wasn't really dad's anyway. She seemed very protective of me, which was nice, but strange. Then again, the whole situation was slightly bizarre, so I guess I shouldn't have been surprised. Who would have dreamed that my dad would find *his* soul mate because of *my* near death experience?

Everything about this situation seemed bizarre after a while. It was surreal, being surrounded by so much pain. My leg seemed to be healing without too much trouble, but the physical therapy was still excruciating. I learned that being pain-free was something I would never take for granted again. Finn too, and it didn't take long to understand why they wouldn't let him move any closer to me.

On the days they worked on Finn's burns, I wasn't allowed to see him and we rarely sent messages back and forth. Colin said he did better than most. He was a soldier, and no stranger to painful wounds. I imagined him gritting his teeth and trying not to let the sound escape his lips. A deep, fierce, guttural cry that pushed through at all costs.

He wouldn't let me talk about it. Every time I brought it up he changed the subject. I wanted to do penance for his pain–to somehow continually keep the apology ever in front of us, but he wouldn't allow me that comfort, as strange and dysfunctional as it was. He knew better. It did neither of us any good.

Our relationship deepened so much during that strange time in the hospital together. At first we rarely saw each other in the flesh, and yet we became each other's distraction and support in an otherwise difficult and painful situation.

The nice thing about being a freelance writer is that you can work from a laptop. The terrible thing about being in pain is that narcotics make writing cohesive sentences next to impossible. Turns out the old me was something of a workaholic, but it was way too exhausting to try to work like I used to. A few lame emails were all I could manage between naps.

I could feel the dependence on the painkillers starting to take hold. It made everything so much easier to deal with. I worried so much less about everything–except of course, the possibility of addiction.

It made me wonder how Finn was doing with it, since he rarely let me talk to him about his injuries. I'd overheard some of the nurses talking in the hall about how he refused the medicine most of the time, and only when they had to clean and debride his wounds did he agree to be knocked out.

I felt like such a wuss by comparison, but then again I'd never had physical pain like this before. The closest I'd ever come to surgery was when I cut my finger on the top of a soup can and had to get three stitches. I had no idea how many stitches I had now, between the leg, the graft site they ended up doing on my leg, and my stomach, but it was a hell of a lot more than three.

One day Finn arranged for us to have a real "date" where the nurses wheeled us down to the atrium so that we could have lunch together. They took our orders and went and brought us our food, then sat at a table where they could see us and had their own lunches to give us a little privacy.

I'd been trying to hold off on the next dose of my painkiller, but it was making me irritable and he could tell something was off.

He leaned in to kiss me and when I tried to meet him in the middle I cried out. He pulled back in surprise and studied my face. "You're hurting, aren't you? How long has it been since..."

I cut him off with a shake of my head. "I'm fine."

"You're not fine."

"I don't want to talk about it." There. See how he likes his own medicine.

"Look at me."

I did as I was told. His eyes were soft and kind, but this was a man who recognized pain when he saw it.

"Why aren't you taking your medicine?"

It took me a while to answer, but his eyes seemed to understand before the words came out. "Because I need it."

"Of course you need it. We both do."

I gave him my no bullshit look. "So are you the pot or the kettle Mr. 'I only take pain meds when they're ripping the skin off my body piece by piece'?"

His face broke as he tried not to laugh. He looked down,

embarrassed rather than proud. "And how is it you know about that?"

"Well, there's nothing wrong with my ears, and there's no shortage of hallway gossip about you. You're like a superhero. I think a few of the nurses are considering proposing."

"Really!" He pretended to straighten a nonexistent tie. "Which one do you think I should go for?"

"I think you could pretty much have your pick–even the married ones. And most of them actually have hair." I crossed my arms over my chest.

He reached over and touched his fingers to my cheek. "I don't want any of them."

I looked back as tears came quickly to the surface. It was getting harder and harder to keep it in check lately. "I hurt. I hurt all the time. The only time I can even get a handle on it is when they give me those pain meds. I need them to survive this pain and I can't stand that. Even worse is that I'm so stressed out about everything else that I look forward to them because they help me to just forget for a while."

"What do you mean, everything else?"

"Losing my apartment, paying off these hospital bills, losing my freelance jobs because I can't seem to put two coherent sentences together? Take your pick!"

He just looked at me as if he completely understood. I thought he would tell me it was ok–that I should go ahead and take the meds now and deal with the addiction later, but he didn't.

We were quiet for a long time. He just sat there rubbing my hand in his.

"Why you don't take them?" I asked.

He licked his lips before answering. "You might say I went off the deep end after Kathleen died. I had a *lot* of injuries, and they gave me a lot of medicine. I didn't want to remember, so I let myself forget. Even after I was released and discharged I didn't know what to do with myself. Nothing was the same. Nothing felt right. I just drifted."

He looked out past me and his eyes twitched a little as he talked, as if the events he was describing were both far from his memory and ever-present. "After a while I started washing it all down with whiskey and painkillers until I couldn't think anymore. I didn't want to think anymore."

When he looked at me, the depth of his pain crushed me. "So the addiction became real for you?"

"In a way, yes. Da came and found me and put me to work renovating one of his bars in an historic section of Dublin. The work was good for me. It gave me something to focus on and something to keep me busy. Then he brought me to the States. Put me to work building Finnegan's."

"He put someone addicted to whiskey and painkillers to work in a bar?"

"Not exactly the way a Yank would deal with it, eh?"

I shook my head. "No, not exactly. We like to think in terms of separation, hoping to break the hold." I made two fists and snapped them up to demonstrate.

Finn got quiet again, and focused on the floor. "Well, we all have our strategies, don't we?"

"But you can drink now. Without it controlling you?"

"Da owns bars all over Ireland. Drinking is a part of our culture. When I went through that rough patch, I'm not sure I was addicted to the substances themselves as much as the act of forgetting."

It was my turn to be quiet, trying to imagine him weak and dependent. I felt strangely relieved knowing he was flawed, even though his coming through the storm made him more superhumanly attractive than ever. He had a strength I couldn't comprehend. Where my losses had made me frail, his had made him tougher, more resilient somehow.

"Do you remember one time on your couch, you asked me 'how do you stop when you want to go'?"

Just the mention of that particular make-out session warmed my insides. "Yeah. I remember."

"Do you remember my answer?"

How could I forget? I'd logged it for use in a future novel already! "That you care more about tomorrow than you do about today. I remember it very clearly."

"Well, that became my ethos. Every time I wanted to wallow in the past or even the present, I tried to look down the road, to the future, and where I would be if I continued on that same path. I still like to have a few drinks now and then, but I don't have the same issues I had before. There were things I needed to discover about myself. Things I encountered in Ireland that I can't really explain to your right now, but some day I'd like to show you."

He seemed to have an intimate knowledge of this stuff. I wondered if he'd seen a therapist too, but maybe that wasn't the way the Irish did things either.

"So your dad walked you through all that–held you accountable?"

"Da took the painkillers away, but he didn't try to stop me from drinking. Like I said, the Irish are a pub culture. Drinking is a very social activity. We drink, we gather, we fight, we laugh. It's all a part of gettin' through. He just...let me get through."

"Somehow that sounds a whole lot healthier than American culture."

"Moving here and starting a completely different life helped me to see a different future for myself. Da got me involved in the planning and designs for some of his newer ventures after we revitalized the pub in Dublin. The more I focused on other things, the less important the need for escape. I got too busy to drink to excess. I could have a couple and stop."

"I've never known anyone who'd fought their way back quite like that. It takes a lot of courage, and no small amount of perspective."

"Well, don't be too impressed. It wasn't pretty back then, and I've had a lot of help along the way."

"But you never went back to the pain killers?"

He shook his head. "At some point you have to choose life."

I was more of the opinion that life chose you. And then it churned you around and spun you till you were dizzy. Choice was an illusion. I was just trying to get through each day with some sort of routine and predictability.

26

*"Great books are weighed and measured by their style and matter,
and not by the trimmings and shadings of their grammar."*
M.T.

Finn was a baffling combination of strength and vulnerability. The more I got to know him, the more deeply my feelings attached to this man whose life seemed so much larger than the life I'd lived. We spent our days in between therapy and meals talking about every possible topic under the sun. There was a rare kiss or some hand holding, but most of our conversations were screen based. 'Long distance', and yet, right around the corner, as it were.

We started discussing books and found that we'd read many of the same volumes. "Tell me your favorite book by Mark Twain."

"I'm surprised you didn't ask me that on our date."

"I meant to, I was just so captivated by your beauty that night, I think I lost my ability to think properly. I assume you've read every one of his books, based on your bookshelf."

"Aha! So you *were* memorizing my bookshelf that night!" I teased, ignoring the smooth comment.

"Not memorizing exactly, but rather fascinated by it. Not to mention the small shrine you've erected for the man, complete with a bust of his tousled head and poorly trimmed mustache."

"That bust was a gift from one of my professors at NYU!"

"So, which book? Shall I make a guess?"

"Go for it!" I crossed my arms. "You'll never guess."

"What, you think I'm going to guess the obvious Tom Sawyer or Huckleberry What's-His-Name?" Finn winked at me, obviously making fun of the association between his own name and Twain's most famous character duo.

Then, instead of guessing, he said something simple that totally shocked me. It wasn't the statement itself that was shocking. It was the fact that he'd discovered something I didn't even know about myself.

He said "You know, it's fascinating the way your books tell the story of your life."

"Excuse me?"

"Our lives are shaped by stories, don't you think? Our own as well as the ones we read in books."

Of course I believed that, but for the moment I was stuck on his comment about my bookshelf telling him my life story. "So you talked to my bookshelf while I slept? What exactly did it tell you?"

He smiled, watching my discomfort with a flirtatious blend of admiration and challenge. "Well, for starters it was impeccably arranged, not just by category but by height within each category and then chronologically as well."

"Chronologically? That's ridiculous. It's not arranged chronologically. According to which timeline? Authors or publication date?" I had to really think about it. Neither one was true. Chronologically it was all over the place, no matter how you looked at it.

"According to *your* timeline. When you read them."

"That's not–" Wait, was that true?

"And" he added. "Every single book was the exact same distance from the edge of the shelf."

I was stunned. Flabbergasted. "You carry a ruler for just such occasions, do you?"

"Approximately." He corrected himself, but maintained a firmly, annoyingly smug assessment of my life through books.

"I don't believe you. I think you're making this up." I had to give him Twain. It was a fairly extensive and prominently placed selection of books, but there was no way he could spout the rest of my titles.

"Would you like me to explain?"

"Please do." This should be good. Although admittedly, I was beginning to sweat.

"From top to bottom and left to right, there were a few children's books. I assume perhaps some favorite holdovers."

He didn't know the half of it. Those books were some of the only good memories I had of my mom before she got sick. She read to Jenny and I at night, and my love of books was born out of those experiences, getting lost in the characters and adventures of people and places I'd never met.

"Then of course the entire collection of Harry Potter, which of course every British child from eight to fifteen is familiar with. Then another collection of all the Tolkien books with smatterings of C.S. Lewis–are you sure you weren't raised in Britain?"

I just sat there shaking my head, trying not to let on just how unnerving it was, having him read me my life story like that.

"Anyway I read all those in my teens. Then the rest is fuzzy but as I recall there were a few classics that most everyone is assigned at University, along with some poetry and philosophy, which most college students start reading on their own when they start having their own mind. And then," he finished "last but certainly not least, was your rapt fascination with the man called Twain."

There was a lump in my throat the size of a small boulder. I couldn't say anything for several painfully silent seconds. I just sat there blinking at him.

"So you see, one can learn a lot about a person by their bookshelf."

I had obviously arranged them by category, because that's what organizational principles teach us. You either alphabetize by title or author, or you arrange by category, but in the order that I'd read them?

It was true, for the most part, maybe not specifically, but at least by general timeframe or age-range. I was stunned at the realization. My need for organization was so deeply engrained that I ordered my bookshelf as a picture of my life. And Finn noticed before I did. He noticed on his first trip to my apartment. As for them being arranged by height and the same distance from the edge of the shelf, well, that was kind of a no-brainer. Everyone knows that's how you arrange your books, right?

By this time I was in a full sweat under my hospital gown. It was running down my rib cage on either side and soaking into the sheets at the top of my butt crack.

"I'm right, aren't I?"

"Yes." My face was hot, I could feel the redness and I wanted desperately to change the subject. "And what would I find if I looked at your bookshelf?"

"You would find a lot of the same books, actually, although I don't have most of my books here. They're in Ireland. I read quite a lot, actually."

I'd never met a man who was over-educated, well-read and interesting to talk to. Not to mention those eyes.

"Now you didn't answer the question."

"Which question?" I wondered. My head was still reeling as I pushed back against a vision of my bookshelves come to life like a scene from Beauty And The Beast and having a conversation with this handsome prince, telling him everything there is to know about me.

"Your favorite book by Mark Twain?"

"Oh, well that's easy. The Recollections of Joan of Arc."

Finn's head tilted slightly. "See now, I was going to guess A Connecticut Yankee in King Arthur's Court."

"That's a good one too!" I smiled.

"Joan of Arc. Huh. I don't think I'm familiar with that one. Is it a novel then?"

"It is."

"And what makes it your favorite?"

"I like Joan of Arc. And I like Twain. So the fact that he liked her made me like him." I watched Finn's eyes move back and forth following my logic and winking at me in the process.

"It's actually the first book I read of his. It's how I made the connection with his writing. I read it when I was a teenager, actually."

"Well then, it's out of order on the shelf, don't you think?" He pointed at me and faked a serious scolding and I had to laugh.

"Actually," I explained. "It's the first one in the collection of Twain books, so not completely out of order, no." I had in fact, consciously organized Twain in the order that I read or was introduced to his books, but hadn't put two and two together about the rest of it. "It's also the last book he ever wrote and apparently his own favorite."

"I see." Finn smiled. "It's strange to think of an author having a favorite book that they've written. I rather assume that's like saying you have a favorite child."

"I don't think Twain cared much about what other people thought. Listen I've got to go. My dinner tray just arrived."

Finn hesitated, watching me over the camera. "Don't worry, Truly. We're going to get it all sorted, and I don't mean your books. One day at a time, alright?"

"Yeah." I agreed, but only half believed myself. "One day at a time."

27

"You cannot reason with your heart;
it has its own laws, and thumps about things which the intellect scorns."
M.T.

The longer they kept us in the hospital the more I realized there was no way around it. I was going to lose my apartment. I'd be forced to move back home, but I started dreading it less, the more dad and I got to know each other.

I have to admit, seeing him with Celia was eye-opening. He was kind and considerate and even a bit handsome, in a rugged sort of way. Different from the Gigi way.

I started to wonder what he was like when we were little. I couldn't remember much before mom got sick. I guess somewhere along the line I'd become so consumed with trying to preserve her memories that he just faded into the background, and that wasn't exactly fair. If my accident was a wake-up call, then maybe it was the best thing that had ever happened to us.

. . .

ONE DAY FINN and I were having Little Debbies and hot cocoa in little styrofoam cups from the cafeteria. He said it was to remind us of our chocolate date and it took pulling a few strings to get me the box of cookies.

I told him about my change of heart, and how I'd been avoiding my dad for the last ten years, but that I was starting to see things differently. He was quiet for a moment.

"What is it?" I asked.

"Do you remember when you asked me about Kathleen?"

"Yes."

He hesitated just long enough for me to brace myself.

"I need you to tell me about Christopher."

I blinked a couple of times, surprised that he even remembered his name. "What do you want to know?"

"The same thing you wanted to know. I want to know if I'm going to have to fight a ghost."

Wow. Talk about blunt. "Do you want to elaborate?"

"Do you?"

I smiled at his candor. "Not really, but I will if you want me to."

"I want you to."

"Can I just ask where this is coming from?"

"The night of the accident, you were a mess because he'd been to see you."

"I told you what happened that night."

"Yes, but what you haven't told me is why one meeting with an ex-boyfriend could make you tremble so violently it makes you throw up, or why you coil back like a cornered animal sometimes, assuming you're going to be struck."

I swallowed hard.

"If he's affected you that deeply then I think I've a right to know a bit more of what I'm up against."

He was right. It was time.

"I'm not in love with him, if that's what you're worried about."

Finn didn't respond, he just waited.

I took a deep breath and tried to think of the right way to explain it to him. Heck, I could barely explain it to myself.

"I thought Christopher was my first love, and maybe he was, but it was definitely one-sided. He never loved me. He never loved anything but himself."

Finn sighed. "I've known a lot of blokes like that. In fact, I've *been* that bloke."

"I find that hard to believe."

"Well, there's a lot you still don't know about me, but right now we're not talking about me."

"It's ok. I'd much rather talk about you." I smirked.

Finn just shook his head.

"I don't know, ok? He...didn't seem to want me, not really, and so I tried everything I could think of to make myself more attractive to him. He always used to talk about supermodels and point out how hot they were so I dieted and exercised and tried to dress well and still he'd call me when he felt like it but then he'd go days or even weeks without a word. I became obsessed with his rejection. I let it define me."

God this was hard. I don't think I'd verbalized all of this before and gotten the words right. It was hard, admitting these things about myself. These weaknesses. But if we were going to be in a relationship, he might as well know now. It's not like my dysfunction didn't bleed through anyway.

"My whole life I've had trouble with throwing up when I get stressed out, so it was kind of a natural progression. It got pretty bad and I lost...a dangerous amount of weight. When he did call, we would go out and he would drink too much and he was rough with me. He was a mean drunk, and sometimes he hurt me, although by that time I was really small and fragile and I think he just didn't know his own strength."

I stopped to take a breath but Finn seemed to have stopped breathing altogether. He was just staring at me, wide-eyed.

"Don't look at me like that! It's pathetic enough, ok? I told you I was broken, right? Remember that? In the limo—before" my voice started to break "before all this happened?"

Finn shook his head. "I'm sorry. I didn't mean to look at you in any certain way I'm just...speechless, I guess."

"Good. Can we stop talking about him now?" I wiped a stray tear from my cheek.

"Where did you meet him?"

I sighed loudly, my frustration obvious. "In a bar. On the Upper West Side. An Irish bar, if you must know. I was looking for a place called The Dead Poet, being the literary type that I am. I was with Kate and we stumbled into this other place and he was bar tending and we got talking about books and—"

Understanding dawned across Finn's features. "And he... dazzled you with his knowledge of John Updike?"

"And introduced me to my first Caipirinha, yes."

"Yet you still drink them. Even after everything."

I felt the color creep into my face. It was even more pitiable to say it out loud.

"Which bar?"

"Excuse me?"

"Which bar did you stumble into on your way to The Dead Poet?"

"Why, does your father own all the Irish bars in town?"

"No but we hire a lot of bartenders. Maybe I know him."

"Let's hope not."

"Which bar?" He said it again, this time more insistent.

"Do we really have to do this?"

"Are you trying to protect him?"

Was I? "No, of course not. I just think it's pointless."

Finn sat there, waiting.

"I don't actually remember. I got very drunk that first night and I went home with him and the next time I saw him after that he had a different job in a different bar and that's how it goes with him. He never stays in one place too long." I stopped. "Or with one person." I added.

"I'm sorry." Finn said simply.

"So am I. You wanna hear something else that's really embarrassing?"

Finn hooked one eyebrow up.

"He was my first real boyfriend. If you could even call him that."

He shook his head. "No. That is not possible."

"It is. It's entirely possible, because it's entirely true. Notice I said *boyfriend*. I've dated plenty of guys, just nothing serious. Very few second dates even."

"And why's that?"

"No one ever held my interest." I shrugged. "When I was in college it was all about grades and partying and to me they were mutually exclusive. I hung out with book nerds and journalists during the week and went to frat parties and hung out with douche bags on the weekends. I never saw myself dating a book nerd and the frat boys and athletes were all about having fun, but most of them could barely carry on a conversation."

"Well, I don't think you were going to the right parties. Where I went to school it was the brainiest blokes that had the most fun. And I must say most of us weren't bad looking either." He grinned.

"I was most definitely *not* going to the right parties."

"Because if you were" he leaned in close "you might have gotten a little more of this." His kiss lit that same fire that kept smoldering in the background of our relationship.

"So where were all you brainy, good-looking, incredible kissers hiding?"

"Oxford." He murmured, still trying to kiss me.

I blinked a couple of times and pulled my head back. "Oxford? You got into Oxford?"

He frowned. "Is that so hard to believe?"

"Well, no it's just–"

"That you've never dated anyone smarter than you?" He smirked.

"Who said you were smarter than me?" I joked.

"Ok, so maybe you've never met your match." He was serious. He was also right.

I'd never attempted to date up. I'd never even attempted to date level. Christopher had been the closest I'd come but his was all sarcasm, meanness, and stuff he'd picked up along the way and overheard in drunken bar rants. He could discuss just about anything and sound intelligent, but he didn't have anything original to back it up.

I had to admit, it was nice, being with someone who challenged me, and if that wasn't enough, I swear, that crooked little smile was going to be the death of me.

Finn interrupted my thoughts. "You know, I can honestly say the same thing."

"What's that?"

"With the exception of one, all of the women I've dated weren't smart or funny or well-read."

"So who was the one? Your wife?"

"She was smart, yes. Very smart. But we never developed any sort of connection. We were just two people trying to find some relief from the horrors of war, and it just so happened that sex was our mutual drug of choice."

"Convenient." I winked.

"It was." He blushed a little. "Until it became...rather inconvenient."

"I'm sorry. That was really tactless."

He grabbed onto my hand. "It's alright. Really. At first it was all fun and games and flirtation and it was just another conquest in a very...long list of conquests."

I raised one eyebrow. "How long is this list?"

He laughed. "I promise you don't really want to know the answer to that question."

"You know? You're probably right. So? Who was *the one*."

Finn hesitated. Significantly in fact. He looked out from our little corner of the atrium, which had become our favorite lunch spot, and then looked down at his lap.

I let go of his hand, realizing with a thud that whoever it was, he wasn't over her. "Well whoever it is, does she realize you're still in love with her?"

He looked up, surprised. "I'm not. I mean, I was. Definitely. But so much has happened since then. She been married for three years now I think. I've met him. He's a decent chap."

There was the three years thing again. My journalistic nose could smell this story a mile off. "So she was the one who tried to convince you there was a better way to do relationships."

He seemed surprised and somehow wounded by my memory of his explanation, as if it didn't belong to me and I wasn't allowed to use it to illuminate the truth.

"So you joined the army, and continued doing things your way, but wound up getting someone pregnant."

I watched the memories move across his features as he tried to reconcile them all. I could see the depth of his struggle, some of which he didn't have a handle on. It was a rare moment of truth for us. His strength and control were always so anchoring. Now it was as if he had come unmoored, and was drifting on rough seas. I reached for his hand again and he grabbed on, but he couldn't look at me.

"There's so much more to this story. It's not what you think."

"Am I wrong?"

He looked up. "No, the events happened in the order you described. I did join the army, partially because of Regan, but partially because I was at a crossroads. I had finished University with two masters' degrees but I'd only ever lived a privileged and perfectly empty life. I didn't know what to do, so I enlisted."

"Enlisted." If he'd been in the army surely he would use the correct terms. "Is the British Army different than ours? With two master's degrees wouldn't you have been an officer?"

"I refused the commission."

"But why? Why would you do that?" This story was getting more and more interesting all the time.

"I felt like two different people. The Oxford grad and the Irish rogue. I guess it was a sort of identity crisis. How could I possibly be in charge of a group of soldiers when I didn't even know how to be in charge of myself?"

"So what did this girl have to do with it?"

He huffed out a breath as if the answer was 'everything'. Either that or the story was so interwoven that it would be impossible to pick apart the threads. "She was the one girl who vowed never to sleep with me; who saw through all of my rubbish. She didn't try to change me exactly, although she did warn me that someday I would learn the difference between shagging and true intimacy." He smiled a little as he talked. She must have been something else. "She had much higher standards than I did, so she just accepted that I was what I was, and that we would just be mates."

"Let me guess. You weren't quite as willing to accept the inevitable."

"That's right." He laughed. "She was older than me and graduated law school before I was finished, but we still saw each other from time to time."

"A lawyer. Smart indeed. And beautiful, I assume."

I watched him swallow with some difficulty. "Quite, yes."

He didn't seem embarrassed by the admission, nor was he keen on trying to hide his feelings. It was refreshing, actually. There are a lot a very beautiful people in this world and there's really no shame in saying so.

Somehow it didn't make me feel threatened exactly. It did make me a little envious, but not of her specifically. Rather, it was the look on his face when he talked about her. The desire that each of us has, I suppose, to be that in someone else's life. Finn said that he loved me, but I doubted his current feelings were anything compared to what he felt for this girl–this...married lawyer who was an ocean away.

28

"True love is the only heart disease that is best left to 'run on'
-It is the only affection of the heart for which there is no help,
and none desired."
M.T.

M y ability to set whatever emotions I had aside and look at things logically–journalistically–came in handy in moments like these, when the man I was in love with was talking about another woman.

"I know what you're thinking." Finn had this uncanny way of looking at me and just knowing things. It was unnerving, yet fascinating. I had stopped trying to deny it and was instead simply curious about his outside-in view of my life.

He started rubbing the top of my hand with his thumb. I could see that we'd been sitting way too long already and he was in pain, but I didn't really want to end the conversation either. I glanced over at our nurses and they were starting to wrap up their lunch items. We didn't have much time.

"You do, huh?"

"Regan and I were never meant to be together."

"You said yourself she vowed never to sleep with you. Did that change?"

His head bobbed back and forth for a minute as he weighed his answer. "Yes and no."

"So she eventually caved to your uncommonly good looks and smooth charm?" I winked at him and he smiled in spite of himself.

"Not exactly. Are you sure you want to hear this story?"

I looked back over at our nurses. They were still chatting. "Yes, but I might need the short version."

"On the night of my twenty-first birthday she announced that we were going to celebrate like Americans. She took me out and, what with me being the shameless womanizer that I was, she decided to honor me with every sex-themed shot that was named in this little pocket bartending book she'd bought me."

I started cataloging the ones I could think of and there were several but Finn started naming them before I did.

"Sex on the beach, blowjob, redheaded slut, slippery nipple, wet dream... The list was long and not very distinguished. Needless to say we were inordinately pissed by the time we got back to her flat. I didn't intend for anything to happen, but it did, and it changed everything for me."

"Changed how?"

"All those things she'd been telling me for years about how sex and love were different, about getting lost in another person, I'd decided it was all bollocks. When I was with a woman I just wanted to...well, shag and be done with it. Not that I didn't want to please a woman, or didn't know how to. I'd become quite good at it actually, but it was the intent that was wrong. I came at it from a place of selfishness. Pleasing just to get what I wanted."

"Well, with all that practice." I laughed. Sarcasm was my friend in situations like these. I tried not to imagine making love to Finn, but I could tell from the way he kissed me that he knew just how to please a woman, and the thought made me warm all the way down to my toes.

"Yes, well nothing I had done previously prepared me for the act of exploring intimacy with someone I cared so deeply for. It was as if I'd never been with a woman before, and the entire night was like that."

They had sex all night long? I understood it theoretically, but it was hard to separate myself from that want. Somehow Finn lit that fire in me the very first time he kissed me. I tried to stay on task. "So what happened? Why didn't you end up together after that?"

"She almost died that night. Spent three days in the hospital being so sick from the alcohol that she nearly swore off it completely. Besides, she didn't remember any of it. Not one minute of it. It was as if it had been completely erased from her memory."

"Well what did she say when you told her? Surely your change of heart–"

"I never told her."

"What? Why not?"

"It's complicated. It would have changed our friendship. And she wouldn't have believed me. She would have thought I was either making the whole thing up to get her into bed again. Besides, it didn't change me right away, and I would have had a hard time convincing her I was a different man."

"So you ran away."

"Well, that's not *exactly* true, but essentially, yes. I did tell her years later, but very poorly. She didn't speak to me for a long time after that."

"I'm so confused."

"Even after that experience I wasn't ready to concede her point. I convinced myself it was a drunken, romanticized version of a fantasy I'd had in my head since I was eighteen. That it wasn't real. But still, I wasn't happy with my life or my prospects. I drank too much, and everything seemed meaningless, so I joined the army. Then I met Kathleen and allowed that relationship to quell the loneliness. Until the consequences became, rather painfully clear."

"But it was real. With Regan. Even if it wasn't real for her, it was real for you."

"Yes. It was."

Just a simple, matter of fact answer that left me wondering where that left us? What did that mean for us? "So it's not Kathleen's ghost I'm competing with. It's hers. Only she's not a ghost." I pulled my hand away and put it in my lap.

"You're not competing with anyone." He said. "Because it was real, it made me realize what I'd been missing. Why I felt empty. That's why I haven't been with anyone. I spent so many years doing it wrong. I'm not willing to be that man anymore."

Just then our nurses showed up. His eyes were pleading with me to believe him, but the whole thing was just a lot to process. The only thing I'd ever known was the physical act of having a sexual release. I mean, sure, I fantasized about romance and watched all the girlie movies. I just thought it was all Hollywood.

Did I mention the fact that I wasn't used to dealing with intense relationships? My head was spinning and my heart was aching and I was glad that they brought us back to our separate rooms so I could be alone again.

My thoughts were repeatedly interrupted throughout the rest of the afternoon with physical therapy and occupational therapy and then a visit from the social worker to discuss my discharge planning and the finances of it all. By the time dinner came my stomach was in knots.

Finn left me alone the rest of that day and halfway through the following day. He didn't text me or try to initiate a video chat even. He seemed to know that I would need some time to think about the things he'd said. He didn't rush me, which I really appreciated, but I was starting to feel guilty about ignoring him.

Everything he'd told me, it was all in the past. He told me those things, not to make me jealous, but to help me understand him better. Besides, I was much too practical to believe that he'd gotten all the way to twenty-eight and never been in love or had a serious relationship. Just because I sucked at relationships didn't mean the rest of the world should suffer.

However, that brought me painfully to my own crossroads. I knew there were memories that haunted him, just like mine did. And yet, he wasn't still in England trying to win Regan's heart. He was here. In The States. Trying to win mine. The thought made me smile from the inside out. We were adults, and it was time I started acting like one.

I also needed to be practical. I could either start writing again, or I might lose everything. If I had to be on a payment plan to the hospital the rest of my life then so be it. The problem would be affording my apartment along with the extra payments. I was already in a rent-controlled building, and I couldn't ask dad for a loan.

I decided to get busy writing. I might be stuck in the hospital, but it didn't mean I couldn't be productive. I opened my laptop and pulled up every possible article idea I had stored in various folders. I started querying magazines outside my norm, even wrote a piece about Yale New Haven hospital from a patient's perspective, and sent it to the editor of the New Haven Register.

My productivity lasted about as long as my pain medicine held out. I fell asleep in the middle of the afternoon, feeling a little bit better about my future. After all, what good was it being a freelance writer if you couldn't work from just about anywhere?

I dreamed Finn and I were back on my couch. He was laying on top of me and kissing me softly. Slowly. Then he picked me up and carried me to bed, slowly taking off all of my clothes. His shirt was off and I could feel his strong chest under my fingertips. He took my hands and our fingers intertwined as he pulled them ever so slowly up over my head.

His tongue slid down my collar bones and circled one of my breasts as he whispered his love to me. Every nerve ending ignited as his hands traced their way down the outsides of my arms to my rib cage and then my waist.

He kneeled above me and I tried to move my hands to

unbuckle his pants but they felt weighted to the bed. He looked at me as if he knew what I was thinking and shook his head gently while his fingers slid circles around my nipples and he followed with his tongue. Lower and lower he slid, down out of sight until my entire body convulsed awake. I was sweating and my heart was pounding and it took me a moment to get my bearings. I looked at the clock. I'd only been asleep for about a half hour.

There was something about this man that drew me in. Something that bypassed my fears and outwitted my sensibilities. He was offering a chance at something I didn't understand, and yet I craved it in some unexplored corner of my soul.

Thanks for sharing all of that with me. I know it wasn't easy for you. I pushed send on the text and waited for his reply.

His reply was to call me up on the computer. I opened up my laptop and there was his beautiful face. My whole body was still warm and willing from that dream and he must have seen it somehow because the first thing he said was "Well now, that was worth waiting for, wasn't it?"

"Pardon?" I tried to look away without letting the red creep into my face. It was no use. I just looked back at him and let myself imagine the dream.

I sat there, looking into the eyes of this man that I hardly knew and barely understood, and I let him see the want. The desire. He blinked back his surprise and didn't say anything for a moment, so I broke the silence and spoke the inevitable.

"I had a dream about you."

His face broke into a glorious smile. "Really? Do tell."

I licked my lips absently as I tried to decide how much of it I was willing to share. "Well, it started on my couch and it ended in my bed."

His eyes twinkled softly. "I think I like this dream. What happened in between?"

"I'm not sure. I woke up before it got really good." I pouted. "But if the ending is anything like the beginning–" I shook my head.

Finn wasn't embarrassed at all by my admission. Instead his eyes smoldered with a kindred desire. "Oh, it will be. I can promise you that."

"Are you saying you're considering breaking your streak?" I winked.

"It's never been a matter of if, love, merely when."

"Well, I think physically we've both got a long ways to go before any of that can happen."

"Yes but you're not the only one who dreams about it."

His statement was matter of fact, with an edge of insistence and a dash of inevitability that created a tingling sensation all up and down my spine, landing decidedly right where the dream left off. It was all I needed to convince the stubborn parts of my heart to hope for the possibility of change.

This was no fairy tale, and I was no princess. Finn was not a saint, or even a knight, but he was noble and honest, flawed and beautiful. And he was the beacon that helped my heart know it was safe to put in towards shore. So I steered toward it. Toward him. Waves be damned.

29

"Necessity is the mother of taking chances."

M.T.

By the time I was ready for discharge, Kate, David, Dad and Celia had all gone and packed up my apartment, moving most of it into dad's garage with the use of one of Colin's supply trucks. I resigned myself to the inevitable. Even with the rent-control I wouldn't be able to manage by myself, at least for a while, and keeping the apartment was impractical. If I stayed with dad I could save money for a while, at least until I was strong enough to get another plan together.

Finn was staying in New Haven, and the likelihood of my seeing him was going to decrease dramatically. My care would probably get transferred to a hospital close to dad's house, although the thought of having to visit any of those hospitals again filled me with an unspeakable dread. They certainly didn't hold any good memories for me. Trouble was, I didn't have much of a choice. It wasn't like New Haven was down the street.

I was sitting in Finn's room talking to him about it. He kept trying to cheer me up, when suddenly the door opened, and Celia walked in with dad.

"We have a proposition for you." Celia was grinning at me.

"No, I don't want to be the flower girl at your wedding. Ask Kate. I'm sure she'd be thrilled to wear the ruffled dress."

Finn was horrified. Dad just shook his head, and Celia smiled down at me.

"I think you're going to like this proposal a little better than that one."

"I'm listening."

Dad cleared his throat. "How would you like to stay at Celia's for a little while, so you can be closer to the uh–hospital." He gestured toward our hands clasped together, indicating the obvious.

I was dumbfounded. "For real?"

Celia nodded enthusiastically, as if she'd just planned the coolest slumber party on the planet. "Yes, for real. I could drive you in on the days you have your wound care and therapy sessions, and in between appointments you can visit with Finn."

"They would let me do that?"

"Of course! You'd be just like any other visitor. They're even willing to put a chaise type chair in here to support your leg."

"They would never do this at a hospital in Queens. Must have something to do with *Yale*" I managed through closed teeth. "Either that or someone pulled some major strings?"

Celia ignored my comment. "I've scheduled myself for eight-hour shifts instead of twelves for a few weeks. My apartment is on the ground floor, and I have an extra bedroom and a big second bathroom so the crutches shouldn't be a problem. On the days you don't need to be here you can hang out with my cat and work on your writing."

I just sat there blinking. "But...why?"

"Why what?"

"Why would you do that? Change your whole life around. You barely know me."

She looked hurt by that. Finn squeezed my hand as if to alert me to my tactical faux pas, then came to my rescue.

"What she *means* is, that's incredibly generous, but it seems like a lot of work for you."

Celia sat on the edge of my bed and took hold of my other hand. "I want to help, and I want to be a part of this story. Your dad and I are moving forward with our relationship, and you're a part of him. I know you haven't exactly been coherent the whole time, but it's not like we're strangers anymore."

I thought about that. How many times had I woken up over the last few weeks only to find Celia at my bedside?

"Think of it as a halfway house. Literally. As in, it's halfway between your dad's house and the hospital. Cheaper than a hotel, but still easy to get back and forth to New Haven. Besides that, it's temporary–just for a few weeks, until you can hobble a little better, and Finn gets released. What do you say?"

"I can't pay you any rent or gas money or anything. I don't even know how I'm going to pay for all these hospital bills."

"Well, you certainly don't eat much, and I won't be going anywhere I wasn't going anyway. Believe me, it'll be nice to have some company. Living alone can get old."

Didn't I know it. At that point I was blinking back tears and Finn squeezed my hand again. I couldn't even speak. I just nodded my answer.

Celia smiled.

Dad smiled.

Finn didn't even look surprised.

"Hey–did you know about this plan?"

His head jiggled ever so slightly. "I may have been alerted to the possibility." Finn winked. "I do have my own selfish reasons for wanting you closer, you know. I've gotten rather used to our little *chats.*"

When he said the word *chats* like that, I knew exactly what he was referring to. Unfortunately so did dad. He stuffed his hands into his pockets and blushed a little, looking away as if some noise in the hallway had captured his attention.

I'd never seen this side of him before, I guess because he'd never seen me with a guy. At twenty-five, I wasn't used to being daddy's little girl. It was new territory for me, but I kinda liked it.

"I don't know what to say. Thank you so much."

Celia was still holding my hand. "It's my pleasure. I'm going to go let the discharge planners know what's happening."

"Ok."

In the space of ten minutes, I'd gone from miserable to ecstatic. I wouldn't have to be without him after all–at least, not as often, and the inevitable move back into dad's house could be postponed. Finn seemed content, and I was elated. Dad and Celia looked happy, and after all the craziness, things had found a way to work themselves out.

It seems safe to say we had a great little group forming, unlikely as it was. Looking back, I'm starting to wonder if that's just how these things go–like military men who meet in trenches and in foxholes and end up being lifelong friends. New Haven was my foxhole, where dad came back into my life and Colin and Celia joined our ranks, but Finn?

Finn was another story.

30

"Experience.
The only logic sure to convince a diseased imagination
and restore it to rugged health."
M.T.

Celia's apartment was in a trendy neighborhood in Stamford, Connecticut. It was cute and impulsively clean. A lot like mine, actually, although a heck of a lot bigger. I guess charge nurses make a decent salary. When I asked why she lived in Stamford but worked in New Haven she told me her ex-husband lived in New Haven, so she moved as far away as possible while still being able to get to the hospital.

"It's about an hour drive, but that's not really an unusual commute around here. A lot of people in this complex commute to the city each day."

"So what does your ex do? In New Haven I mean."

"He's a doctor." Her voice was staccato, but it started to click.

"At the hospital?"

"Yes."

"What kind of doctor?"

She stiffened. "He's a trauma surgeon."

"Oh." Then the light came on. "Oh! You mean–did he operate on me?"

"Initially, yes."

"And Finn?"

"No. Aside from the burns, Finn just needed his ankle fixed. Your injuries were a bit more complicated."

I thought about that. It did make sense. "How long were you married to him?"

"Six years."

"And then?"

She shrugged. "I got tired of the lifestyle."

"Which lifestyle is that?" After all, I had never been married, much less to a doctor. How was I supposed to know what it was like?

"Well," she began puttering around the apartment, straightening things. "Doctors are pretty anal. Surgeons even more so. Trauma surgeons are right up there with heart and brain surgeons. They're the best of the best. For a reason."

"So he's a perfectionist."

"To put it mildly."

I laughed. It sounded a bit like Christopher. Although he was more 'generalized asshole' than perfectionist, he was still incredibly critical and entirely intolerant of opinions other than his own.

"Of course, if I were a patient I'd want someone just like him operating on me." She sat back down on the couch. "Incredible surgeon, lousy husband."

I nodded. I could see how that could be true. "So you still talk?"

"Professionally yes. Personally no."

I looked around her apartment. It made a little more sense now. Not only did she probably make a decent salary herself, there was probably alimony in the picture as well. "So, can I ask you something?"

She leaned forward and put her elbows on her knees. "Sure. Shoot."

"So why my dad? He's about the farthest thing from a Trauma Surgeon you can get. I mean, he fixes cars, not people, and he drinks cheap beer, not good scotch."

She looked straight at me in all seriousness. "He has a kind heart."

Hmm. Not what I expected to hear, but if there was one thing I'd become acutely aware of over the last several weeks it was that. I'm not sure why I hadn't seen it growing up, but it was there now–undeniably so. The next thing Celia spoke was pure truth.

"And kindness trumps good scotch any day of the week."

I nodded.

Finn was kindness personified, and it was incredibly attractive. The fact that he seemed to have money when I had none didn't even play into it, other than the fact that it made me self-conscious at times. Maybe it was that way for dad and Celia too.

After a month in the hospital Celia's apartment felt like a palace, anyway. I had privacy, solitude, and a place to think and heal without being assaulted by all the 'stuff' I knew I'd have to wade through eventually at dad's place.

She tried to make me feel as comfortable as she could. A spare bedroom was prepared and my clothes, toiletries and some boxes of files and mail had been brought there for me to sort through and try to make sense of.

It was weird–knowing all of them had gone through my stuff. Someone had looked in every corner and cabinet, every bookshelf and drawer. I tried to catalog all of it in my mind, to see if there would have been anything shocking or revealing, but I doubted it. Most of what was really important to me was either encrypted on my hard drive or locked up in my heart.

My physical therapy and wound care were scheduled for Mondays, Wednesdays and Fridays, and Celia saw to the rest personally. It was pretty incredible – l couldn't imagine what it would have been like at my apartment or even dad's place, trying to arrange for rides and caring for myself. The pain was still significant and the wound healing was a very slow process, but each day got a little better, so I was hopeful. The hardest part was worrying about Finn. And finances.

The hospital said they would bill me and I could set up a payment plan once they figured out the cost of my stay. It was a good thing my scholarship got me out of paying back school loans but now I'd be in the same boat as most of my friends from NYU–buried in debt and living with their parents. I suppose debt happens to everyone eventually. It couldn't be the end of the world, right?

I spent the first couple of days trying my best to re-establish my identity. Replacing my credit cards wasn't a problem because they hadn't actually been stolen, just destroyed by a fire. The DMV was a little dicey, because I had to find and mail in a bunch of proofs of identity in order to get a replacement license, but it wasn't like I'd be driving anywhere for a while, so the waiting didn't bother me.

Just as I was signing on to my email, a Skype call came in. From Finn, of course. Who else would I be talking to? It was a tough day, pain wise, and I was glad for the chance to take my mind off it and concentrate on something else.

I'd stopped wondering how I looked. While video chats presented something of a vanity challenge, we'd both seen each other at our worst, and I still thought he was the cutest guy I'd ever laid eyes on.

"Hi there." He started.

I could tell he was in pain today too, so I tried to lighten the mood. "On a scale of one to ten, if ten is the worst pain you've ever felt, what's today?" I held up my hands as if I were ready to write down his answer in a hospital chart.

"I have enough people asking me that all day long, and I'd rather not think about it, if you don't mind." He tried to shift in his chair but it was obviously difficult.

"Oh come on." I teased. "You show me yours and I'll show you mine."

He smiled. "Well, if it's show and tell you're proposing, I might have to change my mind. What are you willing to show if I tell?"

"Hmmm." I thought about that. "Well, I'm not sure there's anything exciting under these sweatpants and I haven't shaved in weeks." He laughed. It was good to hear him laugh. I looked at the box next to me. "How about if I show you a part of my past?"

He blinked a couple of times. "That would be lovely."

"Ah ah ah!" I held up my finger. "Your number please."

He sighed and tried to shift again. The look on his face said seven but his mouth told me "Five."

I poked through the box dad and Kate had brought me and pulled out a small photo album. It had pictures in it from when I was a baby up through middle school. I'd kept it with me since the night my mom died. She had it with her in the hospital. Mine and Jenny's. I'd kept Jenny's too.

I pulled it out and held it in my lap, trying to will back the wall of emotion that came with it. I pasted a smile on my face for Finn's sake. "Are you ready to see the cutest kid on the planet?"

"Of course."

I turned the book open to the first picture, and held it up for Finn to see. His smile was immediate. "My, but you've gotten fat. Are you sure you didn't eat a basketball?"

I spun the picture back around to look at what he was commenting on. It was my mother–one of those sideways pictures women take to show how big their bellies have gotten. "I'm not in this picture!"

"Sure you are. You're right there!" He pointed at the screen. At the basketball. "And now I know why you're so beautiful."

I looked at my mother. So young and so full of life. Literally. She was beautiful, but not in a flashy way. She was a beautiful *person*. And she really did glow.

"Thank you."

"You're welcome." Finn smiled. "Can I see another? Maybe once you'd made your grand entrance into the world?"

I turned to the next page. It was a picture of my dad, holding me. Our noses were touching and his head looked giant in comparison to mine. He looked happy too. Maybe we were a happy family way back when.

I suddenly realized that Finn was waiting for me to show him the picture. I looked up with glassy eyes and he smiled at me, so tender it nearly broke my heart. I turned it around, and all the joking was gone from his voice. "That will be me some day."

Most guys would have been relieved, I would think, when an unexpected pregnancy turns out to no longer be an issue. But his situation was different. This wasn't a voluntary abortion or even a miscarriage. It was murder. A casualty of war. But there was nothing casual about a broken heart.

And yet, after everything he'd been through, he was still willing to hope for the future.

"You'll be a great father Finn." I said simply, straight into the camera.

He looked up at me and sighed, his eyes still rimmed with pain and unshed tears. "And you will be a beautiful mother."

"Me? I don't even know if I want kids."

His face registered the shock of that. Maybe Irish Catholics had no box for such a statement. "Well you will be, some day."

I swallowed, trying to make light of the overwhelming pressure slamming into my chest. "I thought you said those activities were *off limits*, mister. You can't make babies if you're just walking in the park, eating sandwiches you know."

"Well, we won't always be walking in the park." He smirked a little, implying the obvious. It sent a shiver through my insides. Even in pain he was thinking about sex. That had to be a good sign.

"Let's hope not." I laughed. "I, for one, am very much looking forward to...*not* walking in the park with you."

He swallowed with some difficulty, and I could almost see him running through the scene in his head. I liked that it was a struggle for him, but not in a sadistic way. I just liked that it made

me feel so wanted. It made me look forward with a kind of antici-
pation I didn't usually get to experience.

"Can I ask you a question?" I wondered.

His head shook a little as he pushed the thoughts to the side.
"Absolutely." He winked at me and my heart melted just a little
again.

"I've been insatiably curious about something since the day
you said it."

I could see the wheels turning in his mind, trying to figure out
what I was referring to. "Hmm. Insatiable...I thought we weren't
going to talk about how much I wanted to–"

"Reign it in there big guy!"

"You started it."

"It's about your apartment."

He stopped and looked at me, waiting for me to finish.

"You said we couldn't go there because it was where you
dreamed us."

His eyes turned toward the floor and he didn't look up for a
long time. "You're going to think I'm crazy."

"No I'm not."

He was silent for so long I started to think he wasn't going to
answer the question, so I decided to break the ice. "Well, how
about if I tell you about one of my dreams first. It has to do with
the night of the accident."

His eyes narrowed and he leaned forward a little, obviously
intrigued. "Please."

"Well, this story starts the morning you called me from
Ireland."

"Ok." Finn nodded in the affirmative.

"I woke up from a dream that really shook me. I couldn't
remember the dream, but I woke up with my heart pounding,
drenched in sweat. Have you ever had that happen?"

Again he nodded.

"Well, I didn't think much of it at the time, because I had no
idea what it was that had scared me. I pretty much dismissed it."

"Right."

"Until the night of our date."

Finn's head tilted slightly, as he tried to predict what I was going to say.

"When I heard the pounding on the door that I thought was Kate."

His face went slack. He knew what happened next.

"Right before I heard the door, I'd been dancing past the mirror–"

"Dancing?"

I laughed at myself and waved him off. "It's a long story, and that part's not important."

He smirked. "Okaay."

"I like, lost my balance or something and as I twirled past the mirror for a split second I thought I saw someone behind me and I froze, remembering a piece from that dream. All I saw was this black silhouette of a man standing behind me. His huge hands came around my throat and he was trying to choke me. In the dream, obviously–not in real life."

Finn was nodding along as he listened, almost as if he was walking through the dream with me.

"But then there was someone pounding on the door, and I couldn't tell if it was real or part of the dream. When I heard it again and came out of it I scolded myself for being silly and getting all freaked out like that. But when I pulled open the door, the threat was real. It was Christopher."

His eyebrows went up. "Wow."

I took a deep breath and blew it out, once again marveling in how creepy it had been. "Yeah."

He just sat there shaking his head.

"So, what do you think?"

"Did the dark figure in your dream have a face?"

"Not that I could tell, no."

"Did it say anything? Could you tell if it was a male or female?"

"Judging from the size and look of the hands I'd say definitely a male. And no, it didn't speak."

"Did you?"

"I couldn't. It was like my mouth was glued shut. I couldn't even scream."

Finn cleared his throat but it was more like he was mumbling to himself rather than talking to me. "Something dark from your past was trying to threaten you."

"Wow. You're pretty good. Are you going to read my palm now?" Sarcasm. Always sarcasm. What the hell was wrong with me?

Luckily, he ignored my comment, but the bile started churning in my stomach. I just stared at him, wondering how much more of the dream I couldn't remember. "And what makes you such a dream guru?"

"I've been interested in dreams my whole life. In the Celtic culture, dreams are very important."

"Oh." I hadn't expected that. I was being a smart-ass and he was being serious. I'd never met anyone who put much stock in dreams, although it was hard to deny the obvious. That dream felt absolutely real – and it stayed with me in a way that most dreams don't. Even as I talked about it I could feel the cold hands closing around my throat. I shuddered.

"It was so real Finn. I still remember it so vividly."

"Some people believe that those lucid, vivid dreams are more like visions."

"You mean like foretelling the future?"

"Maybe, but not necessarily."

"Well Christopher did show up right after that."

The look on his face was one of concern. "Yes. Yes, he did."

"What is that look for?"

"I just wonder what would have happened if your neighbors hadn't shown up."

I thought back to the way he'd made me feel. How my body responded to him without my permission. He had some kind of a hold on me and it wasn't right–had never been right. I had wondered the same thing, I just hadn't said it out loud. "You don't think the choking in my dream meant literal choking, do you?"

"No. I mean, probably not. Dreams are mostly metaphor–symbolic representations of things in our lives. It's the vivid, lucid dreams that get dicey. He may not have been there to kill you, but I'm not convinced that he meant you no harm."

The Brits were entirely too fond of double negatives. I hated having to play mental hopscotch just to keep up with a conversation. "So you think he *did* mean to hurt me?"

"I think he's a man with control issues who preys on the weaknesses of others. I think he got triggered by something completely unrelated to you and was looking for an outlet for his anger. I think he came to you, either accidentally or on purpose, intent on somehow releasing that anger. Physical abuse, sexual domination, mental manipulation–anything to make him seem larger and you smaller."

That about summed Christopher up. I thought again about how big his hands seemed around my waist, proving his size and strength. His smooth, cutting compliments and his hungry stare. I was always just a means to his end. Nothing more.

"So, I told you my crazy story. It's your turn. Tell me about your dreams."

31

"When in doubt, tell the truth."

M.T.

"I've always been a person that–" Finn took a deep breath "strange things happen to."

One eyebrow popped up. "Uh huh...What kinds of things?"

He shook his head. "I see things."

"What do you mean, you *see things?*"

"I get a lot of dreams."

"You mean you *have* a lot of dreams?" The inner editor in me hardly ever shut up.

"No I mean I *get* a lot of dreams."

"Do you eat a lot of pizza?"

"I'm being serious."

I tried to stifle the snide remarks–to shut my mouth and just listen, like he does. It was surprisingly difficult.

"This has been happening to me for as long as I can remember. For a long time I thought it happened to everyone, but apparently it doesn't."

"Thought what happened?"

"That my dreams tend to come true."

"Excuse me?"

He looked into the camera for a couple of minutes, trying to gauge my reaction. "I don't tell this to very many people. Just my family."

"Ok well–I might still think you're crazy, but it's too late now." I smiled, but waved him onward. "Continue."

He started massaging him temples. "I don't know how to explain it really. I just–sometimes I have these dreams, and then they really happen, exactly like I dreamed them."

"You're being serious."

"Yes." He nodded.

"Like–since you were little?"

"From my earliest memories. Other strange things too, but the dreams were the most disturbing. Like the first time I met one of my uncles I'd dreamt about him and then when I met him, I asked how he liked being a conductor–only he'd never told me he was a conductor. In the dream I saw him conducting an orchestra for The Nutcracker Ballet."

"Well, maybe you heard your parents talking about it."

"He didn't get the job conducting The Nutcracker until two weeks after we had that conversation."

"Ok that is weird. So how old were you then?"

"Seven."

I blinked a few times. "Seven?"

He nodded. "But sometimes I don't remember them until they start happening–like a déjà vu. Other times I wake up and remember a dream really vividly. I write it down and catalog it, then some time later–sometimes years later, I will have forgotten that I even had the dream until I walk into a place and it suddenly reminds me."

"Wow."

"And then I know what's going to happen, as it happens–for at least a few minutes."

"That is really, *really* bizarre."

"I know."

"And so what does that have to do with me?"

He hesitated for quite a while. "It goes back farther. To Ireland, when I was at my grandmother's house trying to come off the booze and painkillers. I had a lot of hallucinations, and–"

"And?"

"I saw your face in her mirror."

My heart stopped momentarily. "You what?"

"I saw the face of a beautiful dark-haired woman in the mirror. It was fast–just a flash. At the time I thought it was just another hallucination. But there was a scent that went along with it. A unique scent."

"Like a perfume?"

"I don't know. But then after I moved to New York I had another dream. Of you and I at my apartment. You were in a navy blue dress."

My skin started to crawl. I couldn't swallow. Couldn't breathe.

"And in the dream, I knew you'd never been there before–to my place–and yet, you and I were very familiar. And I knew in the dream that were were making love for the very first time."

He looked scared as he talked, as if I was going to shut the computer off and shut him out of my life any second. In all honesty the thought did cross my mind.

"You have to understand. I didn't think you were real. I thought you were a figment of my imagination. A girl from my dreams. Then back to the night of the Yankees game. I wasn't going to go and then I got this feeling that I needed to go. When I saw you, I couldn't believe you were real."

"Ok, before I was curious. Now? You're freaking me out."

"After you hit me, I looked up and saw your gorgeous face and the whole dream came rushing back to me, which is why I was fairly stumbling over all my words trying to talk to you."

"I don't remember any stumbling."

"Oh, there was stumbling, believe me. We'd only just met, and not a very proper meeting at that. How do you think you would have responded to my telling you I'd had a dream about you and I having sex in my apartment?"

I started to laugh. "You might have gotten punched a second time!"

"See?" He rubbed his chin again for effect.

"So let me get this straight. Are you saying that because of these dreams or visions or whatever you call them, you knew we were going to go out that night? Did you think we were going to end up back at your place? I thought you'd sworn off the whole 'one night stand' thing."

"No. I knew it wasn't for that night."

"So you're saying you knew we would get together? In general?"

"Eventually, I hoped we would."

"That is just too weird. So you gave me your card that night and you weren't worried whether or not I would call you or show up again."

"Oh I was worried. Every moment of those three days I spent looking over my shoulder, hoping you'd show up."

All of a sudden I understood even more than he was telling me. "Oh my God!"

"What?"

I couldn't even speak the words. It was too much. I just sat there shaking my head. "That's impossible."

"What's impossible?"

"Is that why you crawled through the fire to save me?"

"I crawled through fire because I'm in love with you."

I was still shaking my head, incredulous. "But they have to happen? The things you dream?"

"I don't know."

"What do you mean you don't know?"

"Well, there are a lot of dreams I've written down that haven't happened yet."

"But has any dream you remembered in the moment like that

failed to come true the way you remembered it?"

He shook his head. He knew what I was getting at. "Not so far."

"So that's why you've been so calm all this time–reassuring me while we've gone through this ordeal? Because we haven't been to your apartment yet?"

"No. I just believe that everything is going to work out."

"This is weird. And a little creepy"

"I don't mean to scare you. In our culture things like this happen. We just accept that we don't always know why."

I'd never put much stock in alternative energies and all that jazz. "Is your whole family that way?"

"Just my father's side. My grandmother came from a long line of seers and priests, going all the way back to the time of the ancient people of Ireland."

"Fascinating." I never knew either set of grandparents, nor did I ever care enough to even ask about them. Finn seemed to have a family tree with roots reaching back to the beginning of time. "So your father doesn't dream like that?"

"No, but he can sometimes tell things about people by touching them."

"He what?"

"It's like he gets a sense of someone; who they are as a person. He can do it without touching them as well, it's just that touching makes it clearer somehow. Like when you shake someone's hand."

I couldn't believe I was playing along, but Colin really was a touchy person, and yet there was something reassuring about him. "He has a very calming presence."

"Aye. That he does."

I smiled. "You're a lot like him."

It was Finn's turn to smile. "I'll take that as a compliment."

"You should."

"I can't control it, you know, and it's not like it happens every day. Sometimes I go months or even years between significant dreams. So when they do happen, I pay attention."

"But the dream I had wasn't like that, was it?"

"It could have been."

"But I'm not like you."

"Maybe not exactly the same, but I think everyone dreams. And I think dreams like that–the ones that feel incredibly real and stay with you–are always something to pay attention to."

"It seems like a big, strange, twisted fairy tale or something. These things don't happen to real people."

"Sure they do. They happen all the time. You're just finding out about it now."

I supposed that could be true. After all, I'd led a fairly sheltered life, considering I lived in NYC. I didn't have many friends, and kept to myself reading old books when I wasn't thinking about how to structure my life so it all made sense. The fact that there was a great big world full of *non*-sense out there shouldn't surprise me in the least. This was everything I'd always tried to avoid.

What did I know about the history of other cultures and what happens in other countries? I'd never traveled outside the US. Hell, I'd hardly been out of New York State. Ok, a couple times to the Cape and once to Florida with Barbie And The Basketballs, but that was a drunken spring break that barely counts, seeing as I barely remember it.

"The real question is, now that I've told you, do you still want to date me?"

"You mean now that I know, beyond a shadow of a doubt, that you're crazy?"

"Exactly."

His smile was my undoing. I couldn't resist it if I tried, even if he was crazy. I was in love with him. I didn't know much, but of that I was sure. "Yes." I replied. "Of course I do."

From the moment I met him, my life had never been the same. Finn came from some other reality, but my brush with death had changed my perspective of reality. Suddenly taking a chance on a relationship with someone I might never understand seemed plausible and exciting, even if he didn't fit into any of my boxes.

It might just be the beginning of my end. Still, there were worse ways to go.

32

"Grief can take care of itself;
but to get the full value of joy
you must have somebody to divide it with."
M.T.

F inn was in a walking boot before I even got my cast off, and after one more grafting surgery his burns were healing well. He was out of the ICU and in a step-down sort of a unit, but he wasn't going to make it home until after the holidays. Luckily the room was still large enough for me to get around in on my crutches. It would be another couple weeks before I could start trying to bear weight on that shriveled up little leg of mine, so I enlisted Celia's help and organized a plan.

On Christmas Eve Celia took me to the hospital with her. It wasn't a therapy day for me, so Finn wouldn't be expecting me. We went to his room when he wasn't there and decorated it with the help of the nurse's aid on the unit.

I mostly supervised, but we hung some twinkling lights over the bed, put a small fake tree on the nightstand and I even filled a stocking with candy and set it next to the tree. We closed all the blinds so the room glowed softly and we threw a Christmas quilt over the small couch under the window. I pulled out a little portable speaker and put on some Christmas music, then put on my Santa hat and planted myself on the loveseat. Celia deposited my bags in the corner and kissed my cheek.

"See you tomorrow love."

"Tomorrow?" Finn was standing in the doorway and his face registered the shock.

"Yes. I'm sleeping over." I grinned.

"You're what?"

"You heard me."

He looked at Celia as she was leaving and she just shrugged her shoulders as if she had no idea what I was talking about.

"I've brought snacks and board games and Christmas movies and even–" I reached into one of the bags and pulled out a small wrapped package "a present."

He hobbled over and tried to look inside the other bag. I slapped his hand playfully and asked him to sit next to me instead. The darkened room with the soft, twinkling lights made it seem almost festive.

He sat slowly and tentatively. His movements were still pinched by the dressings and the new skin on his back, but he'd become an expert at hiding it. He sat on the edge of the couch and held both of my hands.

"You are a sight for sore eyes." He smiled.

"I couldn't let Christmas go by without seeing you. And I'd rather spend it here than anywhere else." I leaned forward and carefully placed my hands around his face, then kissed him slowly until he relaxed bit by bit. God but that man could kiss, even in pain.

I pulled away just so I could catch my breath, but he pulled me back into him and took my mouth with a hunger that made me tremble.

He looked into my eyes for the longest time. "When this is over and I have full use of my body, I am going to make love to you from sunset to sunrise."

"It's going to be a while before our bodies are willing to cooperate with a fitness regimen like that." I smiled. "But I like your enthusiasm!"

He took a finger and traced it slowly from my jaw down my neck, and across the front of my clavicle. "We'll start slowly." He picked up my hand, kissed my palm and then started sucking on one of my fingers until my breath caught in my throat. "Besides. There are other parts of me that work just fine."

His tongue gently made its way along my bottom lip and I ran my hand down along his inner thigh. I could feel him next to my fingertips but I didn't dare push it. I had no idea what he could tolerate or when the next staff member was going to walk through the door. We needed to keep it PG, but his mouth felt so amazing. Everywhere it touched, it lit a fire.

"When did you say they were discharging you?" I breathed out.

His insistence deepened and he took my mouth again. This time I ran my fingers through his hair and felt his strong chest, my breath coming in shorter gasps. One of his hands came up under my shirt and felt my breast through the thin bra I was wearing.

The loveseat was small but he slid me back against the armrest and laid himself carefully on top of me. He was hard and I was ready, but we were in a hospital room and between our casts and boots and bandages we made quite the pair. Still it was romantic as hell in its own way.

"I know we can't make anything happen just yet, but I wanted to feel you underneath me." He started to move slowly. "I want to show you what it's going to be like one day."

There was nowhere for me to grab that wouldn't hurt him, so I just laid there and let him move against me.

"I want you to feel my love." He kissed me, pressing into me, and I nearly exploded.

I kissed him again and again, feeling the weight of him, the warmth and depth of his emotions. I let my mind imagine the real thing as we laid there consuming one another through our kisses until he started to grunt and the sweat beaded up on his forehead.

"Ok stop." I said. "Come on. Let's get you laying down properly in bed."

He didn't argue, but instead he extricated himself slowly from my arms and I helped him as best I could. He laid down on his side and patted the space next to him.

"Are you sure?"

"Positive. Perhaps we could watch one of those movies you brought?"

I figured out the television and sat down on the edge of the bed, pulling the Christmas quilt over us as I snuggled into him. The movie played and he kissed my neck and whispered in my ear and we fell asleep like that.

Later on a couple of nurses came by to check on us and offered us some of the pizza they had ordered so we sat up and played Monopoly and ate pizza into the wee hours of the night. It was surprisingly quiet on the unit that night and we snuggled back into his little bed around two a.m.

"Merry Christmas Finn."

"Merry Christmas love." He kissed the top of my head and pulled me in close. I must have fallen right back to sleep because the next thing I knew it was morning and the phlebotomist was there to draw Finn's blood. I vacated my warm little spot next to him and used the bathroom to brush my teeth, pulling the hair out of my face and into a clip, although at this point in our relationship, pretense was pretty much out the window.

Finn did the same, and we met back on the loveseat, where I was sitting, waiting for him. I held up his present.

"You didn't have to get me anything."

"I know I didn't have to. Remember, it's the thought that counts."

I'd actually spent a fair amount of time on this gift. At Celia's I had a lot of time to journal about these last months, but nothing I came up with could explain the way my world had turned itself all the way around and upside down, and yet I wasn't willing to let go of any of it. I had spent far too long trying to order my world and the people in it. I'd made way too many assumptions and been proven wrong time and time again.

Mark Twain once said "It is wiser to find out than to suppose." I supposed it was time for a new world order. It was time to find out.

I'd struggled with what I could give a man who had everything. A man who had lived through so much pain and yet had saved my life. There was nothing that could match that except everything, which was exactly what he'd given me.

Inside the small box I had simply placed a small red paper heart. He looked at it, then looked at me. "Is this yours?"

"It is." I smiled. "It's not very strong yet, as you can see. But it's getting there."

"It's beautiful. And I mean that in every possible way." He leaned over and kissed my cheek. "Thank you."

"Be careful with it."

"I will. I promise."

The End

REVIEWS / NEWSLETTER

Leave a Review

Thanks for reading *The Truth About Truly*! Your support makes it possible for this independent author to continue creating.

If you liked what you read, won't you please take a quick moment, before you move on to another great book, to **leave an honest review?** Your feedback is truly invaluable. It's the reason most people will choose one book over another, so I'd really appreciate your feedback. Thanks so much!

∾

Newsletter

Love this book and want to sign up to receive updates on new releases? **You won't get ever get an email more than once a week,** and honestly it will be **more like once a month.** I don't sell or give your email to any third parties, nor do I use them for any other purposes. Just updates.

You have my word. Opt out at any time.
Sign up for updates here:
http://createdtofly.com/**newsletter**/

ABOUT THE AUTHOR

Lynda Meyers is an award-winning author, nurse, yoga instructor, reiki master, motorcycle enthusiast and world traveler. She has written fiction, non-fiction and poetry for newspapers and magazines and currently makes her home in the upper left corner of the United States.

To learn more, visit: www.createdtofly.com

LYNDA
MEYERS
finn
again
The long-awaited prequel to *The Truth About Truly*

ALSO BY LYNDA MEYERS

BY LYNDA MEYERS

Haven't had enough of Finn?

Read Book 2: *Finn Again*

Finn McCarthy is half Irish, half English, and fully fantastic.

Raised in the pubs and educated at Oxford, he never did know which half to favor. His Irish half loves women and booze, while his English half is wicked smart and damned polite. And then there's Regan, the one girl who never did succumb to his charms.

When a world at war beckons, Finn answers the call, but there are some casualties even a soldier can't prepare for. To heal his wounds he must banish his demons, a journey that leads him to a sleepy fishing village where the mysteries of his Celtic roots take hold. He begins to accept his past, only to discover that his greatest battle might take everything he's got left.

War...Does things to a man. But Finn isn't just any man.

EXCERPT: FINN AGAIN

CHAPTER I

The Irish are always quick with a story, especially if they've been drinking, which for a lot of us is most of the time. Or maybe for most of us it's a lot of the time. Either way, drinking and story-telling seem to go hand in hand.

I know this better than most. I grew up in the pubs.

My father was a famous footballer in England. He even played for the national team, then met my mum in a pub just outside London when the team came back to celebrate a particularly fine victory.

If you asked him, he would say it was love at first sight. If you ask her, it was mayhem that night, and she simply had too much to drink. At any rate, fall in love they did, and though her father didn't approve, they married, and he whisked her off to a house in Ireland where they had me and my baby sister, Eiran.

My father took his fame and his earnings and began opening restaurants and pubs of his own all across Ireland and a few in England as well. For a long time, we didn't live rich, but we always lived well. Eiran and I spent our summers and breaks from school traveling with our parents all about the countryside, so he could keep an eye on it all.

While Da conducted business, Mum was always carting us off to the nearest city or township to see whatever history may have existed there. We must have visited every museum, art gallery and exhibit known to man, but it was her way of keeping us occupied and instilling a bit of culture in us. It also taught us a fair deal more about history than most of our professors knew in school.

After my granddad died, Mum spent more and more time with my grandmother at their estate outside London, but Da mostly stayed in Ireland. They never stopped loving each other, they just got along better when they weren't living together, and neither one was willing to give up their lifestyle for the other. Mum preferred England. She said it suited her better and that was probably true.

Besides, by the time we were ready for prep, my grandmother insisted on sending us to boarding schools in England. She said it was time we learnt some of the finer points of life, and Grams wasn't someone you argued with. Mum agreed, and Da stayed out of it.

I think Grams was convinced it was all a matter of breeding, and as such you could breed things out of a person. The Irish pub culture had never set well with her, but like a thoroughbred that just knows how to run, I swear it was there, in my blood. So was football. Except for me it was Gaelic football I came to love.

Gaelic football is probably unlike any other sport you've seen. It's a combination of soccer, rugby and basketball - kind of like Quidditch, but without the broomsticks. I played every chance I got–in the schoolyard and on club teams and even at college. Of course, I often wound up at the pubs afterward, even before I was of age, and if my mates and I got kicked out of one place, I'd bring them over to one of Da's pubs and we'd figure out how to get served anyway. As you can imagine, that made me one of the more popular chaps around, especially with the girls.

As it happens, girls don't have much of a tolerance for beer, and almost none for whiskey, but at fifteen, I'd developed quite an appetite for all three. Da would look the other way when I came home langered, or even drive the girl home if it got too late. After all, he'd been a boy once.

Da understood, but Mum was appalled.

If I was staying in England, she never heard me come home. The house was just too big, and her wing was on the opposite side of the courtyard. Most of the time I snuck in through the servant's quarters and made my way through the back kitchens. I'm certain she wasn't oblivious to my habits, but all that good breeding she talked about forced her to pretend I wasn't sick with the Irish flu next morning.

Still, I knew better than to bring girls home to Gram's house. The one time I tried, I was lectured on honor and decency until I thought I might suffocate. We learned the ropes fairly quickly, Eiran and I. When we were in England, we acted like good little Brits, and when we came to Ireland, it was usually to have some fun.

We had it pretty well sorted.

Sort of.

Eiran loved Ireland and embraced the culture. She did well in the English schools, but as soon as she was old enough for university, she headed back to Dublin to attend Trinity College for nursing. Nursing fit Eiran. She was a softhearted sort who was all the time taking in wounded animals and the like. Ended up marrying one of her patients, as a matter of fact, but that's another story.

It's not that I minded English schools. I felt very comfortable in England and could easily switch accents and mannerisms depending on the crowd. When I was at Eton I fit easily with the Brits, but home in Ireland I fell right back into step with all my mates. Clearly, I was half Mum and half Da. Two more different people could not exist, and yet they did. They inhabited the same body.

Never did get over my penchant for women or whiskey. I loved them both in equal measure, and often at the same time, so that worked out famously for a while. Attending an all boys' boarding school can make meeting girls something of a challenge, but we always seemed to manage.

For all my shenanigans I still finished top of my class at Eton and went on to Oxford. That made Mum and Grams very happy, and since Grams was paying, it paid to make her happy. I was studying computer science and business with moderate results and females with great success, the former being a probable result of the latter. Still, girls back home were a lot more fun than most, so while I was at school, I spent more time with my mates and while I was home, I spent a lot more time chasing skirts.

On holiday, my routine went something like this: Get off the train, walk home, change out of my dress blues, walk down to the pub and meet up with my mates, who were almost always there ahead of me. Whoever got in last had to buy a round immediately, so I always made sure I had plenty of money with me.

Walking to the pub assured that I wouldn't have to drive home, of course. Stumbling was the preferred method of transport for intoxicated persons and, as it turns out, is a lot less nauseating than being trapped in a moving vehicle.

One particular break I actually made it first to the pub, so I sat down at our favorite spot at the bar and proceeded to revel in my success. I had just ordered a shot of Jameson's with a pint of Guinness to chase it when the door opened, and in walked the most beautiful girl I had ever laid eyes on. At eighteen I thought I'd seen it all. I thought I knew beauty, but this girl was nothin' like I'd ever known. Blonde hair and gray-green eyes that could peel the paint off a fence.

She sat down next to me, and I swear my stomach flipped over on itself. I offered to buy her a drink, but she refused. In fact, I tried every trick I knew, but she'd have none of it. Eventually she looked straight at me and smiled.

"Do you find this amusing?" I asked, putting my elbows up on the bar.

"Do I find what amusing?" She mirrored my actions.

"Are you going to let me buy you a drink or not?"

"Are you even old enough to drink, young Finn?" She winked at me as if she knew something that I didn't, and yet I couldn't place her.

"Do I know you?"

"Well, I don't know 'bout that but sure I know you Finn McCarthy. I used to watch you get your nappy changed."

My head rocked sideways. "Excuse me?"

She smiled again. "You really don't remember, do you?"

"Believe me, if you were in a memory, I'd have it with me right here." I patted my chest.

"Save it for a girl who's actually going to shag you, will you?" She flagged down the bartender. "I'll have what he's having."

Tom winked at me. "All right, miss."

She turned toward me and crossed her arms over her chest. "He doesn't think I can do it does he?" She inclined her head toward Tom without taking her eyes off me.

"Do what?" I matched her gesture in mock salute.

She was neither impressed nor amused. "Resist your charms, of course."

"I have charms?"

"Don't you?" She smiled as she downed the whiskey, then nodded toward mine, which I hadn't touched yet.

I followed suit, banging it down on the bar to signal Tom for a refill. "That all depends." I wiped my mouth.

"On what?"

"On who the hell you are and why you've seen my mickey, of course." I smiled again and took a long sip of beer.

"Well, don't worry, I'm sure it's grown since then." She sipped her beer and looked straight ahead, leaving me to wonder just what kind of game we were playing. It's not that I disliked this game, I just wasn't sure what the rules were exactly.

I studied her face, which was artfully proportioned. "*Please* tell me we're not related."

"Would that be so awful?"

"Only if I had my heart set on shagging you. Otherwise no." I smirked.

She laughed heartily. At least I could make her laugh. That had to be worth a couple of points.

She let out a long sigh, smiling all the while. "My older sister Maggie used to watch over you and Eiran. I tagged along a few times. Perhaps you don't remember."

I searched my memory banks and found nothing but a lanky, buck-toothed, flat-chested young sprite who couldn't possibly be the girl sitting before me now. She had to have been a few years older than me, but still, this couldn't be the same person.

I just kept staring at her. "Well, braces for sure, but if you're the person I'm thinking of, I'm not the only one whose parts grew in nicely."

She grinned intentionally, revealing straight, white teeth.

"Regan?"

She nodded once with some satisfaction. "Nicely done. I see Eton taught you a bit of deductive reasoning."

As if on cue, the bottle of Jameson's showed up. "Ready for another?"

Tom poured us both a shot and walked away, shaking his head.

She held hers up in salute. "To fully grown parts!"

"I'll drink to that."

Two shots of whiskey in as many minutes and I started to feel the burn, but she looked as if she could match me all night long. I noticed that a few of my mates had come in, but when they saw me with a beautiful girl they knew enough to leave me alone. They settled into a booth in the back to watch the show, and I was determined not to disappoint.

"So, how do you like Oxford?" She asked, still looking straight ahead.

"Better question." I leaned forward on the bar. "How is it you know so much about me?"

She hesitated. "You caught me. I've been stalking you for years now. Got a thing for younger men, you see."

"Oh yea?" I raised one eyebrow. "And yet you refuse to shag me. How tragic. For you, I mean."

Her laugh relaxed into a huge grin. "Maggie saw your da last year at Michaelmas. He said you'd been top of your class at Eton and looking at Oxford."

"Well that does make more sense."

"But besides that, I just saw you on campus the other day."

"What?"

"I'm home on holiday as well."

"You're at Oxford?" I hadn't meant it to sound condescending, but I'm afraid it did. Either that or sexist.

"Is that so hard to believe? Did you think maybe you're the only one with smarts in this town?"

"Well, no of course not I just–how old are you?"

"That's hardly a proper question to ask a lady!" She pretended to look offended and got Tom's attention by tapping her shot glass on the bar a couple of times. After he filled them, she looked at me and said, "Good thing I'm not a proper lady..."

We held our glasses up and toasted before taking the shots in unison.

She wiped her mouth in a decidedly unladylike fashion and continued, "I'm twenty-two, if you must know. I've just started my law courses. Undergraduate in History with a minor in Economics."

"You're attending law school. At Oxford?"

"What can I say? I liked the gowns."

I shook my head, laughing. "So how is it?"

"What's that?"

"Law school."

"It's all right. Why, what are you studying?"

I was tempted to say whiskey and women, but I was pretty sure she already knew that part. I looked her over again. She was unbelievably gorgeous. "Computer science and business."

She nodded. "And don't be lookin' at me like that. I think I've made it clear I don't date underclassmen."

I leaned toward her then, bringing my face close to hers. "If you really knew as much about me as you think you do, you'd understand how much I hate being told no."

She wasn't put off by the proximity of our noses in the slightest. "Perhaps if you heard the word more often, it would help you get used to the feelin'."

I smiled the way a man should smile at a woman–with genuine compliments and sincere admiration. "You are absolutely breathtaking."

This girl would have none of it. The only reaction that registered on her features was one of disgust bordering on pity. "Aye, but that's just a word, isn't it? And a feeling. And nothin' much else between two strangers. It might get you through the evening, but you'll be just as empty when the daylight hits. I've no desire to be your warm place for the night."

Ouch. "I do like a girl who can speak her mind."

"And I'd like to have some real fun." Her head tipped toward the table where my mates were gathered. "So why don't you introduce me to your friends back there, and we'll have some drinks and play some darts, eh?"

She started to get up, but I put my hand down on hers. I just couldn't go down without a fight. "You really have no desire to sleep with me? Not even once? You know, I might surprise you."

She tipped her head and looked me up and down, then shook it decidedly. "No. Not even a little bit."

A burst of raucous laughter erupted from the table in the back and my face lit up crimson. I couldn't remember the last time I'd been turned down. Regan was already headed toward my friends and I'll be damned if she wasn't even better lookin' from the back. I put some money on the bar for Tom, shrugged, and followed after her.

By the time I got to the table they'd obviously introduced themselves to one another and there were congratulations all around, presumably for her supernatural ability to resist my advances.

"Don't worry love, he needs his pedestal to crash out from under him once in a while. Those Oxford boys can be quite taken with themselves." Daniel assured her.

"Don't I know it." She laughed. "But I've got to give him points for trying, so tell you what – the next round's on me!"

Cheers and glasses went up all around the table and an hour or so later the entire lot of us was inordinately pissed. The boys cleared out one by one, until Regan and I were left talking to Tom. I couldn't for the life of me remember where her family lived, but if I'd known I would have offered to see her home. Truth be told, I was just hoping to have more time with her, whatever that might mean. We walked out of the pub into the cold wind, and she wrapped her jacket tighter.

"Can I walk you home?" I put both hands up in self-defense. "I promise, no advances. Just a gentlemanly offer."

She hooked her arm through mine. "Sure."

I have no idea how long we walked but the conversation was somehow deep below the surface and the laughter came easily. I wanted to kiss her right there on the street, but I couldn't figure out how to do any of it and still maintain her respect, which I felt strangely desperate for. We ended up on the other side of town before she pointed to a door in the middle of two shops. "This is me."

I looked up to see an apartment above one of the shops. "So you don't live at home anymore?"

"Too many brothers."

"Ah yes. Noise can be quite a factor when you're trying to memorize historical data."

"And when you've a scholarship to keep up, that data becomes very important."

"Well" I stuffed my hands in my pockets. "It was very nice... running into you again. After all these years."

"You too." She grinned. "And it's too bad I'm so drunk."

"Why is that?"

"Because normally I'm marvelous at keeping secrets." She giggled.

"Secrets? What am I missing?"

"I've made a bit of money tonight is all." She pulled a small wad of bills out of her coat pocket along with her keys and unlocked the door, stepping into the small vestibule to get out of the wind, and motioning for me to do the same.

"I'm sorry?"

"Your friends." She shut the outer door behind us and started up the stairs. "It wasn't the first time I've met them."

My mouth dropped open and I ran up the stairs after her. "No!" I spun her around. "They did not!"

She doubled over, laughing heartily. "I must say, it was rather convenient that I happened to have a bit of history with you, not that you remembered of course."

Incredulous, I raked my hands through my hair.

"I mean, I actually did used to help mind you and your sister." She looked down at my pants, unashamed. "And I have, in fact, seen your mickey. Granted, it was a very long time ago, and it wasn't very impressive back then." She smirked mercilessly. "But they did pay me to say no to you."

I put my hand against the wall to steady myself. "No wonder no one was about when I got to the pub." It all made so much sense. "There I was, congratulating myself for getting there first when all along they were waiting for the sheep to wander off alone so they could send in the big bad wolf!"

"Aye." She laughed.

"So, wait a minute then" I said, putting my other hand up against the wall, effectively closing her in between my arms. "If that was all a game..."

Her eyes looked up at me from under heavy lashes. "You're still too young for me, Finn McCarthy."

"Says who?" I swept her up in my arms and kissed her solidly. Her words may have said too young, but for a moment there, her mouth said something altogether different. Still, she pushed my shoulders away in a physical reiteration of her earlier comment.

"Hey now! I thought we were doing just fine." I tried to lean back in, but she turned her head just in time.

"I know part of it was a game, but I was serious too, Finn. It's not about your age, not really. I'm just not interested in being someone's *just for tonight*."

She waited to gauge my reaction. I just sat there blinking, so she kept talking.

"Listen, you're very attractive, a surprisingly good kisser, and have...quite obviously grown into your grown-up parts." She pushed me a little farther away. "But I hope you can understand."

"What if I told you I wasn't looking for a *just for tonight*?"

"Then you'd be lying to the both of us. You're eighteen Finn. You don't know what you're lookin' for. I'm twenty-two and I'm barely gettin' the hang of it. Can't we just be mates?"

I sighed. "I can't say I've ever had a mate I wanted to shag as much as you, but uh–I suppose we could give it a go."

"Well, in that case, would you like to come in for a cup o' tea?"

"Let's not push our luck, shall we?" I stepped back. "I'm very drunk, and I am only human, after all."

"Now that's the spirit!" She handed me a slip of paper with her number on it. "Ring me up some time and we'll tip a few more." She slipped inside her apartment and began to shut the door before adding, "Mate!"

I leaned back against the wall and took a deep breath. This was going to be interesting.

Buy the Book...

STEEL JOURNEYS
LYNDA MEYERS

THE ROAD TO

Patagonia

ALSO BY LYNDA MEYERS

Join Abby Steel on a series of breathtaking international adventures with Steel Journeys - an all-female motorcycle touring company where she calls all the shots. From huts to hotels, it's never the same adventure twice.

To some people, home might be wherever you lay your helmet, but for Abby Steel, home was wherever she laid her ass. Today it's a Harley. Tomorrow it might be a BMW or a Triumph or a Honda. Home was whatever bike fit the terrain. Home was wide open spaces tucked under an expansive sky.

Home was the road.

It took a lot of miles to work through the hurts of her past, but she's finally built a business she can be proud of. Women from all walks of life come to join in her adventures, for all sorts of reasons. Equal parts badass and life coach, Abby genuinely cares about the women on her tours, and they respect her for it.

The Road to Patagonia finds Abby back home in California on a break between trips, when an unexpected visitor threatens to bring all the blocks tumbling down.

STEEL JOURNEYS: THE ROAD TO PATAGONIA

EXCERPT

Abby Steel hadn't seen the inside of her own apartment in over three years. There hadn't been any need to come home really, so she just...didn't. Life on the road kept her busy and building her own business had taken way more time and energy than she'd anticipated.

She looked at the compulsively clean apartment and was thankful, once again, that her sister came and dusted the surfaces once a month. It wasn't as if she'd left it dirty, but time and dust had a way of accumulating in equal and inevitable measure. Lauren had also been nice enough to retrieve her mail from the post office when it no longer fit in her box, getting rid of all the junk mail and opening anything that seemed important. There wasn't much. Abby had very few bills outside the business, most of which were handled remotely.

At this point, she was thankful for familiar surroundings and the chance to recharge. Three years was a long time to be away. It was time to reconnect with her roots and what was left of her family. Riding back from Alaska, many miles had been spent dreaming about long showers and luxurious baths with unlimited hot water. The grime that had built up under her fingernails would need to be soaked and scrubbed, her hair untangled and brushed—things life on the road rarely allowed for.

It would be good to see Lauren and her nieces in the flesh, instead of over video chat. She was excited to share stories of her adventures and show off her pictures, but seeing them would have to wait until she had energy for endless questions from curious little girls. She sat down in one of the comfortable side chairs in the living room with a glass of water and a stack of mail, but barely got through half of it before falling asleep.

When she woke up, the sun had dipped below the horizon, shrouding the apartment in a kind of eerie glow that reminded her of sunsets on the Spanish plains just outside Sevilla. She closed her eyes and let the scene linger in her mind, colors bursting across the open sky with the sweltering summer heat billowing up inside her leather jacket. Riding there had been nothing short of magical. A lot of places felt that way.

It was the magic that kept her on the road. Each new place had its own set of challenges, its own set of charms. The challenges faded, but the charms remained, decorating her memories and dangling from her heart.

For Abby, the constant drifting from place to place created an unusual sort of routine that was comforting in its uncertainty. Lauren thought it was crazy, never knowing where she was going to sleep or what dangers might lurk around the corner, but one person's danger is another person's thrill. She and Lauren, they were wired differently, that's all.

California's Napa Valley had been home for thirty-three years, but she left the small-town of Calistoga with an insatiable need not just to see, but to fully experience all the world had to offer. By that time, she'd already seen most of the US, and a good portion of Canada, but those had all been shorter trips—three weeks at most.

Culture shock becomes something of a nonissue when you're constantly changing cultures. Eventually, the life she'd left in California was no longer the ruler by which she measured all of her other experiences. Instead, her old life became just one of many other foreign concepts, all blended together in a beautiful mélange. Living abroad had changed so many of her perspectives that her old worldview seemed distorted by comparison.

Leaving the confines of the continental United States and choosing to travel the world turned out to be a polarizing decision. Three years later, she felt like a completely different version of herself.

Being back in her apartment, surrounded by all the furniture and artwork she'd left behind was its own sort of culture shock. They were her belongings, of course, but all the things she thought she would miss had eventually faded into the background. They'd been replaced by people, places, smells, and tastes of a life too vibrant and varied to be contained within four walls.

The life she had built before was there on the walls and in the furniture, blended into the color scheme. They defined a person she wasn't sure existed anymore. A part of her recognized it, was even comforted by the deep familiarity, but an even bigger part wondered if it was possible to go back in time. Time seemed to have gone on without her.

Maybe coming home wasn't a matter of choosing now or then, but rather, allowing the new to inform the old, and the old to make space for the new. If her life was a tree, like the sadhu in India had told her, then she could never hope to become a different tree. The new experiences would instead have to be grafted onto the trunk, eventually growing together into a unique expression of life.

Steel Journeys was a company she had founded all on her own, most of the seed money coming from her inheritance. Lauren had used her half to build a house in the suburbs and was raising two beautiful daughters. Abby chose to pay off debt, buy a condo, and set off on the adventure of a lifetime. She'd spent the past three years researching the best roads, the best views, and the best options for lodging in dozens of countries, taking copious notes and pictures, giving out business cards, and forming business relationships.

Cataloging it all had been a labor of love, born of passion and drive. Each new place had its own rugged truths waiting to be discovered. She filled several paper journals with notes and sketches, cross-referenced with digital galleries.

She couldn't recall precisely when the idea for the business hit her—it was somewhere between Bangkok and Ho Chi Minh City. Like a reformed smoker she suddenly, desperately wanted other women like her to experience the freedom she had seen, felt, heard, smelled, and tasted. That was the dream—to form a women's motorcycle touring company and take it global.

"What, the entirety of the United States isn't enough for you?" Lauren had asked.

The answer was simple. It wasn't enough. It would never be enough. Wanderlust was embedded deep in her DNA—so deep, in fact, that she wasn't sure where it ended and she began.

Lauren was happy being a soccer mom and living in the suburbs. She was a card-carrying member of the PTA. The only cards Abby carried were a Visa and her gun permit. She didn't carry her gun internationally, of course, but traveling solo had taught her a thing or two about self-protection. Tucked into remote corners of the globe, far from big cities and police patrols, the rules were different. Street smarts were learned, and she had learned plenty.

It *was* a long time to be away, but for Abby, home was a concept, not a place. To some people, home might be wherever you laid your helmet, but for Abby, home was wherever she laid her ass. Home was her saddle, which for the last three years had been a Harley, and before that a BMW, a Triumph, and a custom café racer she'd rebuilt with her dad. Home was the wind in her face and wide-open spaces tucked under an expansive sky.

Home was the road.

This homecoming—this apartment—was one more stop along the way. It was the obligatory reset point on a map filled with pushpins. Except, of course, this room was tastefully decorated, with a comfortable bed, down blankets, and the best sheets money could buy. That bed was calling to her, and the rest would have to wait.

She woke the next morning with dirt on the sheets and little balls of dirt surrounding her jeans, which were hastily removed and crumpled up in the corner like a one-night stand. Perhaps a shower might have been the better choice before bed, but it was still a hundred times cleaner than most of the places she'd lived recently. Dirt was a part of life, and the only thing it damaged was a person's sense of expectation. She put it out of her mind and padded toward the bathroom.

The requisite extra-long shower, complete with a double scrubbing of her hair, ears, fingernails, and feet took longer than strictly necessary. Lauren was expecting her, but after three years, what was another thirty minutes? When she felt reasonably satisfied with her results, she filled the bathtub with lavender-scented Epsom salts and soaked, with the sun streaming through the glass block window.

As she soaked, she listened to pan flutes and meditation music that reminded her of some of the temples and monasteries she'd visited in India. She only spent a few weeks there, barely scratching the surface of just one region, and there was still so much to see and explore. Indian people were very kind to her, and she admired their deep spirituality. It was definitely on her *must-return* list.

She emerged from the bath and pulled a long, clean, white T-shirt and some yoga pants out of the closet. "Well hey there, guys! I haven't seen you in forever!" She paused for a moment, staring at the sheer volume of clothing neatly arrayed before her and shook her head. After surviving for so long on two perpetually wrinkled shirts and one tank top, it all seemed so extra.

Still, it felt amazing not to be wearing jeans or leathers, and *not* sweating into a helmet for a couple of hours was a delicious thought. Most of the time she wore her thick brown hair up or braided to keep it out of her face. She decided to blow it out a little and let the ends curl up naturally with some leave-in conditioner.

She'd barely noticed how long it had become. Upon closer inspection, it was desperately in need of a trim, but split ends would have to wait.

Life's sense of urgency was something that had mellowed over the miles. Time was slower in other parts of the world. Life was about the experience. Relationships. Good conversations. Being present in the now was something she was still working on, but an area where she'd seen a hell of a lot of improvement.

It was satisfying to think that some measure of growth and change and wisdom had come over time. Everything had fallen into place, and she was finally doing exactly what she wanted with her life. When she opened the back door to let in some fresh air, even the birds sounded happy. The way the morning was going, nothing could harsh her mellow.

Except maybe her ex-boyfriend showing up at her door.

Read the book...

LYNDA
MEYERS

Letters
from
the
Ledge

ALSO BY LYNDA MEYERS

Still reeling from the suicide of his best friend Tess, seventeen-year old Brendan struggles to overcome addiction and identity issues. Walking the ledge outside his Manhattan apartment has become its own sort of drug, as he stands night after night with his arms outstretched, ready to fly away.

Sarah can see him from her window and begins journaling about a boy on a ledge. Paige and Nate, a young couple in another building, can see both teens from their fire escape.

None of them know the others are watching, but a strong desire for freedom resides in each of them, and as their lives begin to intertwine, that desire will be tested.

Three buildings. One city block. Three stories. One common thread.

Sharp, humorous, and deeply layered, this chronicle of a suicidal teen's survival explores the reality of addiction and other tough issues, but does so easily, through the use of multiple perspectives, intelligent dialogue and authentic characters. Equal parts romance, contemporary drama, and coming of age, this highly engaging and intensely beautiful novel challenges our cultural perceptions in the battle for balance, deftly uncovering the hopes, dreams and fears that keep us from falling, and ultimately teach us how to fly.

This is a work of fiction. Names, characters, places, and incidents are the product of the author's imagination or are used fictitiously. Any resemblance to actual events, locales, or persons, living or dead, is entirely coincidental.

The Truth About Truly

Copyright © 2019 by Hallway11

All rights reserved.

53469445R00192

Made in the USA
San Bernardino, CA
14 September 2019